GROOMED FOR DEATH

MARY ANNE WOLLISON
&
MICHELLE COOKE

BLACK ASH
BOOKS

Published by Black Ash Books
www.blackashbooks.com

Cover Art and Design
© Michelle Cooke
Other art available from Michelle Cooke
www.quickbrownfoxcanada.com

Paperback ISBN: 978-1-7777527-0-5
eBook ISBN: 978-1-7777527-1-2

Version 1

FICTION / Mystery & Detective / Cozy / General
FICTION / Mystery & Detective / Amateur Sleuth
FICTION / Mystery & Detective / Women Sleuths

Also by Mary Anne Wollison

Non-fiction:
Affairs: The Secret Lives of Women
Feed Me or Else
Prime Times: Life, Love, and Sex after 50

Fiction:
Code Talkers
Saving Cash
Black Lake
An Island for Two
Legends of the Bay

Anthologies:
Danger Zone
Homes

ONE

Is *it bad luck to take a dead guy's job?* I pushed the thought away
and tried to focus on the bright side. I was starting a whole new
career, one that would give me the means to maintain my daughter's
happiness and reclaim my independence. It was too bad that Morty
Feldman had to die to make that happen.

I parked on Main Street and retrieved a cardboard box out of the
trunk. On the sidewalk outside the Yorkdale Weekly office, I took a
deep steadying breath.

The old, two-story brick edifice was prominent on Main in the
town of York Ridge. It had been painted white some time ago, but
the paint was flaking in some places. Still, the dark green and gold
lettering of the newspaper's name on the front window had a "shabby
chic" charm. I opened the heavy glass-and-wood door. Brass bells
jingled overhead.

My eyes went straight to the matronly woman who sat at a solid
oak desk behind a reception counter. A rectangular, metal sign quietly
announced she was B. Pittman. She didn't look up but continued to
shuffle file folders. I waited for her to notice me. Maybe she was half
deaf and didn't hear the bells? Her face was as stern as the starched
white blouse which disappeared into the vee of her buttoned gray
cardigan. I guessed that under that big old desk was a pair of sensible
shoes, probably lace-ups with crepe soles.

I took the opportunity to survey my surroundings. Two squat metal chairs, meant for visitors, sat under beige vertical blinds. Between them was a low coffee table, almost completely covered with past editions of the Weekly. On the walls were framed awards for journalism, along with head shots of the staff, starting with L. Braithwaite, Publisher. Sympathy cards marched in single file along the wooden counter beside a florist's papier-mâché vase filled with white roses frayed and yellowed at the edges. An antique wall clock with a short brass pendulum tocked every passing minute. Still the woman shuffled papers. The silence gaped before me. Finally, I put the banker's box on the counter and cleared my throat. No reaction from B. Pittman.

"Hello?" I said, before I exploded with impatience.

She peered over the rim of her wire-framed glasses. "One minute. I'm busy. The new editor's coming this afternoon and I have to get these files ready for him."

"That would be me."

Her lips compressed to a thin, colorless line. "I don't think so. Our new editor is Darcy Dillon."

"That's right. I'm Darcy."

"But ... you're a woman."

"Can't fool you." I hoisted my box back onto my hip. "I brought a few things for my office."

I was rewarded with a frown. "Never heard of a woman named Darcy before."

At that point, Lorne Braithwaite, my new boss, barreled into the reception area wearing a smile and a zippered cardigan. He thrust out a hand. "Darcy! Good of you to come so late and on a Friday afternoon. I was hoping we could get you settled in so you're ready to hit the ground running tonight. I see you've already met Miss Pittman."

More like Pit Bull. "Yes, briefly."

"Come. I'll show you to your office." We swept past Pit Bull, and I could feel her eyes frosting my back. Would it be too much to have someone in reception that was actually receptive?

"This has been a shock to all of us," Lorne said, as he led me down the corridor. "Miss Pittman is having trouble getting over the loss of Morty. She worked for him for over twenty years, but she'll adjust, just give her time." I caught up to him, and he leaned closer and lowered his voice. "She's very old school, but she'll grow on you." I tried not to picture it.

I walked around Morty's old desk, noting overlapping rings where he hadn't bothered to use a coaster for endless cups of hot coffee. File folders were stacked in a plastic bin in the right corner beside a multi-buttoned phone. Centered on top was an oversized desk calendar. Each square was filled in till it got to the end of the first week of the month. After that, they were blank. I eyed the black leatherette chair and then looked up at Lorne. "Is this where …?"

"He died? Yes."

I shuddered.

"Just slumped over, no warning, still holding the phone. Miss Pittman found him, poor dear. They did an autopsy, standard procedure I believe, and a thorough search of his office, too. Not sure why they needed to go to those lengths; I'm sure it was his ticker. I'll probably go the same way," he said, giving his head a small shake. "Anyway, the chair has been replaced, and the desk was scrubbed down."

Gross. "Can't wait to get started," I said, depositing my box on the floor but still not taking a seat.

Lorne took that as his cue and grabbed a few file folders. "This week's paper has been put to bed, so you can focus on next week's edition. You can include the Grand Prix event at King Equestrian where we met. Apologies for just throwing it at you like this, but no matter what happens the news goes out." He pointed to a whiteboard on the wall where town and county events were noted in green marker. "Tonight, there's a ratepayers' meeting at the hall. Tomorrow, there's the opening of the Malfaro Conservation Area and qualifying races for the Yorkdale County fair."

I was distracted by Morty's last entry on his desk calendar. "B.M. 5 p.m." *Yikes. Was this guy so old he was recording his bowel movements?* I looked up to see Lorne staring, and I tried to recall his last words. *Ah yes, qualifying races. Somewhere.*

"Horse races?" I asked.

"I knew you'd think that. No, crowd pleasers for the young ones. Demolition Derby, ATV, there's a bunch. Miss Pittman will give you the contacts. And this file has some story ideas Morty was working on before he …"

Miss Pittman trotted in without ceremony. She slapped a pile of papers onto the desk. Tiny red plastic flags peeked out from between the pages. "You need to fill out these forms. I've marked the sections to sign. I expect these on my desk by Monday." She paused briefly and then as a kind of afterthought added, "Hope you have a great life insurance plan." She turned on a sensible heel and left as abruptly as she came.

Was editing going to be hazardous to my health? I frowned at Lorne, but he gave a small shrug and looked away. I was beginning to wonder if Morty really had a bad ticker or if there was more to the story. Almost immediately I heard the doorbells jingle again, and then a woman's voice sang out. "Hey, Miss P. You're lookin' good. Is the new boss here yet?"

Twenty seconds later, a striking brunette wearing the tightest knit dress I have ever seen poked her head into my office and flashed a gorgeous smile.

"Darcy?" she asked, stepping into the office on six-inch stilettoes. "Sorry to interrupt," though she didn't look sorry at all. "I'm Cynthia Davis, your photographer. People call me Cyn."

I could see why. "Sin" was right. She was something. I reached out and shook the perfectly manicured hand she offered. Bold white lines and swirls danced across coral nails. I had expected someone a lot more rumpled, wearing a canvas vest with lots of pockets. I couldn't imagine where she'd keep a camera in that outfit. She air-kissed Lorne's cheeks before swinging a hip onto the corner of the desk. One stiletto shoe swung back and forth, revealing a little more thigh with every wave of her foot.

"How about you and I blow this pop stand? I'll buy you a coffee and we'll get to know each other," she said. She glanced at Lorne and winked. "You're okay with me stealing her?"

"Sure," he said. I had a feeling Cyn got her way a lot with men. I'd have to remember that.

She leaped from her perch. "Okay, good. Give me a few minutes. I've got to get some files for tonight. Then we can head over to The Blackbird Café, two doors down. My friend Amelia and her partner run it. We can walk."

In those heels, I doubt I could have, but it would be good to get a break from Morty's creepy office and Sergeant Pit Bull for a while. Less than half an hour here and I was already uneasy. We agreed to meet again in fifteen minutes.

Lorne pulled at the crêpey skin of his neck, and a downcast look replaced his ready smile. He looked all of his seventy-some years. "I'm counting on you, Darcy. These weeklies are dinosaurs. We need new younger blood to get us into the digital age, an online presence. I doubt we'll stay in business another six months without it."

What? I tried to keep the surprise off my face. So much for this being my new cash cow. Lorne hadn't been overly forthcoming about their financial woes when we talked yesterday, nor the need to launch the paper into the digital age.

"Well, I like a challenge, Lorne." This wasn't going to be the snooze I thought it was. And since I couldn't afford for this job to be temporary, I would have to get up to speed quickly.

While I waited for Cyn, I unpacked my box. One wall of built-in bookcases had been cleared of Morty's personal items, evidenced by the dusty outlines where things had sat. The only relic from Morty was a half-full bottle of antacids. I hoped it wasn't an omen. I took a tissue from my purse, and after wiping away the dust on the shelf, with a shiver I realized it might be the remnants of fingerprint powder. I placed a framed photo of my daughter Kiera and her horse Amigo with their first-place ribbon, front and center. I flanked it with two panoramic shots, one of my parents' home in Ireland and the other of Kiera and me in a lavender field in France, taken two years ago. I added a small fern in a terra cotta pot. I stood back and surveyed my handiwork. It barely made a dent. The office, like the exterior, had never been updated. The dingy beige walls bore down on me. It would take more than a few mementoes to cheer this place up. Morty's ghost lingered in the creaky joints of the room, just like the rank smell of his cigarette smoke clung to the faded drapes.

I took a bracing gulp of air. I couldn't let this spook me. I needed to begin making some hocus pocus to keep Kiera and me in funds, and at the same time save the paper, and purge a ghost.

TWO

Cynthia and I trudged down the sidewalk. Well, I trudged. Cyn minced. I felt like every inch the clod beside her.

"You survive The Pits?"

"Pardon?"

"Miss Pittman, a.k.a. the Pits. God forbid you move a paperclip; she'd have a nervous breakdown."

I pulled a face. "I prefer Pit Bull. Does she have a first name?"

"Belle, I think."

"Ironic, isn't it?"

Cyn laughed. "You and I are going to be BFFs in no time."

The Blackbird Café was set back from the street, which allowed for a patio out front. A wooden placard over the door bore a giant image of a menacing blackbird. Its beady eyes followed me as I walked in, trailing Cyn. The inside was not what I imagined. I expected country music; I heard the beat of African drums instead. White-washed walls were lined with original artwork. Underneath were tiny cards noting the artist, the medium, and the price. The counter was cluttered with pamphlets advertising gallery openings, stacks of gluten-free cookies, and flaky homemade pies bursting at their seams. Goodies galore exploded near the cash. Mismatched tables shared space with iron bistro chairs with hard seats. "There goes the waistline," I muttered to myself.

A diminutive figure in a black vest and T-shirt appeared behind the counter, half hidden by the biggest espresso machine I had ever seen. Spiky pink and lavender hair poked out from under a gray fedora.

"Cyn, what can I getcha?"

"Decaf, skinny, lactose-free latte with extra foam," Cyn rhymed off.

"And you?" She glanced at me, giving me the once over.

"I need a minute." I searched the bric-a-brac and finally found a blackboard where a scrawled script listed the day's fares and prices. Where was a regular coffee among the lattes, mochas, espressos, avocado wraps, wheat-free muffins, and lentil soups? I wasn't in the mood to decipher chalk-scribbled hieroglyphics. "Coffee, black," was all I could land on.

Amelia grunted, slopped coffee from a nearby pot into a mug and pushed it towards me. She then turned to the espresso machine, and with the comfort of a mad scientist at work in her lab, she concocted Cynthia's drink. Meanwhile, Cyn made introductions. Amelia nodded at me. I thought it might be a greeting, so I smiled back. Best to be friendly in hostile territory.

Cyn was fishing for some bills in her purse when a young buxom blonde dashed past us for the door. Cyn eyed her as she left.

"I do believe that was Tasty Tanya," Cyn said.

"Herself," Amelia barked.

"Strange."

"Even stranger that she had coffee with Clive," Amelia said, one eyebrow raised.

"Clive Carruthers?"

"Yeah, and she didn't look none too happy about it, either."

"I wonder what's up."

Amelia just shrugged.

I had no idea who they were talking about. It was a small town, but I'd been fairly isolated out on a county road for the past decade, and when I did go out it was to stables and horse shows with my daughter.

We made our way over to a table under an enormous portrait of a black-and-white cow and sat in the chairs, which proved to be as uncomfortable as they looked.

"Best place in town to nose out a story," Cyn whispered. "Besides, the latte's to die for." She pulled out her cellphone and jabbed her pointed nails at the keys. "Do you have a Twitter username I can reference in my tweet?" she asked without looking up.

"Uh, no. Who are Tasty Tanya and Clive Carruthers? I think I saw her at the horse show earlier this week when I ran into Lorne, and he offered me the job."

"Interesting. Well, the bombshell is Bruno Malfaro's main squeeze. Tasty Tanya is her stage name." I tried to picture what stage. Cyn continued to text. "You really should, you know. It's a great way to connect to a fan base. I have two hundred thousand followers."

"What?"

"Twitter. You really should tweet."

Two hundred thousand? "What do you tweet?"

"Fashion advice, mainly, from my days as a model. Usually, I post pictures of myself in the outfit of the day."

I get it. Two hundred thousand horny men. "I'll think about it." I had to bring the paper into this century, but I wasn't sure doing it in bursts of 140 characters or less was the way to go about it. However, Cyn's prowess with social media gave me a glimmer of hope. Maybe I could start with a Facebook page. "Do you mean Bruno Malfaro of Malfaro Developments?"

"Yeah, the big cheese himself." She tapped away. "Right now I am announcing your start at the paper. I could post a photo of you to go with it." She eyed me in the same way Amelia had. "The black linen suit is a little conservative, but it does make your auburn hair pop. If you tried a little more color, though, like a scarf around your neck, those green eyes of yours would look amazing."

"Why don't we hold off a while? I'll make a point to dress for the occasion." *Not ever!* "So, why are we interested in Tasty Tanya meeting Clive Carruthers for a coffee?"

Cyn finally dropped her phone onto the table and let out an exasperated sigh. "We really have a lot of work to do to get you up to speed. For starters, one of tomorrow's assignments involves the opening of the Conservation Area donated by none other than Bruno Malfaro. Clive will be there since he's head of The Environmental Defense League. You have heard of them?"

"An environmental group trying to protect conservation lands?"

"Good. So, Clive and Bruno are at loggerheads because Clive believes property developers like Malfaro buy off opposition to get around bylaws so they can build on protected land. I have to wonder why Bruno's fiancée is meeting Clive and if Bruno knows. Sort of smacks of sleeping with the enemy, doesn't it?" She gave me a skeptical look.

"And how is this newsworthy?"

"I don't know yet, but something smells funny. Clive is always after something, and he's an absolute sleazebag. For Tanya to meet him the night before the grand opening …"

"What's Tanya's story?"

Cyn's eyebrows flicked. "She's a stripper—ex-stripper, I should say—who danced her way onto Bruno's pole." She chuckled at her own joke. "Anyway, now she lives in a completely different world and doesn't admit to her old life."

"Could she and Clive just be friends?"

"Oh sweetie, you have been out of the loop, haven't you?"

"I'm a little out of the loop, I admit. But I gather Clive must be after some favor, and he must have some chip to bargain with for Tanya to risk meeting him." I looked up like some expectant ten-year-old. I was rewarded with a spectacular grin.

"You're a quick study. So now we keep our eyes and ears open for any developments from those two." I nodded my understanding. "By the way," she continued, "how do you know Lorne?"

"We met recently at a horse show where my daughter's riding coach was competing. Seems Lorne was in a rush to fill the position, and I'd written some articles for him before. I guess there weren't too many candidates on short notice. Morty sounds like a hard act to follow."

Cyn pressed her lips together. "Good old boy, Morty. He lived and breathed the Weekly, his home away from home. You know he died at his desk?"

"Yeah, it gives me the creeps. What happened?"

"Odd thing. Healthy as a horse, then boom, he just keeled over." She tapped her coffee mug, and her look was far away. "The Pits, I mean Pit Bull. Love that nickname. Anyway, she found him. Saw the office lights on late and went in to check. Stiff as a board. Probably only time she saw him stiff …"

I grimaced.

"Sorry," she said. "First time I ever felt sorry for her. Whole thing's weird. The police spent several hours going over his office. Anyway, the cause of death hasn't been revealed, and no one knows why. Lorne said they've finished the autopsy."

I wasn't sure what to say about the whole macabre affair, but I really needed to lighten things up. "To be continued … what about you? A newspaper photographer. How did you fall into that line of work?" I took a sip of my coffee, now wishing I'd asked for cream, but there was no way I was going to ask the crusty Amelia for anything extra. Overbearing women annoyed me, especially in the hospitality industry, where I thought rule number one was to be hospitable.

Cyn snapped back to attention. "In another lifetime, when I lived in New York City, I was a model. I figured I better learn about the photography business behind the camera before my looks left, and I had no career," Cyn said matter-of-factly. Her looks had definitely not left her. She was exotic, but I couldn't place her origins. She had dark hair, almond-shaped eyes, and a touch of color to her skin that made her complexion glow—a far cry from the pasty white I would turn midwinter. She dressed about a decade too young from what I could see, and I was seeing a lot. "I mean I'm comfortable in front of a camera, but it's more interesting to be on the other side where the real action is."

"Like that oh-so-exciting ratepayers' meeting we're going to tonight?" I asked with a smirk.

"Smartass," she said, and smiled broadly. I felt as if I was gaining an ally at the newspaper already, and for the first time today I felt a sense of calm. It was to be short lived. I had to run to drop Kiera off for her riding lesson at the barn.

❧

"Were you nervous?" Kiera asked as she strapped herself into the passenger seat.

Terrified. "No, just excited. I haven't worked in an office for over a decade." I pulled out of the driveway of our century farmhouse and onto the gravel road. "Are you sure Nacho is fine with driving you home?"

"Mom, you asked me that five times already. He says he's good." She dug lip gloss out of her purse, smeared it on, and rubbed her lips together.

Mmmm, I'd love him to run me home some night. Stop it! At forty, his dark hair, Mediterranean complexion and muscular physique made him Magic Mike material, but Ignacio "Nacho" Rodrigo, besides a coach, was a father figure to Kiera. Under the circumstances, it would be best for everybody, myself included, if I kept my fantasy just that. I didn't want short-term gain for long-term pain. Been there, done that.

I turned into the long driveway which was flanked by two old stone pillars. Each bore a small oval plaque with *Maple Lane Stables* etched in black on cream. Kiera's riding lessons were held inside a huge arena beside a dozen paddocks. I parked under a majestic maple already starting to turn color and snatched my purse out of the back seat.

"You don't have to walk me in."

"It's past the end of the month. September's board is due, remember?" The boarding fees were more than I could afford, but I was determined that because of my divorce, at least this area of Kiera's life would continue to run smoothly for as long as possible. Nacho and his barn had been the only one with next to no drama. It was run by a man who really did have the goods and was honest – a rarity in the world of horse trading, and competition for big money and fame.

The barn smelled of fresh hay, wood shavings, and horse sweat. I gingerly picked my way down the hallway, aware that this was hardly the setting for dressy clothes. I hoped I didn't pick up horse scent and carry it to the meeting with me. At least, I didn't have to worry about horse crap on my trusty black pumps. Nacho kept a fastidiously clean barn.

Kiera turned left towards Amigo's stall and the tack room where she had her locker. I was just about to wave goodbye when she called out, "And I've got a ride to the party and back, too." *What party?* She darted into the tack room before I could launch an inquisition. *Teenagers.* I shrugged off my irritation for the moment and headed for the viewing room where I knew I'd find my invoice.

As I swung the door open, I was almost broadsided by a cement truck of a man who barged past me without a word. He barreled down the aisle, a shock of white hair and full-length camel-hair coat disappearing around the corner, before I could even catch my breath. There was something familiar about him I couldn't place, but my glance had been too brief. I tugged my shirt down and straightened my sleeves, wishing once again that I was back in jeans and a T- shirt: much more my style and about twenty times more comfortable than the tight blouse and belt.

Nacho was in the arena exercising Pinball, a seventeen-hand, dark bay Warmblood. The muscles of the stallion rippled as horse and rider leaped effortlessly over frighteningly high jumps in an equestrian ballet. I caught Nacho's eye as he turned smoothly and passed by the viewing room window. I melted at the sight of dimples that formed in his tanned cheeks when he smiled at me. And then he winked. *Damn, I hope I'm not drooling.*

Without warning, Nacho and Pinball galloped fiercely for the door. Nacho leaped off Pinball in one fluid movement and ran, gesticulating wildly. Pinball trotted away, steam rising from his rump. I could not see anyone else, but I could hear the muffled timbre of Nacho's voice. Any second, I expected steam to rise off Nacho, too. I had never heard him irate before. Peeping Tom that I am, I pressed closer to the glass and caught the tail end of his words.

"… ruined. I will stop you, whatever it takes!"

Yikes. Time to leave. I pushed away from the glass, grabbed the invoice envelope out of the tray, and scurried out of the room. I didn't even bother to try and find Kiera to say goodbye. She was off in her own world now, anyway.

THREE

The morning sun was just peeping through orange and yellow tinged trees. I had already been up for ages dithering over last-minute details and, of course, wardrobe. I decided on a short plaid blazer and dark brown wool pants. Perfect autumn attire, I thought, for the opening of a Conservation Area. I decided to wear my hair down instead of pinned up in a claw clip as I often do.

"Kiera, get a move on. It's already seven! I told Cyn we would be at her place by ten after," I yelled to the closed bedroom door.

"I know. This so sucks," came the cranky voice that only a freshly woken seventeen-year-old can deliver. *Give me strength,* I thought, quietly cursing Will, my ex, for leaving me to cope alone.

When she appeared in the kitchen a few minutes later, Kiera looked surprisingly polished, her sleek blonde hair tied into a ponytail, her lean legs clad in tight pants and knee-high boots, a sharp contrast to her jagged mood.

"Why do you have to work weekends? I thought you were the boss. Can't other people do the reporting?"

This was one of those times when I thought of recording her whiny voice. Years from now, I could lock her in her room and make her listen to herself. Poetic justice. Instead, I conjured up an extra dose of patience, reminding myself that this, too, would pass.

"That's the way it is with small-town newspapers. They don't have the budget for a huge staff. The editor has to wear many hats."

"I don't see why I can't have the car. You had it last night."

"I was working, Kiera. At the job I took to keep you in riding lessons, remember?" And I was at the most boring meeting I'd ever attended. The only useful tidbit was that Council was making significant cuts in funding to environmental groups.

"But it's so early, I don't have to be there for another two hours."

"You could have tried coming home from the party a little earlier, too."

That comment got another scowl. I slammed my purse down on the counter and fished around in it for my car keys. So much for patience in the morning. I'd tried. "I won't be home till later this afternoon. Cyn and I have lots to cover. You'll have to ask Rena to drive you home if Nacho can't do it."

"Whatever."

Something was definitely bothering Kiera, more than normal teenage angst, and I wondered if it had anything to do with Nacho's explosion the afternoon before. The secret with Kiera though, was to wait. At some point she would end up telling me. Today I chose to ignore my own advice. "So, how was the lesson?"

"It sucked! Mom, I am so unhappy." Tears gathered in her eyes.

My heart sank. "When did this start? I thought things were going so well."

"Me, too, but in the last few weeks ... I don't know. I must suck as a rider. Nacho even lowered some of the jumps. He acts like he doesn't care if I show or not."

"Let's not leap to conclusions. You don't suck at riding or Nacho wouldn't bother with you. You're one of the youngest riders at an A-circuit barn, and he is one of the top equestrians in the country. Why don't we have a talk with him and find out if there's a problem?"

Nacho was a former Olympic rider on the Argentinean show jumping team. He'd traveled the world training horses before putting down roots in the County. Clients trucked their horses miles, for only a few hours with the renowned coach and trainer. He always delivered for both riders and their horses with his almost sixth sense of what worked. I also knew Nacho wouldn't waste his time on Kiera if he didn't see promise in her. He had always been a straight shooter.

"Will you talk to him? I can't do it." She wiped the tears off her cheeks and started smearing peanut butter onto the bagel I'd set out.

"Of course," I assured her. *And the sooner the better.* My kid didn't need trouble at the barn. It was her haven and her motivation to keep going on. It had saved her from depression and things I preferred not to think about. "You'd better eat that in the car, honey. I don't want to be late."

Cyn was more than ready when we swung by her place. She bounded outside, molded into skin-tight jeans, low-cut striped top, and black leather booties with three-inch spike heels.

"I'm a morning person," she said as she folded herself into the back seat. She tucked her long dark mane behind her ears and pulled a pair of Ray Bans out of her sac. "But I'm really good at night, too." She winked before she pushed on her glasses. I glanced at Kiera, sitting beside me in the front. She rolled her eyes. I gave her the evil eye. Translation: keep your mouth shut.

"Unfortunately, neither Kiera nor I are morning people," I said, and slipped the car into reverse to back out of the driveway of Cynthia's village bungalow.

By the time we reached the stables it was seven-thirty, and the sun was not quite halfway up the trunks of the feathery white pines that lined the drive. We passed the outdoor sand ring and open paddocks. A miniature donkey brayed a rude welcome from behind a split rail fence. A few annoying guinea fowl had the misconception that they owned the driveway, and I found myself tapping the steering wheel while I waited for them to clear the path. One car was already parked outside the barn next to a horse trailer.

"Looks like Rena is here already."

"Mom, that's a Mercedes. No way it's Rena's. Anyway, she doesn't start till eight on weekends."

It was odd that someone other than an employee would be here before the horses were fed and turned out. "I'll come in with you just to make sure everything's fine," I said, turning off the car engine.

"I can take care of myself, Mom."

"I'm sure you can." I opened the car door anyway.

Then we heard it: a banging sound from the barn, and the distinct whinnying of an agitated horse close by. I frowned. "Something's not right."

Even Kiera went from disgruntled to worried. "It sounds like horses kicking in their stalls. Something must be upsetting them." She flung open the passenger door and hurtled out of the car.

The white barn door was closed. "This sounds like a riot," I murmured, as we drew closer to the sounds of even more horses in a chaotic chorus. I held back. I'm not big on being stampeded, which is what I feared.

"We're not going to know if we don't look," said Cyn, boldly flipping the latch on the door.

"Maybe you should …" I didn't get the sentence finished before the door burst open, smashing into Cyn and throwing her to the ground. Out charged a huge chestnut horse as if on fire. He bolted down the lane between the paddocks, bucking and whinnying. Kiera screamed. I gasped. Cyn yelled "Oof!" I leaped to where she was lying in the muck.

"Oh my God, Cyn, are you all right? Are you hurt?"

She was panting, too stunned to reply. I dropped to the ground and gently touched her shoulder. "Are you okay?" She looked up at me and managed a nod.

"So sorry Cyn. Mom, I'm going to grab Dante to make sure he doesn't hurt himself," Kiera said and fled towards the paddocks.

"Is that a good idea?" I called after her. "He looked crazy."

"I have to get him locked into his paddock so he doesn't take off down the road."

I helped Cyn to sit up and assess the damage. Her wrist was sore from where the door had hit it. It wasn't broken, though, and by a sheer miracle the door hadn't slammed into her head.

"Lucky the ground is soft here," she said, "but look at my jeans! Crap, there's mud and hay all over them."

It wasn't only mud, but I wasn't going to elaborate. "I'm sure they'll wash up."

"But they're brand new! And they're 'rag&bone'."

"You could have been killed by a rampaging horse and you're worried about your jeans?" I offered her a hand. "Come on. We should move away from the door just in case." She grunted as she stood.

Kiera raced up to us carrying a saddle. "Dante's calmer now. He went into the paddock and started grazing. But it's weird that he was partially tacked up. Mom, I'm going to check on Amigo."

"Not alone, you're not. Something's still bothering those horses." I looked at Cyn. "Do you want to wait for us in the car?"

"Hell no. I want to know what's going on."

I had to give it to her; she's a trooper. Lesser women would have tottered off on their three-inch heels, never to return.

"This time I go in first. And watch where you're walking in those kamikaze things," I said, pointing at her booties.

"Hey, careful what you say about the Louboutins."

The troops fell in behind me. The only source of light was the weak sunlight through the windows. It took a minute for our eyes to adjust to the dimness. I walked warily, checking the shadows in every corner. Any second now I expected more crazed horses to charge down the aisle and wipe us out. I fought the urge to turn back.

Kiera, bringing up the rear, made a left-hand turn and reached for a bank of switches. Light flooded the aisle and stalls on that side of the barn. It seemed to have a calming effect on the animals although there was still a lot of foot stomping.

"Amigo's down here," she said, and headed off. Cyn followed where it was light, her heels clicking on the cement floor.

"Okay, I'm going to the other side to check on the others." I tried to sound more confident than I felt. Horses make me nervous. They're huge and powerful, and I lack Kiera's self-assurance around them. And this wasn't a barn full of old nags: they were the crème de la crème, the rock stars, the ones skilled enough to do the National and Grand Prix circuits. I crept along, trying to make as little noise as possible, not wanting to further upset these expensive, high-strung animals.

This hallway was still shrouded in early morning shadows. Small slivers of light slithered through cracks in an exterior door, but the hall to the right loomed in absolute darkness. I inched my way past the viewing room and tack room. There were still snorts, whinnying and an occasional staccato burst of banging on stall walls. Goosebumps covered my arms and I shivered.

Something soft brushed my leg, and I muffled a scream. I stumbled over a lump and careened into the wall, knocking the wind out of myself. Until then, I hadn't realized I'd been holding my breath. I looked down and slumped with relief.

"Fred, you silly cat, you scared me half to death." I reached out to pet him, but he gave me the evil eye. He stalked away, tail twitching.

I rounded the next corner and stopped dead in my tracks. I must have made some noise I wasn't aware of because a voice called out to ask if I was okay. I could barely speak. "D … don't come down here. Stay there … where you are. P … please."

I groped blindly for a light switch and finally located one on the wall to my right.

Oh my God, this isn't happening. I stared, openmouthed, hoping it was a hallucination, something I'd conjured up out of the shadows and my fear. But no, it was real, and suddenly it was very clear what had upset the horses. In the exact center of the aisle, the body of a man dangled, suspended from the rafters, arms hanging limply at his sides. He wore riding pants, and leather riding boots but no helmet. Leather reins were wrapped around his neck and ran upwards toward a ceiling rafter. The man appeared to be maybe mid-sixties. A lock of pale hair hung over his forehead, partially hiding his face. His head was cocked at an odd angle. The blood had drained from his face, his lips appearing dark blue in comparison. He was so pale, so colorless. Definitely dead.

I took a whole bunch of deep breaths. A million thoughts raced through my mind. *Who is he? Was it suicide? Why here? Should I call the police? Or Nacho?* And stupid things like, *if I touch him, will the police think I killed him?* And, *if I get him down, could he start breathing again?* I walked in small circles focusing on only my feet. I stopped abruptly. I knew what I had to do—keep my daughter away.

Suddenly Cyn was behind me. "Looks like we know why that horse was loose."

"How can you be so cool?" For the first time, I noticed my hands were shaking. Actually, my entire body was quaking with shock.

"Unfortunately, I've seen it before. Death, I mean. And I'm not really all that cool ... because I know him."

"*What?*"

"Mom?" I snapped to attention. Kiera was calling from the other side of the barn.

"Stay there, honey. I'll be right there."

She must have heard something in my voice. "What's wrong?"

"Be there in a sec." I looked at Cyn and silently asked the question.

She leveled a look at me. "It's Bruno Malfaro."

FOUR

"**B**runo Malfaro? The developer we were talking about last night?"

"One and the same."

I grabbed Cyn's arm. "Wait here a sec. I've got to make sure Kiera doesn't come wandering down this aisle."

I tore off in the direction of Amigo's stall. Kiera was still brushing her horse, talking to him in soothing words.

"Whose horse was that, the one that was loose?" I asked as calmly as my racing heart would allow.

"Dante? He belongs to Marco's grandfather."

Like I was supposed to know who Marco was. I looked at her questioningly.

"Marco, Mom. Marco Malfaro's only been Heather's boyfriend for, like, six months." She made a face.

Right. I'd forgotten that Kiera's best friend had been dating a boy named Marco, and that meant Marco's grandfather must be Bruno Malfaro.

"Anyway," she went on, "Marco grooms and exercises Dante, but I never see his grandfather ride him. He probably comes during the day when I'm at school." She stopped brushing and stared at me suspiciously. "Why? What's happened? Is Marco hurt? Heather will freak."

"No, no." I was quick to placate her. "Nothing's happened to Marco. There's an older gentleman … he's been hurt. I have to call 911."

"Is he going to be okay?"

I shook my head. "I don't think so, sweetheart. But you stay here, okay? I don't want you to go down there." For once she didn't challenge me, and I gave a quick but silent word of thanks heavenward. As I walked back to the grisly scene, I pulled out my cellphone with shaking hands and dialed 911, giving all the information as I knew it. Then I phoned Nacho, but I got his voicemail. I left a message telling him I was at the barn and that he should come as soon as he could. With any luck, he was already on his way.

I returned to where Bruno Malfaro's body still hung from the rafter and came to an abrupt halt. "Cyn! For Heaven's sake, what are you doing?"

Cyn lowered her camera and looked at me. "My job."

"Photos, Cyn? It seems so tasteless. And we could never publish them. Ick!"

Cynthia rolled her eyes. "Give me some credit. I was afraid people might show up and disturb things before the police could get here." She reviewed her shots on the tiny camera screen, making little grunts of satisfaction.

A voice called out and we both jumped.

"Nacho? Is that you?" The stable manager's voice echoed through the halls. "Sorry I'm late. I'll get the rest of the guys out."

Clearly, Rena thought Nacho was here. I scooted around the corner before she got too far.

"Rena, it's me, Darcy Dillon," I called out. "Kiera's Mom. It's just me, Kiera, and my colleague here." *And the dead guy.* "Can I have a quick word with you?" I walked quickly toward where I had heard her voice.

Rena was about twenty-nine, a slender blonde who'd had a love affair with horses most of her life. She was thrilled to be in a stable the caliber of Maple Lane. Her ambition was to breed and train horses, and she was eager to learn all she could from Nacho. She called him "the best mentor and jumper ever." She looked at me sideways as I approached. "Sure," she said cautiously. "What's going on? Has something happened to Nacho?"

"No, Nacho's fine as far as I know, but I do have something disturbing to tell you." I brought her up to speed, wording it as delicately as I could.

"Mr. Malfaro? I can't believe it." Suddenly, she bolted, and I ran after her. She went straight for the area where Bruno had apparently hung himself. "He's d ... dead!" Her hands flew to her face, and she spun around.

"I'm afraid so. Rena, do you know any reason why he might have wanted to kill himself?"

"No! I just saw him last night. I mean, he was pissed at something, but *this* ... this just doesn't make any sense."

My mind went back to the scene I had witnessed yesterday. Was Bruno the man Nacho had been yelling at? Did that mean Nacho was somehow involved in what happened next? I didn't like the sound of this at all. Over the past two years, Nacho had become the most important part of Kiera's life and, by extension, mine. I felt an urgent need to find Nacho and press him for details.

I put an arm around Rena's shoulder and led her away from the scene. But I desperately wanted to know more, so I asked her to elaborate.

"Nacho and Mr. Malfaro had been arguing. I didn't really hear their conversation. Mr. M. is always so rude to everyone. I don't know how Nacho has put up with him for so long. I'd have told him to leave and take his damn horse with him."

I sensed there was more, but the barn door opened then, letting in a triangle of light and the sound of screaming sirens. A good-looking, sandy haired man strode towards us. He had a casual, broken-in feel about him. I liked the look of him right away. His confident gait and upright carriage made me think of Game of Thrones, where Jon Snow strode in, rescued the little lady and took her off to a little castle in Winterfell in the northern woods. This was a man who would have your back. Even Rena looked impressed.

"It's Sheriff Armstrong," Rena said.

I signaled him with a wave of my hand, and he closed the gap in a few long strides.

"Hi," I said. "I'm Darcy Dillon. I made the call to 911. This is Rena, the barn manager."

If he had been wearing a hat, he would have tipped it. "Dillon?" His eyes narrowed as he moved the name around in his brain. He seemed to be about to say something else when Cyn interrupted.

"Well, hey there, Sheriff. I see the posse's arrived." Then she grinned. "How are ya, Adam?"

"Good, Cyn. I didn't expect the press to be here so soon. You got insider information or something?"

She explained the circumstances which had brought her, Kiera and me to the barn, and then she introduced me as the newly hired editor of the Yorkdale Weekly. Sheriff Armstrong asked her and Rena to wait in the viewing room and asked me to take him to the scene since I'd been the one to make the 911 call after discovering the body.

I refrained from looking directly at Bruno, although his silhouette was always visible, at least, from the corner of my eye as I watched the sheriff go about his business. He clicked on a pen and wrote something down in a pint-sized notebook. He seemed to be totally in his cop zone. I didn't know how many times he'd seen corpses, but he certainly handled it with aplomb.

"I'd like Rena to use the other door to remove these horses out of here. Not just for safety's sake but for theirs. Horses are very sensitive to death. There will be a fair amount of commotion that can be unsettling for them."

"I'll tell her. It will give her something else to focus on. She's pretty shaken up."

"Hopefully, she can keep it together long enough to get the job done. We can't move the body till the Medical Examiner does his thing."

"I hope so, too. I certainly don't want my daughter moving the horses. She's only seventeen. She shouldn't have to deal with this ... this scene."

"I get that. I wouldn't want my son to go through this, either. Not ever."

I looked into his unperturbed face. "So, how do you know so much about horses?"

"Grew up on a farm. Always had horses. Excuse me." He spoke briefly into the two-way radio that was clipped to his lapel, then looked back at me. "I'm sure you want to get your daughter home, but I need to ask her a few questions and get statements from you and Cyn. Sorry about that, but I'll be as quick as I can."

"Kiera normally works on Saturday mornings. The horses will still need exercising." I could feel the onset of a mini panic attack. I wanted my kid out of here, but I knew her first priority would be the horses.

"I'm going to keep activity around here to a minimum today. We have to thoroughly search the area so I'd rather Kiera went home when we're done interviewing her. I'll have a word with Nacho about letting her take the day off. Speaking of Nacho, where is he?"

Well, wasn't that the question of the hour. "Sorry, I don't know. I've tried to call him, but he's not picking up." A scowl crossed Armstrong's face that made me nervous for Nacho. "He could just be sleeping in, or already on his way in. Um, Sheriff, why do we have to give statements? This is a suicide, isn't it? We can't possibly know what happened that Bruno Malfaro would want to hang himself."

"Fair enough question. What we have here is called a 'suspicious death'. We can't rule anything out. Once the ME gets here, we should have a clearer picture of exactly what happened. I wouldn't worry about it; it's procedure."

But worried I was. Why would a guy as successful as Bruno want to kill himself? Could it have anything to do with his girlfriend's rendezvous with Clive Carruthers? But what bothered me most was the argument between him and Nacho.

Two uniformed cops slipped past me, one carrying a roll of yellow caution tape, the other carrying a professional-looking camera, much like Cyn's. The first one proceeded to tape off the area as per Sheriff Armstrong's orders, securing the entire corridor, as well as the corpse. The second began snapping shots of the scene. The sheriff also charged them with the collection of evidence in the immediate area.

"Why evidence?"

"Routine."

I began to wonder if there was something going on that I wasn't aware of. It seemed like overkill for a case of suicide.

I checked my watch. There was no way Cyn and I were going to make it to the qualifying races now, and we were due at the opening of the Conservation Area in three hours. Clearly, interviewing the donor of the land was out of the question since the man happened to be hanging from the rafters about fifty yards from where I stood.

Where the heck was Nacho? I felt like a lunatic stalker, but I redialed his number, only to get voicemail again. I hoped he was just holed up with the flavor of the month, although another part of me hoped that wasn't the case. Could something have happened to him related to Malfaro's death? Did Bruno go after Nacho in the wake of their fight, and then commit suicide? Or worse, could Nacho be somehow responsible for what had happened here? My thoughts were making me crazy, and I tore around the corner as if I could leave them behind.

Cyn was entertaining Kiera in Amigo's stall. It became apparent, listening to their conversation, that Cyn wasn't just a pretty face; she was a fairly worldly woman. Finally, Kiera spotted me.

"Mom! Did you know that Cynthia was a model for Victoria's Secret? She went to photo shoots in the Bahamas and Antigua! I never met anyone before who was a model."

"I didn't know, but I bet Cyn's got all kinds of interesting stories to tell." So far, she'd done a great job distracting my daughter from the horror in the barn, and I would have to remember to thank her later.

"And the awesome part is she thinks I have the body and face to model! She said I could do that to pay for my horse shows. That's so whack!"

Whoa! I hadn't counted on that. I flashed a look at Cyn. "We'll talk about that later, okay?" Kiera deflated right there in front of me.

"See? I told you. I knew she'd never let me do it," she said, addressing Cyn.

"Not fair, Kiera. This is not the time or place to discuss it, but we will. I promise." Her eyes glazed over. I knew I'd lost her attention.

"How long before I can leave? I don't want to hang around here now. It's gross."

So, Cyn had told her about Bruno Malfaro—good. One less thing for me to wrestle with.

"I don't blame you, honey. Sheriff Armstrong said he would make it fairly quick, but he needs to ask you a few questions before you go." I hoped he was a man of his word. I wanted her long gone before they took the body out in a black vinyl bag.

"I can't help thinking about Marco. I couldn't imagine how I'd feel if Grandpa died this way." Kiera pushed past me. "Anyway, let's get this over with, okay? I just want to go home."

I wasn't about to let my kid face questioning on her own, so we sat across the table from Sheriff Armstrong on a well-worn leather couch. Armstrong had usurped the viewing room for his purposes.

Kiera was nervous; she played with her hair, constantly twirling the ponytail with her index finger. I felt crummy that I couldn't protect her from this.

"When were you last at the barn before today?" he began.

"Last night."

"Was that the last time you saw Mr. Rodrigo?"

"Yes, he drove me home. My mom had the car." She slid a look in my direction.

"And do you remember what time that was exactly?"

"Seven," said Kiera with conviction.

"Was the barn closed at that time?"

"No. The barn stays open till eight-thirty, except for Sundays, when it closes at six. But lessons were over for the day."

"Was anyone else here when you left?"

"I don't know. I don't remember," Kiera said, biting on her bottom lip.

"Who makes sure the barn is secure for the night?"

"Usually Nacho, or if it's not him, the last person out is supposed to turn out the lights and close the doors."

"Would Mr. Rodrigo have come back last night?"

I definitely did not like where this was going. Was Nacho actually under suspicion of something?

Kiera squirmed in her seat. "I don't know where he was going after he dropped me off, but everybody here is really good about closing up. I mean, the horses are really expensive. So if Nacho didn't do it, it was probably Rena."

"Thanks, Kiera," Sheriff Armstrong said, smiling now. "I know this isn't easy. Remember not to mention this to anybody, okay? We still have to notify Mr. Malfaro's family. I'll let your mother know when it becomes public knowledge. Now, do you mind waiting outside while I talk to your mother alone? Then you two can go."

I dug the car keys out of my purse and handed them to Kiera.

"You can take the car, honey." I briefly explained to Armstrong that I had only stopped at the barn on the way to an appointment, and that I hadn't really planned on going home. Cyn and I had a job to do.

"But how will you and Cyn get back?" Kiera asked.

"Don't worry about us. We'll call a taxi or something. Just get home. And drive carefully."

"I'll make sure your mom isn't stuck for a ride," said Armstrong. "Walk your daughter to the car, if you like. I'll talk to Rena in the meantime." I was really starting to like this guy. A class act.

I flashed him a smile. "Thanks." I led the way through the maze of horse stalls, making sure Kiera didn't take a wrong turn and wind up face-to-face with Bruno. At the car I gave her a quick hug as my emotions got the better of me, but she was having none of it. She shook me off and dropped into the front seat, leaving me to get back to being a newswoman instead of a worried mother.

When I returned, Cyn was reviewing the photos on her digital camera. "I've got lots. Pictures of Bruno, the barn, the stalls inside and out, just in case they're needed. You never know." She popped out the memory card. "Do you have a pencil or something not permanent?"

I rifled around in my purse. "Sorry, I only have this," I said, and held up a pen.

"It'll have to do." I watched Cyn write the date and then the initials B.M. on her memory card.

B.M.? "Oh my God." An epiphany exploded in my head. Morty wasn't tracking his bowel movements. Bruno Malfaro had been his last appointment. Ever.

FIVE

Before Cyn and I had much of a chance to say anything to Sheriff Armstrong, the Medical Examiner tapped on the viewing room door and summoned him to follow. I got up and paced, too agitated to sit still while we waited. I circled the viewing room. A small desk and rolling chair, a large filing cabinet, and one vinyl guest chair pretty much filled one corner of the room. Nacho's laptop sat open on the desk. Two comfy leather couches and a picnic table overlooked the arena, while a side wall contained a counter with microwave and small flat screen TV. The walls were covered in framed photos of prize horses and their owners, as well as several shots of Nacho at the Summer Olympics.

"Cyn?" I called, and she clicked her way over to where I stood in front of Nacho's desk. "Um, Nacho's computer is open, and it's on. Think you could watch my back while I have a peek?"

She rubbed her hands together in glee. "Ooh, you've got *cojones*. This is gonna be fun."

"I'm just trying to find out where he is."

"By snooping. I love it."

"Just go stand by the door and give me some sort of signal if someone comes, okay?"

I touched the keys and found Gmail logged on and open.

Unusual. Most people logged off; Nacho may have been in a hurry when he left. My ears were tuned for the slightest sound, and my palms dampened as I clicked the mouse on his Inbox.

The most recent message was from '*tastygirl*' and read: "I'm alone. Hurry before I start without you." No signature, not even initials. I tried to control my imagination. It could explain why Nacho had rushed off without shutting down his laptop. And maybe he slept in, or exhausted himself. There were a slew of emails from tack shops, the vet, and horse associations, but I was drawn to the more provocative conversation thread, of course.

I took a gulp of air and clicked on the Sent box, realizing just how badly I was invading his privacy. I wondered if this career in reporting the news was going to mean all my morals would be compromised. I was a little bit surprised that my fingers didn't drop off immediately from committing a criminal act.

I scanned the messages, aware that my subterfuge could be caught out any second now. The theme was the same in each: Nacho had had it with the bastard. I had no idea who the bastard was. And then my heart sank. "Your brute of a boyfriend is taken care of, or should I say husband-to-be. Now I'll take care of you." What did that mean? Taken care of. By *taken care of* did Nacho mean *dead*? It seemed obvious: Bruno had to be the brute he referred to, given their argument the day before. By extension, that made the email correspondent, '*tastygirl*', Tasty Tanya. Did Nacho drive Bruno to kill himself? Or, worse than that, had Nacho had a direct hand in his death? I felt sick.

I felt even sicker when I read the reply. "Think of the ring as a financial investment. I have a plan to have my cake and eat it too." Before I could speculate further, I heard voices. I put things back how I found them and scooted over to the couch. Cyn peeked over her shoulder and gave the high sign. I nodded.

The paramedics had arrived to take Bruno away. I could hear the rattle of the metal gurney as its wheels clacked on the concrete floor. Cyn wanted to go and snap a few shots, so I followed her out the door. Another rush of the heebie-jeebies racked my body when I spied the black bag being lifted up and strapped to the table.

I whispered in Cyn's ear. "What do you think the chances are the ME will talk to us?"

"Well, let's just see what I can do to convince him, shall we?" She sauntered away and returned less than a minute later with the gray-haired Dr. Sermer, who couldn't seem to take his eyes off her cleavage.

"The only thing I can give you right now is what I told Sheriff Armstrong. Time of death was at least twelve hours ago, sometime last evening."

I did some quick mental math and realized that it had probably happened shortly after Kiera had taken her lesson. I wished I could remember when that last email had been sent to *tastygirl*.

"And I can't determine cause of death until after the autopsy," Sermer continued. "Anything at this point is strictly assumption. And that information will go directly to the Sheriff's department, not to a reporter." He coughed and looked at us sternly. Clearly, the cleavage wasn't getting us any leverage.

"You mean it's not by strangulation, or asphyxiation, or whatever you call death by hanging?" I asked, hoping for a crumb.

The good doctor shrugged and made a face that seemed to indicate this wasn't quite an open-and-shut case. "No comment," he said. He gave us a flourish and with a sheepish grin backed out with a gentlemanly, "Ladies."

Within minutes Sheriff Armstrong returned. "Darcy, Cyn, I'll need your statements now," he said. "After that, I can give you a ride back to town, or home, or wherever you are going. Darcy, you first?"

This was a first for me. I'd never been interrogated by police before, but Adam Armstrong exuded such an air of competence and respect that I was hardly flustered. In fact, I almost lost my train of thought while looking into those clear blue eyes. I explained how I'd come upon the body and the upset the whole business had caused the horses, but I skipped over the unpleasant scene I'd witnessed at the barn the day before. Omitting the information wasn't sitting all that well with me, but, after all, I had not seen who was arguing with Nacho. At least, that's what I told myself. I had no intention of pointing the finger of guilt in Nacho's direction until I'd had a chance to talk to him first. Still, omitting information made me feel shifty. Both my butt and my conscience squirmed somewhat under the Sheriff's cool gaze. I got out of the room and let out a huge sigh.

I waited outside the viewing room while Cyn spoke with Armstrong, but I didn't have to wait long. She couldn't tell him anything he didn't already know.

We climbed into the Sheriff's cruiser under a bright blue sky. At least, the day had *that* going for it. It seemed odd to see the guinea fowl pecking away and the horses idly grazing in their paddocks as if nothing had happened.

"You're on Ridge Road, is that right?" the Sheriff said.

"You know?"

"Husband's last name Van Dyke?"

"Ex-husband now," I corrected him. Had we met before? With those clear blue eyes and that rugged jaw, I'm sure I would have remembered him. "How do you know so much about me?"

"Oh, we police have our ways," he replied with a smirk. "Actually, my son Andrew is in the same grade as your daughter. I knew your name had a familiar ring." Then he added, "It's my business to be familiar with all the farms around here."

"Farms are police business? Do tell."

"Weed. Marijuana grow-ops proliferating at an alarming rate. Inside, outside, doesn't matter. We have to monitor activity on farmland as well as in town. You know those low-flying planes that are decked out with aerials, look like spy planes?" I nodded. "Reconnaissance."

"Wow. The things you learn," I said. I turned around in my seat and spoke to Cyn. "Did you know about that?"

"Yup. Morty reported a few busts."

"Not enough, though," said the Sheriff. "I hope you won't be quite so timid."

"Darcy's not afraid, Adam. She has balls!"

I wasn't sure what I was supposed to not be afraid of, but it did occur to me that suddenly I had found myself involved with death and drugs, both in the same day.

"Speaking of Morty," I said, "have you heard any news on his cause of death? I heard there was an autopsy."

"Why do you ask?" he said, looking at me intently.

"I hadn't received any news how he died. It's natural to be curious, seeing as I am taking over his position at the paper, and I should report to our readership."

The Sheriff nodded in understanding. Just when I thought he was going to say something, my cellphone rang.

I looked at the number and inwardly cringed. I hit 'ignore' and dropped the phone back in my purse. It rang again, and Armstrong gave me the eye.

"Aren't you going to answer that?"

"Oh … sure. I didn't want to be rude." He waved away my apology, an invitation to go ahead with the call. I answered, trying to sound as casual as possible.

"*Mi amiga*," Nacho crooned.

"What? Can you hear me? Hello, can you hear me now?" I tilted my head as if to get a better signal. "I'll have to call you back on the land line in a few minutes," I shouted, then hit 'end'. "Bad reception," I lied. The heat rose in a flush on my face. Could they tell?

The cruiser rolled up my driveway and stopped by the side porch. I leaped from the car. "Thanks for the lift, Sheriff."

"Call me Adam. I think we're going to be seeing a lot of each other."

I smiled my thanks. "Cyn, I'll meet you at The Blackbird at eleven-thirty, okay?"

"Sure, we can ..."

But I'd already turned to go. "Hey! What's the rush?" Cyn called, as she tucked herself into the front seat I'd vacated.

We really had to figure out a system of signals to each other. "Gotta pee," I lied again. Every second that passed ratcheted up my worry threshold. I waved and did a pretend potty dance for dramatic effect and dashed to the side door. I had to speak to Nacho—now!

Six

As soon as I got in the door, I peeked out the window to ensure the Sheriff was pulling away before I redialed.

"Darcy, what's up?" Even in these circumstances Nacho's deep voice managed to unnerve me. Something in the way his accent reinvented my name made it sound exotic ... even sexy. *Damn, how could I think like this now?*

"Where the hell have you been?" I was clutching the receiver so hard my knuckles turned white. I hadn't meant to sound so shrill, but the emotion I'd been holding back all morning finally broke through the dam. "Everyone's been looking for you!"

"Why? What's going on?"

"I don't want to talk about it over the phone. Can you swing by my house?"

"You're worrying me."

"You *should* be worried. And I probably shouldn't be talking to you, but you're my friend and I want to help. Are you close by?"

"On Seventeenth, close to the barn."

"Don't go there. Come straight here. Promise?"

"I'll be there in less than five minutes," he assured me, and we disconnected.

I pulled the coffee maker toward me and filled the reservoir with water. As I scooped coffee into the filter, my hand shook so badly that grounds spilled onto the counter. I growled my annoyance and wiped them up, tossing the dishcloth into the sink.

"Hey, Mom."

I swung around. My own kid had startled me half to death. I was really going to have to get a grip before Nacho got here. Kiera peered at me with a puzzled look on her face. It had only been a couple of hours, but I thought she already looked older, maybe just a bit wiser. Perhaps it was just a mother's paranoia.

"How are you doing, honey? Sorry you had to go through that."

"I'm fine, Mom. I feel bad that Mr. Malfaro's dead and all, but I didn't really know him. It's Marco I feel sorry for." Her cellphone chirped, and she pulled it from her jeans pocket. She'd let her hair out of the ponytail, and it fell across her face, hiding her expression. She punched a few letters and pocketed the phone.

"You're not telling anyone what happened, are you?"

"I'm not a moron, Mom. I heard what Sheriff Armstrong said."

Why do teenage girls have to be so touchy? I thought back to when I was a teenager and all the crap I probably put my own parents through, and my indignation quickly passed. What goes around comes around.

"I think I'd like to model the way Cyn did. It sounds cool, and it would pay for my shows."

Damn Cyn for bringing up the subject. "It's a rough business, especially for young girls. They get chewed up and spit out."

"I can handle myself. I'm not a little kid." The petulant look on her face reminded me of her when she was four.

"No one said you were. I just don't want you to get hurt."

"Hurt?"

"That business is very competitive, and the people in it are predatory."

"You don't think I'm pretty enough, do you?" It was a statement, not a question. *Why does she always go there?*

"That's not what I'm saying at all! You're gorgeous. Cyn wouldn't have even suggested it if you weren't. Anyway, right now your priorities should be school and riding, not working for a living. There's lots of time for working."

"But I'm already seventeen. I knew you'd never understand." She snatched a bag of chips out of the cupboard and slammed the door.

I heard the crunch of gravel and peeked outside. Nacho's pick-up truck was coming up the driveway. "We'll talk later. I have something I've got to do."

More slamming—this time the fridge door after she pulled out a can of Coke. The doorbell rang. Kiera looked out the window. "What's Nacho doing here?"

"He doesn't know about Mr. Malfaro yet. I'm going to break the news."

She made a face. "What? I can't tell my friends, but you can?"

"This is different? It's his place, and it would be terrible to walk in there without a heads-up. He'll find out soon enough anyway."

"Sucks to be you."

Ain't that the truth.

Kiera ran to the door and opened it wide.

"Hey, *bonita*. You finished your riding already?"

"Nope. Not yet. But I gotta go. Mom wants to talk to you. Alone." She high-fived him and bounded up the stairs like a long-legged foal. I wanted to follow her, hide under my bed. Not a great quality for a news editor

I was alone with Nacho in tight quarters. That six-foot frame clad in tight everything made the temperature rise about twenty degrees in the foyer. Yummy didn't begin to describe the effect he had on me. Yummy and now something else—suspicious. I faced him and for a second allowed myself to drown in those gorgeous chocolate eyes of his. I hoped he couldn't read my mind; I was probably looking at him like he was a prize cupcake.

"Am I in trouble? Should I come in?" His face wore a cocktail of emotions.

His words shook me out of my trance. Time to get down to business.

"There's no easy way to break this to you, Nacho, but Bruno Malfaro is dead." I couldn't get a handle on the look that flitted across his features—shock, and then what? Relief? Maybe.

"How? How do you know?"

"There's more and it's not pleasant since it involves your barn ..."

"What?" His eyebrows shot up and his shoulders tensed.

"It sucks, as Kiera would say, to tell you this ... suicide ... hanging by his reins in the corridor by his horse's stall." Nacho stood completely still and silent, as if frozen, except for a slight twitch in his eye. Was he was searching for words? Thinking back to last night? I couldn't tell so I pressed on. "Nacho, why weren't you answering your phone? Everyone—especially the police—was wondering where you were."

He inhaled sharply and let the air out slowly. "I was somewhere I shouldn't be, but that's another story." He ran his hand through a mass of lustrous dark hair that has fueled many a fantasy. I couldn't help but wonder if that somewhere involved Tanya. Two deep grooves appeared in the bridge between his eyes. "I'd better get to the barn, pronto. I guess you must write about this, yes?"

"His death?" He nodded. "Yes, I have to, but I don't know how much Lorne will actually let me tell. Malfaro Developments is big advertising money for the Weekly, so this might require special handling." I had to ask. "I heard you arguing with someone yesterday, Nacho. What was it about?"

He didn't see that coming. His head snapped up abruptly while his eyes narrowed in a feral look. He didn't answer right away but seemed to pull himself together. "Nothing you should concern yourself with. Nothing that would have anything to do with Bruno's death either, if that's what you are implying." His eyes became hooded. *In other words, mind your own business.*

"Sorry, I had to ask. I didn't mean to upset you."

"No offense taken. I need to go." He did a one-eighty and pushed open the screen door. I followed him outside.

"The police are still at the barn. They've cordoned off the scene. They'll want to question you, too."

"I can handle it. There's nothing to tell. Suicide. I never would have thought. It's going to get messy." He strode down the flagstone path to his truck. He drove off in a hurry.

My pulse and the temperature dropped dramatically. I went inside and discovered I'd forgotten to turn the coffee maker on.

~✦~

I parked near The Blackbird and pulled out my cellphone. At that moment I was not in the mood to put up with Amelia, the bad-ass barista, no matter how great my need for java. I texted Cyn. *I'm outside and I'll drive. Ready?*

Two minutes later, she strode out of the café. She sure knew how to make an exit, as well as an entrance. She undulated like Marilyn Monroe in slow motion. Skin-tight jeans had been replaced with skin-tight leopard-print leggings, a taut black T-shirt and fitted black jean jacket. A wide black belt around her waist accentuated the fullness of her boobs. Again, the whole package was stacked on four-inch-heeled black booties.

"Wow," I said when she swung open the car door. "You won't have any problem getting people to look at you when you want to take their pictures."

"Hey, I love animal prints. I relate to them. I'm natural." *More predatory.*

We drove together to Hickory Hollow Sideroad, just on the edge of town, where about twenty acres of Bruno's land that he couldn't develop was to be designated Malfaro Conservation Area. I had read that it would offer hiking trails, observation posts, and a huge picnic spot. Volunteers would act as guides, pointing out various natural phenomena in the wetland, pond, and grassy areas.Local folks had nicknamed it Malfaro Bog and thought it a clever way for Bruno to avoid paying taxes on land that would otherwise sit empty.

And then it struck me. According to Morty Feldman's calendar, he and Bruno had met a little less than two weeks ago. Now they were both dead.

The sun delivered on its earlier promise of a wonderful September day of clear skies and balmy temperatures, with just a smidgen of crispness in the air. The forest and wetlands beckoned people to hike amid trees in autumn color. If I hadn't been here on business, the setting would have soothed my soul; instead, duty called.

We got out of the car and Cynthia tossed her cellphone to me. "Take my picture so I can tweet it. Great backdrop for this outfit, don't you think?"

I took three shots and handed the phone back. "Here you go, for your faithful followers." She typed a message and attached the photo to her tweet. I just rolled my eyes. Then she hefted her camera bag onto her shoulder and we set off down the path, which was not much more than a rutted, soggy driveway dotted with clumps of wet grass.

Cyn grumbled next to me. "Bloody muddy swamp is all this is if you ask me."

I looked down at my sensible walking shoes and just smiled. "Looks like you gained a few inches."

She bent to pick off about two pounds of muck from her heels, treating me to a view of leopard-spotted, bootylicious behind. "Nobody likes a smartass," she replied, wiping her hands on a tissue. "Besides, the men—they love the shoes."

I shook my head and kept trudging in the direction of the

ribbon-cutting site. "Lips are sealed, remember. I haven't heard that the Malfaros have been notified."

Colorful balloons were weighted down to the ground, and streamers looped like Christmas garland between low-hanging tree branches. Next to a red ribbon that spanned the space between two wooden uprights, a number of conservatively dressed suits stood around, looking like they'd taken a wrong turn and ended up at a circus. Mayor Floyd and the suits, whom I assumed were council members, stared at us as we approached. One couple stood out from the crowd. The guy had shoulder-length hair, a silver nose ring, and a tattoo that snaked up his arm. Dressed in blue jeans and tank top, and accompanied by a woman with a full-length Indian print skirt and long unkempt hair, they definitely did not belong with the other group. There was only one other woman I could see. She carried an old-fashioned clipboard and wore a worried look as she checked her cell. I guessed she was P.R. for Malfaro Developments, given that she wore the company crest on the lapel of her taupe polyester suit. I approached her first and stuck out my hand.

"Hi, I'm Darcy Dillon, editor of the Yorkdale Weekly, and this is Cynthia Davis, our photographer."

"Janet Turner, Public Relations for Malfaro Developments. I had hoped Mr. Malfaro would be here to answer your questions. I'll try him again. There's still about ten minutes before we get started. I'm sure he's on his way."

I was sure he wasn't on his way to anywhere but the morgue. Obviously, she hadn't heard the news yet. Cyn looked at me wide-eyed and wandered off to the clutch of men who surrounded Mayor Floyd. They greeted her like they had just discovered some rare exotic specimen that needed closer examination. Janet continued with the usual blah blah party line of how swell Mr. Malfaro was. I knew I should be paying more attention to her, but I couldn't quite focus, knowing what I did about his fate.

I finally extricated myself, telling her I needed to interview the

Mayor. Getting his attention wasn't easy, as the voluptuous Cynthia kept snapping his photo. Clearly, this guy liked the attention he was getting. Political campaigning 101: smile for the camera.

"Darcy Dillon, editor of the Weekly. Perhaps you could tell me, Mayor Floyd, what the new Conservation Area means to the people of York Ridge."

He gave me the once-over. From his look, I'd say I passed the sniff test. "My pleasure, Darcy," he said in his too-smooth voice, and then launched into a rehearsed spiel about community teamwork and generous donations.

I turned my attention to the councillors, hoping for something more than a sound bite. Hippie dude, along with his female sidekick—the back-to-the-land type with well-worn Birkenstock wannabes—rushed up to me, invading my space. I took a step backwards, but not far enough away that I couldn't smell the garlic left on his breath from his lunch. He thrust a finger in my direction, insistent on presenting the militant philosophy of the Environmental Defense League on environmental issues. That kind of fanaticism could only hurt their cause, I thought. I was born with back-to-nature genes, and this guy still unnerved me with his diatribe.

"And bloody Malfaro is a no-show. Typical. No conscience, just tear up the land without a second thought. No consideration for anyone or anything but themselves. It's a joke if you think Malfaro Developments even has the environment on their radar. And I hope you're going to print that."

"And you are?"

"Clive Carruthers, and this is Jillian Hamilton. We represent people who care about our world and this county in particular."

My eyebrows raised. I couldn't picture him and Tasty Tanya sharing the same space, much less having coffee together. What a combo—Tasty Tanya and Tasteless Clive. I couldn't help but wonder if their recent rendezvous had something to do with Bruno's demise.

I interrupted him. "Clive, why don't you give me some comments on the benefits of the Conservation Area, rather than your opinion of Mr. Malfaro, and maybe I can get you some coverage."

He stroked his scraggly goatee and realized I might be on to something. He launched into an explanation of how the Conservation Area gave them an opportunity to monitor the frog population. "Frogs are the best indicator of the health of the environment ..."

Someone tapped me on the arm. "Sorry to interrupt," Cyn whispered, "but the suits are getting restless. We should get on with the dedication and the ribbon cutting. Think there's anything we can do to move this along?"

At that point, Janet Turner took a step closer. The clipboard was tucked under her arm and she was actually wringing her hands. "Could we wait a few more minutes for Mr. Malfaro to arrive? I can't imagine what's keeping him."

"The councillors and I have other things to attend to." Mayor Floyd, too, had wandered over to our little group. Clive and Jillian glared at him and backed away.

"Just a few more minutes?" Janet pleaded.

"A few more minutes and no one will be here," the Mayor answered with authority.

She withered and gestured for us to go ahead. The Mayor was more than happy to take Bruno's place as the Keeper of the Scissors, and he grinned broadly. Then Miss P.R. had a brainwave. "But we need someone besides the Mayor and council to help cut the ribbon. Darcy, would you please assist?" she asked. Everyone looked at me expectantly. Trapped. Against my better judgement, I agreed. Anything to get this over as soon as possible. A brief speech, a round of applause, and we were finished.

From the corner of my eye I could see Janet Turner tapping the call button on her cellphone. I practically yanked Cyn across the grass as I headed for the car.

"Hey, watch the threads."

"Come on. Miss P.R. is on the phone, and I'm guessing from her expression that she's just now hearing the news. I don't want to be here when all hell breaks loose."

We fled for the car, but we were far from avoiding all hell breaking loose.

SEVEN

The bells hadn't even stopped jingling on the door of the Yorkdale Weekly office before the Pit Bull pounced.

"I've already had a call from the Fall Fair organizers that you missed the qualifying races," Miss Pittman huffed, her hand holding her throat. Cyn and I hadn't even made it through the door yet. "And you cut short the event at the Conservation Area as well. Morty, God bless his soul," she said, making the sign of the cross over her ample bosom, "was a professional newsman. He never missed a community event. Just wait until Mr. Braithwaite gets ahold of you." The beginnings of a smirk played at the corners of her mouth.

The Pit Bull had definitely missed her calling as a prison warden. She must have been that smarmy kid at school who not only took delight when other kids got in trouble, but actually informed on them.

"There's been an accident," I said. Her smugness was replaced by a puzzled look.

"Well, they think it's a suicide," Cyn interjected.

"What? Who?" said the Pitt Bull. Her gaze shifted back to me.

"Bruno Malfaro was found this morning at Maple Lane Stables hanging from the rafters. He was the one who donated the land for the Conservation Area."

Her hand flew to her mouth. "Oh my! I never would have guessed he'd do something like that. I always figured he'd die in his sleep with a smug look on his face. Either that or have his pudgy little neck wrung by another." I winced at that too-close-to-home graphic image.

"What do you mean?" I asked, curious at her reaction.

"It's no secret he made many enemies in town. He was not very well-liked."

"But he donated all of that land for the Conservation Area."

"Pul—leeze. Everyone knows that land is mostly swamp. He couldn't build on it so he used it to curry favor with the Council to push through other development requests. Oh, listen to me, talking ill of the dead," she said, not looking remorseful whatsoever.

I wanted her to continue while she was on a roll. "Do you know any more about Bruno? I saw Morty had an appointment with him just before he died."

The Pit Bull went rigid. Her face drained of color as if she'd seen a ghost. A shiver went through her before she hastily grabbed the phone and began punching in numbers. "I really need to call the Fall Fair Committee and tell them you were unavoidably detained."

The Pit Bull had turned away and already begun talking on the phone. Cyn and I exchanged glances. Cyn gave an imperceptible shrug. "What do you need me to do?"

"I'm thinking you could print out the photos you took and make a copy of the original files for Sheriff Armstrong. He said he'd come by once he was finished at the stables. We'll have to figure out how to report this. A suicide ..." I said, absentmindedly smoothing my hair, "and he was a prominent figure." I'd naively thought editing a small-town paper was going to be uneventful.

I walked into my office and dumped my bag on the top of the desk. I suddenly remembered it was Morty's desk and picked it up and put it on the floor. I shuddered. I felt surrounded by death. I dug out Morty's notes from the desk drawer to see if I could glean any further information. Cyn came down the hall with a handful of printed pictures. A shiver went through me at the thought of reviewing them.

"Problem?" she asked.

"Uh, no, I was just thinking it might be a good idea to grab lunch while we can. I haven't had anything since six, and a coffee is long overdue. Should we head over to The Blackbird?" Anything to avoid Morty's ghostly vibes. I couldn't quite stomach them today.

"Sure, let me grab my purse."

"Bring the photos with you. I'll have Miss Pittman tell the Sheriff to meet us over there."

At the front counter, the Pit Bull refused to meet my eyes. "The Fall Fair Committee will send over some photos and a write-up for the next edition," she informed me in an uncharacteristically subdued voice. I guessed any further Bruno Malfaro inquiries were out of the question.

The Blackbird was humming with the noise of the lunch crowd. This time I thought I recognized the twangs of an Indian sitar playing in the background. We squeezed into a table at the front with mismatched chairs and one potted plant too many perched on its surface, to take advantage of the light from the front window. I glanced around to see if anyone could see what we were doing since I didn't want anyone seeing the shocking content of the photos. Since the door was inset into the café, our table had two walls and the window, while the table closest to us had a bench seat that faced the other way. A fern or two provided some privacy from prying eyes. It was a perfect setup for our purposes.

Amelia called out from behind the counter, "What'll you have, ladies?" I couldn't see her, as the enormous silver espresso machine on the counter shielded her face, though small tufts of pink spiky hair stuck up from behind it.

"Whatcha got?" Cyn asked.

"The usual." *Oh, that's helpful.*

"I'll have the grilled vegetable salad and my usual latte," Cyn replied.

"Ham and cheese on rye for me." I figured it was basic enough to be on the menu. I was too preoccupied today to decipher the chicken scratch on the chalkboard.

"Nope," Amelia countered from her bunker behind the coffee machine.

"Pardon?" *How could I go wrong with a ham sandwich?*

"No meat," she said without any explanation or elaboration.

"No meat?" I repeated, dumfounded like some mynah bird.

"No meat! Don't eat it; don't sell it, and don't wear it."

"Oh, I should have said something," Cyn cut in. "Amelia and her partner, Lou, are vegetarians."

I'd never seen the mysterious Lou. I wasn't even sure if Lou was a guy or a girl. These days you can't assume anything when someone refers to another as their partner. And with a name like Lou …

"Sorry, cheese sandwich will be fine."

"Out of cheese," Amelia boomed.

Merciful heavens. "What do you have?"

"Sprouts and avocados. It's on the board!" I'd clearly not figured out the rules on my first visit.

"Oh, okay." *Ordering lunch shouldn't be this stressful.* "The sprout and avocado sandwich sounds great."

"To drink?"

Please make this end. "I'll have the same as Cyn. Thanks." It was going to take some getting used to Amelia's gruff nature. Cyn seemed to favor this place, and it was just so handy. Until I got over my issues with my desk I was likely to be here a lot. On the other hand, I had enough stress in my life already.

My chair had a homemade pillow on the seat. I adjusted it to get more comfortable. Cyn handed me a few photos, and we spread them out to get a better look.

Everything had happened so fast this morning I really hadn't taken everything in, and I'd avoided looking at Bruno's dead body. Now, I felt my stomach turn queasy as I stared at photos of Bruno with a rope around his neck.

"What are we looking for here?" Cyn asked.

"I'm not sure. We definitely won't be using any of them in the paper, of that I'm sure. Maybe we'll get an idea of what he was doing there. I don't know, but there could be a clue in these pictures. Kiera said Dante was saddled. That doesn't make sense. If you were going to kill yourself, why saddle your horse first?"

"Honey, I wouldn't saddle a horse for any reason," Cyn said looking at me from under extended lashes. I smiled. She was starting to grow on me.

"Cyn, your lunch is up," Amelia barked from behind the counter. Cyn wedged herself out of our private corner and tottered over to the counter.

I thought back to earlier this morning. Sheriff Armstrong suggested Bruno might have used the horse to reach the rafters. Once he had the reins secured in place, all he had to do was slap Dante on the haunches to make him bolt. The dead drop would break Bruno's neck. Dante was a big horse, definitely tall enough to give Bruno the height he needed, while the ceiling in that aisle was fairly low. It would have been doable to reach a rafter while in the saddle. But Bruno was not a young man. The horse could have been difficult to control in that small space without using the cross ties to secure him. It seemed so elaborate, especially if you were simply concerned with ending your life. And the question that nagged the most—why the barn?

Cyn returned from the counter with a food tray and shimmied back into her chair.

"What are you thinking?" she asked.

"That things don't add up." I reached for my sandwich. The contents looked like green swamp scum on bread. I closed my eyes and took a bite. *Very healthy.* I grimaced as I chewed. I was holding one of the photos in my other hand and spotted something. "Look here." I turned the picture around to show Cyn the ladder leaning against the back wall in the hallway where Bruno had been found. "Why go to the trouble of bringing out your horse and tacking up to reach the rafters when there was a ladder right there?"

"Are you looking for an angle to report this?" Cyn queried with raised eyebrows.

"No, not at all. I've been thinking things don't make sense. Not that suicide should make sense."

"I'll tell you what doesn't make sense," Cyn said, grabbing the photo. "He's wearing riding gear. For me, personally, if I were to kill myself, I'd do it in my best outfit. Those pants hardly flatter his figure."

She had a point. Just like the saddle, why bother? Rena had seen him argue with Nacho earlier. Had he been in riding gear then? Did he stay there? Did he return? And then the light bulb went on and I jerked, slopping some of my coffee. The camel cashmere coat. It was Bruno.

"Steady there," said Cyn, as she grabbed some napkins.

The door opened and Amelia called out, "Afternoon Sheriff, what can I getcha?"

"Coffee, lots of it."

Cyn pivoted in her chair and waved with well-manicured nails sporting leopard spots.

"Ladies," he said, as he approached our table.

I slid over to another chair to make room for him beside me. Cyn shot me a look which I chose to ignore. I was divorced, not dead. Immediately, his gaze went to the photos on the table.

"Are these the ones you took earlier?"

"Yes, and this is for you," Cyn said, handing him a USB stick she had copied the files to.

He picked up the stack and flipped through them. His phone rang, and he pulled it out of his pocket, silently mouthing an apology as he answered it.

"Sheriff Armstrong." His brow furrowed. "Who found it?" he asked, then paused. "Make sure it's bagged and sent to the lab. Have them run tox on it and have it compared."

He slowly put his phone back in the clip on his belt. "Turns out a syringe was found in Dante's stall. Somehow my guys missed it. Rena found it when she was finally allowed to muck out the stall. I'm having the Medical Examiner run a tox screen against the body to see if it matches the substance in the syringe."

"What does this mean?"

"It means we may well be investigating a possible homicide."

EIGHT

I gulped. "Homicide? But couldn't he have injected himself with that?"

"Could have, Darcy; however, he wouldn't then be hanging himself. You can't die twice. The cause of death could have been an overdose, strangulation, or a broken neck."

Sheriff Armstrong ran his fingers through his hair with a look on his face that said he was struggling with a decision. "Remember you asked about Morty earlier?" he said.

"Yes," I said, not sure where he was going with this.

"We ran tox screens on Morty, too."

My head was spinning. I didn't think it made sense that Bruno's death was suicide, but I had assumed Morty's autopsy was just a formality. "So, he didn't die of natural causes?"

"That's right, but I can't go into detail. It's definitely a suspicious death." At that point, he left so abruptly that he created a mini tornado from the breeze as he tore out the door, as well as a tornado of thoughts in my mind.

"Oh my God"! Cyn whispered. I was as stunned as she was. Probably more. A shiver went through me when I realized the implications. A homicide in my own backyard, right where my daughter was riding, and now I was replacing someone whose death was also under investigation. I didn't know what to think. Finally, I spoke. "Two suspicious deaths."

"Caught me by surprise. Seriously, Morty was a good guy. Maybe a bit soft on the news, but it's a small town and he didn't like to ruffle feathers."

"Soft on the news? What do you mean?"

"I know this town is sleepy, but really I always got the feeling Morty was sweeping some stories under the carpet."

"Do you have anything to back that up? What are you suggesting? Foul play?"

"I have nothing, just a gut feeling. I shouldn't be saying anything, since the poor guy is dead," she said frowning. "Anyway, I have no idea who would have killed him. He was old and set in his ways but hardly a reason to off him. There's probably some reasonable explanation."

"I hope you're right. Okay then, Bruno. Who would want him dead?"

She smiled slightly and said, "Who wouldn't? Pardon my French, but he was a prick."

This opinion was reminiscent of the Pit Bull's remarks. "What? How do you know?"

"When I was married to my Sugar Daddy, Bruno and I were in the same social circles.

We weren't buddy-buddy, more acquaintances since we had friends in common. Mostly, I heard about his shenanigans second-hand rather than saw them. I know he certainly had no morals when it came to hitting on me. From what I hear, his morals didn't prevent him from screwing anybody else either, whether it was for sex or money."

"So, I don't get why everyone hung out with him?"

"Darcy, he had money, lots of it, and he threw good parties. People figured they could make money if they did a deal with him. I mean, even Betty Boobs was only with him for his money." She smirked.

"You mean Tanya?" Nacho's words from earlier in the day repeated in my mind. 'Somewhere I shouldn't be …' along with the tawdry emails, which I would keep to myself for now.

"Do you think she had anything to do with this?" Now, I was worried, especially if it involved Nacho or the barn. If Nacho was involved, then my child was in possible danger. I took a deep breath to steady myself.

"No way. She had everything to lose if he died. Rumor has it he gave her a four-carat diamond engagement ring. You know what they say, 'There's one born every minute.' Why are you looking so worried? The Sheriff 's good at his job. He'll check out the usual suspects although with Bruno the list will be long … very long."

"Just surprised, that's all. It's been quite the day," I said, shrugging. I had no intention of sharing what I found on Nacho's computer or what he had said with anyone. I was having difficulty picturing the man I knew as someone who would fool around with someone else's fiancée, let alone hurt or murder someone. "What will happen now?" I asked. This just kept getting "curiouser and curiouser" and closer to home. Why would someone just engaged to a bombshell commit suicide? Unless that person found out their fiancée was unfaithful?

"My guess is Frank will turf Tanya out of the Playboy Mansion pronto," Cyn replied. She put down her cup and stared. "Are you listening?"

"Sorry, yes, just thinking of the scenarios. Anyway, Frank. Frank who?"

"Bruno's son. There was no love lost between Frank and Tanya. The family was horrified when she moved in; it was embarrassing for them."

"I suppose it was. Do you think Bruno put her in the will?" My mind was still running through possibilities.

She threw her head back and laughed. "Wow, never thought of that. Wouldn't that put a monkey wrench in the works for Frank! He would be furious. Looks good on him. He's just as nasty as his old man."

"Maybe he was already furious." I stopped. She looked at me and her eyes narrowed.

"Are you thinking what I'm thinking?"

Maybe not. "Yeah, if you're thinking that Frank would be at the top of that hit man list." I was clutching at straws here, unwilling to tell her the other option that was floating around in my cranium, and that I couldn't say out loud. Nacho could be involved.

"You're not as naïve as I thought," she said. I didn't know whether to be flattered, insulted, or both.

"Looks are deceiving." Just because I looked like I walked out of J.Crew didn't mean my mind was equally conservative. "Now, who else can we put on our list of suspects? Who else would have something to gain from his death?"

"Probably any number of people who didn't want to see some housing development going in next to their farm or land. People around here don't like change too much. They like it just the way it is. I've been here since I was twenty-two and I still feel like an outsider. People are still suspicious of me."

She meant women. They were threatened by her hot looks. I had a small taste of that mistrust and jealously when I divorced; however, I hadn't been looking to hook up, and my main role was always Mom. I was, however, quite capable of changing my mind. Best to keep one's options open.

"It looks to me as if we might have a bigger story than we first thought. Let's get back to the office and see what we can dig up," I said, anxious to find some real solid facts to allay my fears about Kiera continuing to ride at Nacho's barn.

Hopefully Cyn just saw me as being enthusiastic.

In fact, she did look at me somewhat funny, or was I being paranoid again? "What?"

She just shook her head. "This is so not what I expected. Things are going to be very different around the office with you here."

"Okay, I give up. How, and is that a good or a bad thing?"

"Oh, good, a good thing. I mean, now I feel as if I'm really working on a newspaper and not an advertising brochure. Life is going to be very interesting with you at the helm." Her look turned thoughtful. "But be prepared for flak, especially from Simon, the Ad Manager. As I said, people don't like change, and the newspaper is no exception. You might have guessed that the Pit Bull worshipped Morty. Who knew why? He certainly didn't treat her that well."

I felt a bit of a fraud, especially since I had ulterior motives for digging into the story, but my daughter's welfare came first. I, too, didn't want change. I wanted the barn to stay the way it was before Bruno's death. I wanted to keep my image of Nacho as it had been. All of that now felt threatened, and I had no idea how deeply involved Nacho might be in whatever transpired. The sooner the Sheriff got to the bottom of this, the better.

NINE

The weekend flew by. I spent much of Sunday going through old articles about the Malfaro family so I could get a handle on their professional workings and family connections. The Malfaros had their fingers in quite a few pies, of land that is, developing subdivisions here and shopping malls there. There was a certain amount of controversy involved in a number of their deals compared to many other construction companies. Bruno had been recorded on numerous occasions badmouthing the environmentalists.

One particular incident got a lot of play when Bruno was taken in for assaulting a gentleman who had chained himself to a tree on Malfaro land. The land had been slated to be a townhouse subdivision. The development had threatened an endangered specimen of salamander. After the police were called to arrest the man for trespassing, Bruno and the guy ended up in a scuffle, and both were hauled off to the station. Bruno was a very physical man, it seemed. Eventually, all the charges were dropped on both sides, and the story died down. The name of the battered environmentalist was none other than Clive Carruthers.

The townhouses were eventually built although modifications to the original plan were made. Bruno's developments seemed to follow a similar history, with issues raised by certain groups. So far, I hadn't found any links to the mob, but my hunch was that they might be there if I looked closely enough. I wasn't sure I was going to look that closely. Bruno had been unscrupulous at best, and I wasn't sure of his worst.

I squeezed in some time to set up a Facebook fan page for the paper since I was on the internet doing research. I could promote it in my first edition. Even though I was consumed with Bruno, I still needed to keep my eye on the bottom line. I had to keep this job.

Sunday had flown by, and though I let Kiera go to the barn I was on edge the entire time. Now that Monday was here, I hoped I would find out more from the Sheriff. With luck, toxicology results were in, and we would know for sure what we were dealing with. I was also hoping to find out if there was some possible link between Morty's and Bruno's deaths, or at least more details to fill in the blanks.

I decided to drive Kiera to York Ridge High on what was promising to be another spectacular fall day. Too nice, I thought, to be worrying about ugly things like murder.

Yorkdale County was the least likely place for anything as horrible as murder to be happening. Here, fields rippled off in the distance turned golden with wheat and corn while glacial till and rocky ridges snaked throughout the county, topped by tufts of century-old hemlocks and maples basking in the autumn sun. Abundant clear streams crisscrossed the county, nourishing numerous aquifers and springs. Amid green pastures, frisky thoroughbreds dotted the landscape like a scattering of wildflowers, while freshly painted black or white paddock fences marched in rows across the hills, framing the stately manor houses of the rich and famous. Murder wasn't allowed in Yorkdale County. Its citizens would never stand for it.

I'd been worried about Kiera since Bruno's death but had had little chance to talk about it. The drive gave me a chance to catch up. It seemed we always had our best chats in the car, ever since she was little.

"How were things at the barn yesterday?"

"Kind of sketchy. I mean, people were a little freaked by what had happened. Nacho moved Dante to a spare stall to sort of start things fresh. I don't think anyone wants the stall beside where it happened?"

"Did you know Rena found a syringe in that stall when she cleaned up?"

"So?" She shrugged and did a funny thing with her mouth that always made me feel as if I was too ridiculous to live. "There are syringes in the barn. They're not locked up."

"There are?" I realized how little I knew about day-to-day workings at the barn. As Kiera got older, I had thought to give her space and make sure the riding was her thing.

"Nacho keeps them in the fridge in the feed room. I use the ones without needles when I put glycerine in Amigo's mouth so his bit doesn't bug him as much. He loves the taste; it's minty."

"Is that's all they're used for?"

She looked at her phone, scanning through the messages, only half paying attention. She had no idea how much was at stake, and I wasn't about to worry her. It took her forever to answer. "No." She paused and typed something. "The ones with needles are used to tranquilize the horses when they're being groomed or have dental work. To keep them calm."

"Did we tranquilize Amigo for grooming?"

"Mom." A wave of exasperation rolled from one side of her face to the other. "We don't have to. He doesn't spook at the sound of the clippers. He's fearless!" She stopped, and like a storm veering off course, a distant look replaced the disgust of a minute before. "But I don't understand why the syringe was in the stall. We put used ones in the garbage. We don't just leave stuff lying around in a stall where a horse could hurt himself."

"Sheriff Armstrong sent it off for toxicology testing, but I don't know the results yet." Either way, the syringe there made no sense.

"Weird. Wonder what was in it?"

I couldn't answer that, and I thought it best to try a different tactic.

"So, how was Nacho yesterday?" She gave me a sly look at my question. I chose to ignore it and hoped she hadn't noticed my interest. "I mean it's a shock. To have it happen on his premises is nasty."

"He was kind of weird too—sort of grumpy and not himself."

"That's not that unusual under the circumstances."

"I guess he might be worried some clients might leave."

"Would they?" I asked, wishing all would be back to normal soon.

"Maybe, but where would they go? He's one of the best riders and coaches in the world. No one else in the County comes close. You don't want us to leave, do you?" she said, her voice rising.

I didn't know what to say. That I was waiting for the shoe to drop? "You would never have gotten this far or got that horse if it hadn't been for Nacho." She looked relieved. "Anyway, as far as I know there's a waiting list, isn't there, so hopefully he will always have clients. However, I'd feel better if you weren't at the barn alone."

"What? You're not going with me for every ride, are you?" Kiera said, her mouth agape.

"Until we find out what's going on there, unless you have a better idea."

"Whatever, although I think you're being paranoid. Don't you think you are a little too busy with your new job to be following me around?"

"Yes, I am busy, but if you want to keep riding there, you'll have to think of something."

"Okay. Just give me a day. I have something in mind." Maybe she did, maybe she didn't, but I wanted to give her a chance to find a solution other than the drastic one of leaving the barn.

Even if she had a plan, I was skeptical about the fate of the stables. There's nothing like a taint on your reputation with the horsey crowd to make them think twice. I remember one barn that resembled the Mad Hatter's tea party. All of a sudden, all the clients just up and left almost en masse for no apparent reason. These high-maintenance clients were as easily spooked as their mounts. If I was freaking out, I could just imagine how they were feeling.

"Nacho had us all meet in the viewing room and told everyone about the accident. We had a minute of silence, and he said some nice things about Bruno. He told us all it would be business as usual. I thought that was nice since he just didn't ignore what had happened."

"Was Marco there?"

"No, and he's barely talked to Heather all weekend—said his parents were going nuts. But he does need to come soon and exercise Dante."

I had another thought. "His Dad wouldn't be Frank, would he?"

"I'm not sure. Why the twenty questions?"

"Just doing research for an article on Bruno."

I dropped Kiera off at York Ridge High, but I decided I couldn't wait until I got to the office. Kiera had made my curiosity about the syringe go into overdrive. I pulled the car up alongside a trail and called Sheriff Armstrong. He had given me his own personal extension. I felt privileged.

"Sheriff Armstrong." His husky voice came on the line, as reassuring as home. I paused and forgot why I had called. "Hello," he said, to wake me from my reverie.

"Sheriff, it's me, Darcy Dillon."

"Darcy, I thought I might be hearing from you."

Did he sound excited to hear from me? "I was wondering if you got the toxicology results back yet on the syringe from the barn." I tried my most professional voice.

"We did."

"And …" I let silence fill the air. I learned a long time ago that people will fill the silence if you give them long enough. The Sheriff was proving to be a hard nut to crack. I listened to dead air through my cellphone, but it paid off. The Sheriff finally said, "They found trace amounts of Acepromazine. It's a serious tranquilizer. The Medical Examiner is now running tests on the body."

A tranquilizer. I flashed back to what Kiera had said earlier. "Kiera said they use tranquilizers at the stable to calm the horses down when grooming them. Some of them are spooked by the clippers. From what I've heard, it's a common substance in the barn."

"Yes, Darcy, I know. And I hope it turns out to be as innocent an explanation as that. The last thing I need is a homicide on my hands. And of course, I'll let you know when this is a matter of public record."

"Was that the same substance you found in Morty's case?"

"No, Darcy, not even in the same ballpark. I can't say anything about that, and I don't want you to, either. There may be a perfectly logical explanation."

I clicked off the phone and pulled my car back onto the road, heading for the office. I had been hoping it had been glycerine in the syringe, like Kiera had mentioned she used to soften the bit for Amigo. In my mind, things were already stacking up to look like murder in Bruno's case. The saddle on the horse, his riding clothes, the syringe … things just didn't add up in my mind. The circumstances were strange. I was hoping it was my overactive writer's imagination at work. I hadn't a clue what to think about Morty's death. As the Sheriff said, it might have been nothing at all. I parked outside the office and headed inside.

As soon as I walked in the door, I saw Lorne coming towards me from the back offices. He was at the front before I'd barely got inside. The look on his face gave me cause for worry. His shades of gray hair were not quite as coiffed as they had been a few days ago, and his eyes were practically lost in the frown that furrowed his brow. My first week on the job and I could tell I was already in trouble.

"I told you to cover the story, not become the story. What the hell were you doing, cutting the ribbon at the opening of the Conservation Area?" Lorne blasted at me. Clearly, someone had ratted me out, and my money was on the Pit Bull, especially since I could see out of the corner of my eye that she seemed to be enjoying my public flogging. I was on probation, which meant I had better smooth this over fast.

Simon, the weasel ad man, who had barely spoken to me, peeked out of his office down the hall, ears on full alert and expression smug. I could tell he was enjoying this as much as the Pit Bull. The Pit Bull had the advantage of a front row seat, though.

Holding my ground I countered, "They picked me out of the crowd to fill in at the last minute. I couldn't tell them that Bruno Malfaro was going to be a no-show, since I'd found him earlier that morning hanging from the rafters at Maple Lane Stables." I regretted my choice of phrase as soon as the words were out of my mouth.

"What? You found Bruno?" A look of incredulity washed over his face. "I heard about the death, but I had no idea you were the one who found the body," Lorne said, and plunked down in one of the chairs in the front entrance. Catching his breath, he continued, "I didn't realize ... How did you happen to be there?"

I told him that Kiera rides at Maple Lane Stables, which was the reason he and I met, and gave him a brief account of how I found the body. I made myself out to be a little braver than I really had been. Lorne was my boss after all; I wanted him to think I was fearless.

The Pit Bull got up from her desk and headed towards the back.

"Were the two of you friends?" I asked, after Lorne had time to digest my version of Saturday.

"Friends, no, I wouldn't call us friends."

I thought there might be more behind that. *Did I dare ask?*

"Then, just business?"

"More or less. He and his firm have been one of our biggest advertising clients for years. Simon had enticed them to advertise in our paper. They have a double page spread in each edition devoted to their home development sites. Plus, they often take out additional ad space when they have a commercial property for lease."

The Pit Bull returned with a glass of water and handed it to Lorne, who took it with a smile. She shot me a dirty look in the process. After he had taken a few sips of the water he turned to me, and I could tell he was in recovery mode. "You're going to have to write an article about Bruno and his place in the community. The funeral home will have the family provide the obit to them so they can append the details of the service."

"The service could be delayed," I said, thinking of my conversation with Sherriff Armstrong earlier.

"What do you mean? Why delayed?"

"I've been in touch with the Sherriff, and there has been some additional evidence found. They are running tests on Bruno's body. I imagine it will delay its release and could hold up the service."

"Spill, Dillon, what more do you know?" Lorne said, the color returning to his cheeks and a gleam emerging in his eye. I saw this as my opportunity to redeem myself in his eyes and told him about my conversation with the Sheriff regarding Bruno, alerting him to the fact that the actual cause of Bruno's death was still not confirmed.

"So, we may have a murder on our hands?" he asked to confirm he understood. Although he was trying to keep his composure, I could see the alarm in his eyes.

"We won't know until more tests are done on Bruno." Even then I wasn't sure how much the Sheriff would share of his findings, given his secrecy over Morty.

"All right, get on the story," he said, standing and putting his glass on the Pit Bull's desk. "Be prepared for any angle when the results are finally released. I'll want you to tie Bruno's death into the coverage of the Conservation Area opening as well. And see if Cynthia can do something with that photo of the ribbon-cutting to crop you out of it while you're at it."

Oh, great. This was going to take some creative writing to put something decent together. From what I had heard so far, Bruno wasn't all that loveable. Who knew what else I would uncover in the process? Maybe something Morty had already found.

TEN

After the conversation with Lorne, I dug up more info on Malfaro via the Internet. I thought it may be time for a few interviews with those who knew the man and avoid bothering the family for a day or two. I was deciding whom to call when Cyn burst through my office door. "I've got to get out of this place; it's just too claustrophobic. And I thought to myself, why not take some photos of the barn since in all likelihood that's all we'll be allowed to publish."

I made a face. I really didn't like the idea of dragging Nacho's place of employment into the sordidness.

Cyn read my mind. "I know you don't want to do this, but our business is news. You know the old saying, 'If it bleeds; it leads.' This will be your top story this week and maybe for weeks to come!"

"Yeah, I know, but why there? I haven't even got my feet wet. I don't want to be the one who has to interview and drag people into it from the barn. There must be some other places you can photograph that were connected with Bruno?"

"There are, but kiddo, right now you don't have a choice about where he died."

We hightailed it to the barn before Nacho's customers arrived later for their lessons. I thought, at least, I could get a read on the atmosphere around the barn and on Nacho. The place was probably still swathed in crime scene tape. What a mess, and getting messier.

The day was the epitome of Indian summer. With the sun high and the windows down, the weather teased us with the notion that the season was going in reverse and summer was on the doorstep rather than autumn. Cyn had stripped down to a tight white T-shirt that left nothing to the imagination. She was making faces into her cellphone and sticking out her tongue.

"Snapchat filter," she said to my questioning look. "I'm barfing rainbows."

I raised my eyebrows but kept my eyes on the road. *Best not to ask.*

Driving up, the barn looked as benign as always. We weren't there for more than a minute before Nacho came out to greet us. He shook his head and that about summed it up. He just didn't have words for the mess. Before I could even ask him how he was doing, Cyn, whose eyes were positively smouldering, jumped in to introduce herself. I thought I had better intervene before she self-combusted before our eyes.

"Sorry for the intrusion, but there have been a few ongoing developments and we may have to run a photo of the barn in the next edition. I feel horrible about this, but it's part of the job."

"I understand; just do what you have to do. I know it will be a while before this all blows over and life here can return to normal."

Boy was that an understatement. I wasn't going to be the one to tell him the latest and not greatest. I'd let the Sheriff do that, and hope in the meantime it was all a false alarm. My gut, however, told me otherwise. While we were shooting the breeze about how things were at the barn, Cyn charged off around the corner … where angels fear to tread. I didn't need another glimpse to bring it all back. Back she came at breakneck speed, her tits leading the way. "Kiera's right; the place is a little sketchy. It needs a good cleansing!"

"I'm sure Nacho will clean up when he's allowed."

She harrumphed. "I said cleansing, not cleaning! You know, eradicating spirits. Like Bruno's, if he's hanging around."

Nacho and I both looked at her. I was speechless. I expected Nacho to cringe at her choice of words, but he, on the other hand, looked at her as if he had just discovered gold.

"Okay, enlighten me," I said, even though I was afraid of what she might say.

"My grandfather believed in ghosts. He used to take sage and sweetgrass and cleanse places of troubled spirits, sending them on their way to wherever troubled spirits go."

"Does your grandfather still do it?" I asked a little skeptically.

"Naw, he's a spirit himself now. I meant me!"

"Knock me over with a turkey feather. I never figured you for having this talent."

"I'm quite spiritual, you know ... maybe even psychic," she expounded. I bit my tongue.

Nacho smiled. "Some of the native cultures I know in Argentina believe in spirits haunting places. I think Cyn is on to something."

"You understand, guys, that my grandpa only told me about this. I never saw him do it. I follow spiritualists on YouTube and watched how they do it. I did cleanse my place, but that doesn't count. Technically, I'm a virgin cleanser."

That is debatable.

"I would be thrilled if you could do this for me," Nacho said, "and the sooner the better. It would be good for morale."

"Give me a half an hour to get my stuff and change."

I decided to drive Cyn, as I wasn't comfortable being alone with Nacho at the barn. I also decided then and there that Kiera better have a plan to not be alone there either.

"Wow," she said when we got in the car. "That macho Nacho is so hot cheese would melt over him."

I laughed. "And single." *Why did I say that?* She looked as if she had just seen the most tempting cheese pizza of her life.

She fanned herself with her hands. "Maybe I should let him know I have some other talents." She looked at me as if for approval. I shrugged. If she had said that a week ago, my mind would have been screaming, 'Hey, no fair, I saw him first.' But now he had an aura of spoiled goods, and I secretly hoped Cyn wouldn't take this any farther for the moment.

I couldn't believe my eyes when Cyn walked out of her bedroom. She would be right at home in a Vegas Cirque Du Soleil act. Having poured herself into some kind of skin-tight Spanx body suit, she had added deerskin-type chaps, and slung a cowl of hot pink feathers around her neck. Both wrists and ankles were encircled in bracelets while on her head was a fedora hat with earth-toned feathers sticking out of the band. The whole bizarre outfit tottered on skyscraper stilettos. All I could say was, "Wow, that's an original look—really unique. Want me to take a picture for you to tweet?" I already knew the answer. I doubted the image would leave my mind any time soon.

"Listen, sister, I'm improvising here. It's not as if I have a whole spirit-chasing wardrobe in my closet."

"I didn't realize boas were standard fare for spirit cleansing," I said, which got me a look that was reminiscent of the ones I got ten times a day from Kiera.

"Yeah, well, I had it for another activity."

I didn't want to ask what activity. "Those look like claws around your wrists," I said, changing the subject.

"Bingo. They're bear claws. It's all symbolic, you know," she said, doing a little shake with them as a preview.

By the time we arrived back at the barn, I was almost embarrassed for Nacho to see Cyn in this getup, but the only giveaway was his arched eyebrows. Otherwise, he was entirely gracious. Luckily for us, boarders were noticeably absent on such a great day.

Cyn lit her bunches of sage and sweetgrass with a red Bic lighter, and with ankles and wrists shaking and clicking from claws and teeth, she began chanting something indecipherable. She raised her arms, wafting smoke into every corner of the barn and stalls. I stayed well enough back, as I was choking being downwind from the smoke.

After about twenty minutes and when the bundles were getting a little low, Cyn pronounced the barn purged. Maybe it was my imagination, but the place did feel mellower. Either that or I was overcome by smoke fumes. Nacho thanked Cyn profusely and promised her dinner for all her efforts. So, there was a method to her madness after all! And now I had someone else to worry about.

For Cyn, however, that was just the warm-up act. "I can't let all this effort go to waste. I'm all pumped for somewhere else that is in more need of cleansing." With that we made a beeline for the office.

I pushed through the doors of the Yorkdale Weekly Office. It was time to rid my office of Morty once and for all. I knew I was being weird about it. I just couldn't seem to get over the fact the guy had died at his desk, my desk, and under some mysterious circumstances that the Sheriff was unwilling to share. Cyn's hocus pocus at the barn seemed to have put Nacho in a better state of mind. I was willing to give it a try, or I was going to forever be working with my laptop on my knees, afraid to let anything touch the desk. Childish, but I was hoping to give the ghost the boot once and for all.

Cyn paraded through the door of the office, claws clacking and feathers flying. The Pit Bull leaped up from her desk and scurried round it. I didn't know the old gal had it in her to move so fast.

"What exactly are you doing in that getup?" she barked at Cyn. "And you …" she shot a look at me, "you are only encouraging her!"

"I am here to perform a ceremony to cleanse Darcy's office," Cyn said very officially.

"It's already been cleaned. I used Javex and everything!"

"I am going to rid it of Morty's spirit," Cyn said, her arms outstretched, and her head tilted back. I suppose she meant to be looking at the heavens, but from my vantage point she was staring at the ceiling fan which ruffled her feathers as it moved. A few pink feathers fell off her boa and started to float around the room.

After Cyn's proclamation of purpose, the Pit Bull was in a flap. She too outstretched her arms, but she was not convening with the spirits above. She had the more earthly purpose to prevent Cyn from proceeding to my office. The two bobbed and weaved in the front foyer for a good couple of minutes until Cyn got the advantage by spearing the Pit Bull with one of her stilettos. For a moment, I contemplated if the shoes were part of the traditional dress but then quickly followed her down the hall to my office.

Once inside my office, Cynthia closed and locked the door. I could hear the Pit Bull rattling the handle to no avail. Then I heard her retreat as she clumped down the hall. "The Pit Bull's on the warpath."

"No matter, I have ancient magic on my side." Cynthia set to work pulling the sweetgrass out of her Prada purse and lighting it with her red Bic. I coughed from the smoke and looked over to her.

"Are you sure this will do the trick?"

"Honey, didn't you see how things improved at the barn after the cleanse?"

I had to agree; the horses and Nacho did seem less frantic after she had worked her magic. When I thought back to how mellow the barn became, I began to wonder if she was really burning marijuana instead of sweetgrass.

"Maybe you should get a video and put this on YouTube?" she said, enthused with her sudden inspiration.

Perish the thought. "No time. Best get on with it before the Pit Bull arrives with the cavalry."

She nodded and waved her arms in the air, allowing the smoke to spread into all corners of the room. This was a much more confined space than the barn. I worried she would she set off smoke detectors. I concluded that Lorne was way too behind the times to have much in the way of safety features installed. The claws on Cyn's wrists rattled as she started to swoop and swirl around the space and chant something that sounded like a string of hard consonants. Above the din I could hear keys jangling at the door.

Cyn yelled, "Out spirit out!"

Just then the door swung open. A crazed Pit Bull launched herself at Cyn. "Not my Morty!" she yelled. "Leave him in peace."

Thinking fast, I grabbed a bottle of antacids off the bookcase and pulled off the lid. "Cyn, put his spirit in here!" I said, handing her the bottle.

Cyn avoided the lunge of the manic Pit Bull, swooping her arm with the sweetgrass and pushing smoke into the bottle in several little puffs while she continued chanting. She then gave a nod, and I took that to mean it was okay to put the cap back on the bottle of antacids. Lid firmly on the bottle, I handed it to the Pit Bull, who had ceased foaming and was now standing frozen in shock.

The Pit Bull looked down at the bottle and tears formed in her eyes. I was thinking it might have been the smoke, but by the tender way she was cradling the bottle, she believed she held the spirit of Morty in her hands. Good enough for me. She left cooing. Finally, I sat down in my chair and put my feet up on my desk.

"Thanks, Cyn," I said, putting my hands behind my head and taking in a deep breath. I immediately started coughing from the smoke. Quickly I brought a closed fist to my mouth as I hacked away. Morty's revenge. I pulled my feet off the desk.

"My work here is done!" Cyn proclaimed and turned on her heel to sashay out of the office, pink feathers swirling behind her.

I didn't get much of a chance to recover before the phone started ringing. I tilted forward in my chair. It felt good to finally be at my desk. Looking at call display, I could see it was the Sheriff. I had a sinking feeling my mellow mood was going to quickly vanish once I heard what he had to say.

Eleven

"**D**arcy, glad I got hold of you," Sherriff Armstrong began. His tone was all business. I sat up straight in my chair.

"Have you heard back from the lab?"

"That's why I'm calling. On the record, Bruno's case is now being investigated as a homicide."

I paused to take that in. I'd had my suspicions, but now the grisly reality was sinking in. "Someone took the time to stage things to look like a suicide," he continued. "That means it was premeditated."

A shiver went through me. "So, the tranquilizer you found in the syringe was also found in the body?" I asked to confirm what I was sure I already knew.

"Yes. How well do you know Ignacio Rodrigo?"

"Nacho? Why do you need to know?" I could feel my blood pressure rise.

"Now that the case has turned from suicide to homicide, we are putting together a list of suspects."

"As you know, he is the owner of Maple Lane Stables and coaches my daughter." I was wary of how much detail to provide.

"How long have you known him?" This now felt like an official interrogation rather than a sharing of information with the editor.

I did a mental calculation. Kiera started riding at Maple Lane about two years before Will and I broke up, and then continued once we divorced two years ago. "Four years," I responded.

"In that time have you ever seen him demonstrate any violent behavior?"

"No. Never. Do you think Nacho had something to do with this? Nacho has been nothing but kind to Kiera." I was torn, wanting to defend the man I knew and yet repulsed and suspicious of his secret behavior.

"Like I said, Darcy, I am doing my job and that means building a list of suspects. I heard he had an argument with the deceased the day before he was found dead."

"I heard that too," I said without elaborating. I wondered if my nose would suddenly start growing. Technically it wasn't a lie, but the statement was up for misinterpretation.

"He also has access to the syringes, I take it."

"Yes, of course he has access," I said, trying to control my emotions. "They all do. They all use them for grooming," I snapped. I didn't know who to be mad at when I was really just mad this was happening, period.

"Look, both our jobs include asking people questions, so bear with me. We need to run down every lead and every suspect. Do you know where Nacho was between eight and ten last Friday night?"

"No, of course not," I said apprehensively. *And I didn't know where he was the next morning when I tried to reach him on his phone either.* "So, the time frame you just provided, is that the time of death?" I asked, trying to get some facts I could use.

"Yes."

"Would you be willing to provide a quote to the Weekly for our publication this week?" I asked, switching into editor mode.

"We'll be releasing an official statement shortly that you can use," the Sheriff said formally. "I thought you'd want to know since you found the body and," he added more kindly, "I know how important the stables are to your daughter."

Just when I was starting to close up, he had to show me how empathetic and perceptive he was. "Thank you. I really appreciate you letting me know before the official statement."

"You're welcome. Oh, and I need you and Kiera to come in to be fingerprinted. I need prints from everyone who was at the barn on Friday evening, even though I know you and Kiera left well before eight."

"Even children?"

"Yes. So we can rule them out, Darcy."

I had never been fingerprinted in my entire life. He rung off, leaving me with a huge knot in my stomach.

I had no time to waste. I wanted to get to the stables and see what Nacho had to say now that it was sounding like he was a prime suspect. I was also having second and third thoughts about Kiera riding there at all. I slung my purse over my shoulder and ran down the hall into Pit Bull territory. I hoped she wouldn't stop me and question where I was going. I was in luck; she was busy fussing with the bottle of antacids. It looked like she was fashioning a little shrine on her desk. I shook my head and bolted out the door.

From what I could see, things at the stables had gotten back to their normal routine. Horses were out in their paddocks. I could hear the small Bobcat over by the hay storage shed. Rena must be moving hay. I ducked out of the sunlight and into the dark interior of the barn. I watched swallows swoop down from the rafters and glide down the hallways, oblivious to what had happened here only days before. From my vantage point at the head of the hallway I could see that Amigo was head down in his feed. It was a wonder he could jump at all given the amount he ate, according to Kiera. I wondered if he should have been out in the paddock enjoying the sunshine with the other horses. *I should say something to Kiera about it when I get home.*

"Nacho," I called out, and was rewarded with his head of wavy dark locks poking out from one of the stalls. A bright white smile lit up his tanned face.

"Darcy! I am so pleased with the cleansing your friend Cynthia did. Everything has finally been getting back to normal."

I didn't really want to ruin his good mood, but he had already read the look on my face.

"What's wrong?"

Of course, he had figured it out. He worked with animals who didn't speak; he was in tune with any small change in body language. I looked off towards Amigo's stall.

"The police have some evidence back from the lab. Bruno's death was not a suicide." I paused, almost losing my nerve. "They are saying it was murder," I blurted out, and dared to glance back at his face to see his reaction.

"¡*Dios mio!*" I had to guess from his expression that he was thinking his life was in the toilet. His surprise seemed genuine, which was somewhat reassuring.

"Nacho, the Sheriff is asking questions."

"What?" His elegant hands raked through his thick hair where they came to rest as he tried to take it all in.

"He wants to know where we all were on Friday night between eight and ten."

"I can't say."

"Nacho, you don't understand. You are being looked at as a murder suspect! We all are. Everyone here on Friday night has to go to be fingerprinted! We all have to provide an alibi. You will have to tell the Sheriff when he asks, which I am sure will be shortly."

"I've done something bad," Nacho finally said, looking at me.

Oh no. I shouldn't have come and pushed this. I backed away, not sure what to think. My expression, I knew, betrayed my fear, and he reached out to grab my arms. Holding me squarely in front of him and looking directly in my eyes, he said, "No. I didn't murder him, if that's what you're thinking. I was mad at him, sure, but I didn't hurt him."

"Then where were you and what bad thing were you talking about?"

"I'm ashamed of what I was doing with her."

In spite of myself, when I heard the word 'her' I felt myself stiffen. I know it was stupid, but I preferred not to think of him with women. I wanted him just to be Nacho the horseman, pristine like some natural wonder.

"I was with Tanya at the time you are asking about," he blurted.

"Tanya, Bruno's twenty-something fiancée?" I said, unable to suppress the repulsion on my face. Although I thought it, somehow it didn't seem real until he said it. "By *with*, do you mean '*slept with*'?" I asked, making quotation marks in the air.

"Yes." Nacho closed his eyes and sighed.

Crap, I thought, both nasty and stupid, but instead of telling him what I thought, I said, "You will need her to corroborate your story." I was so disappointed to find out he was so sleazy that I was fidgeting to get out of his grip.

"Yes," he said, releasing his hold on my arms. "I'll get Tanya to vouch for me. I am so ashamed that I was dishonoring the man while he was being murdered."

"Please, tell me you weren't at his house!"

"Oh Darcy, I guess I deserved that." I felt uncomfortable, and for the first time I really wished I hadn't taken this job. "We were at a friend of Tanya's—Monica Stanislaw. She was out of town for the weekend."

"Was your truck parked at her place?" I was thinking of ways to verify his story.

"No. To protect Tanya, I parked at the Community Center, and Tanya picked me up. Listen, I know what you think. I know it was wrong, but he was an old man." He threw up his hands as if he couldn't find words to make it right.

"You mean you weren't fighting about her?" He looked puzzled. "On Friday night," I added.

"No, Bruno was putting the place up for sale without even giving me notice. I was caught off guard. It takes time to find another stable. I had wanted to buy this place if it ever came on the market, but I wasn't ready for that just yet. I found out when someone came to look at the place!"

I was taken aback. "So, he was hardly the nicest landlord." But it was another motive for Nacho to get rid of him.

"I was warned about him when I leased this place. I thought it would be different because he rode here." He shrugged.

"Sorry. There is something else. They found a syringe like the ones you use to administer tranquilizers to the horses."

"And?" Nacho asked, puzzled.

"And it had trace amounts of the tranquilizer you use at the stable. That same tranquilizer was also found in Bruno's system."

"Anyone could have had access to that. We keep them in the fridge. Did that kill him? It doesn't take much."

"According to the Sheriff, yes."

"As for the syringe, I'm not worried. I stock the fridge and my prints are on all of them, but it is not locked."

Of course, I thought there were likely prints on the syringe.

"You're right; everything can be explained," I said, but I felt even more uneasy. Not everything had been explained. There had been another nagging thought that pushed in, reminding me of my own lack of scruples. The worst thing was I couldn't even ask. When he mentioned Tanya, my mind flipped back to the email messages and the one from *tastygirl* that read "I've taken care of the brute; now I'll take care of you." Now I wish I'd never read those private emails. I had confirmed Nacho was a slimeball who was going to be kicked out of his own barn by the dead guy whose fiancée he was boffing, and who was also going to vouch for him. No, everything had not been explained—not by a long shot.

Rena came in through the front doors of the barn, and I used that as my opportunity to get going. I told Nacho I'd catch up with him later. I needed to get home before Kiera as she was sure to be home from school soon. I wanted her to find out the news it was murder from me first. I didn't know if the murderer had targeted Bruno specifically, or if it was just a random act by some calculating monster who wanted to see if he could get away with murder. Whoever it was had had access to the barn and may still have. The more I thought about it, the more I needed to get home and talk to Kiera about moving Amigo. If I thought the conversation with Nacho had been uncomfortable, I knew I was in for a four-alarm blaze when I brought this up.

TWELVE

The blast of noise hit me as soon as I opened the door. The virtual cars careening on the screen were so loud that the kids obviously didn't hear a real car. There on the couch were Kiera, her BFF Heather, and a well-built, sturdy young man with a shock of dark hair and broad features. The plastic steering wheels in their hands were as animated as the virtual cars flying around the screen. I walked over and scared the crap out of them, more than I had intended. Kiera paused the game. "Mom! What are you doing here so early?"

"I was about to ask you the same thing."

"Well, Marco needed to get out of the house and Heather wasn't concentrating in class so I invited them over here. Heather and I skipped Data Management with Mrs. Payne. She is so boring. Nobody listens. All the kids are texting. I'm sorry." She looked at me sheepishly. We had had numerous discussions about the infamous Mrs. Payne. Of course, now I was over a barrel with all three looking at me expectantly. I decided to save the lecture on skipping for alone time. *Play nice.*

I extended my hand to Marco. "I don't think we've been formally introduced, Marco. I'm Darcy, Kiera's Mom. I am so sorry about your grandfather. I imagine things are chaotic at home."

He took my hand with a firm grip and smiled. "Yeah, things are pretty bad. My Dad is really shook up. He's had to step in at work for my grandpa, too. I needed to get away. It was too intense!"

I wondered if he knew at all whether it was now a homicide. That would certainly ratchet up the tension.

"Yes, I imagine there's a lot to do."

"Well, it's just that the Medical Examiner's office won't release Grandpa, and Tanya, my grandpa's fiancée, is being a pain in the butt." He rolled his eyes.

"I guess the police have to be thorough under these circumstances, but I don't understand about Tanya." I ignored Kiera's glare that said I'd overstayed my welcome. The newshound in me couldn't help it. Marco was only too eager to share.

"She's insisting that she run the show since she was engaged to Grandpa. Dad said that it's none of her business. We're his family, and we know the kind of service someone of Grandpa's position should have. None of the family ever liked her. Mom calls her a gold digger and other things I can't repeat. She said she only wanted Grandpa for his money. It's a real freak show at the moment."

"Well, people get very emotional when they're grieving. I'm sure in a few days everyone will compromise."

"Tanya doesn't look too much like she's grieving to me. She just keeps worrying about the money and says she's staying in the house. Grandpa was always getting his heart broken by sluts!"

At this last remark, Heather shoved him. "Marco!"

I think the grieving widow might just be my first interview for my article on Bruno Malfaro. This, coupled with the dalliance with Nacho, was the stuff of soap operas, and it sold newspapers. Of course, there was no way I would name names, especially Nacho's.

"Well, I'm just glad you weren't at the barn on Friday night. At least you were spared that."

"Yeah, luckily we go to the movies on Friday nights," Heather piped up. "We normally go to the second show at nine in case

Marco's grandfather wants …" She stopped as she realized what she was saying; her mouth froze in the shape of an O.

"Yeah, normally I tack up Dante for Grandpa, but he never called last Friday so I assumed he wasn't riding," added Marco. That struck me as strange, given I had heard him at the barn on Friday night, and when we found him, he was dressed in his riding clothes.

Kiera just couldn't stand any more. "Mom are you staying or going back to work?" Her eyes looked daggers at me. I didn't want to ask any sensitive questions of Marco and upset them. There must be some explanation that would come to light. I also wondered what Marco was going to do about Bruno's horse.

My conversation about Bruno's demise would have to wait till Kiera and I were alone. I was still on a roll so plan B sounded like my best plan.

"Sorry guys, enjoy your game. I'm off with Cynthia. Kiera, I'll be late tonight, so you can make something for yourself and your friends. There's frozen pizza in the freezer." Kiera gave a nod.

"Say hi to Cyn for me," piped up Marco.

"Don't pay any attention to him," said Heather. "He just thinks she's hot."

"You know her?" I thought Kiera was going to pop a blood vessel so I cut things short. "Okay, I'll go. Nice to formally meet you, Marco. My best to your family. Oh, one more thing," I hastily added. "Are you still going to the barn to look after your grandfather's horse?"

"Of course, at least until my parents decide what to do with him."

"I'd appreciate it if you would keep an eye on Kiera at the barn, with everything going on."

Before he could answer, Kiera snapped. "Mom, I was going to ask Marco. He was my solution. Why couldn't you be patient?"

"No problem, Kiera. I'll make sure we're there at the same time, and if Kiera needs a ride I'll be glad to swing by and pick her up and drop her off."

"Perfect. Can't thank you enough," I said quickly, pleased I had something in place for the moment. I beat a hasty retreat from the family room. I could have sworn I heard Kiera grumble as I left. I had detected a faint smell of weed when I had walked in and suspected the kids, but now that I was alone, I still smelled it. *Holy smoke, I think it's me.* Just what was that concoction Cyn had in the barn that had mellowed the place so dramatically?

A quick phone call and in five minutes I was back on the road driving over to Bruno Malfaro's estate on Hudson Hill Drive. I had never been to his house nor seen his house, and up to now hadn't even thought about this wonder developer. We just didn't run in the same circles. Nor did I run in the same circles as Tanya Beauchemin, a.k.a. "Tasty Tanya" according to her old ads at Club Supersex in the city. Tanya had sounded more than eager on the phone. Perhaps this was her chance to assert her role. I didn't know what her angle might be. Too bad for her that they hadn't married. She was probably on some shaky ground.

I found the black wrought iron gates. Black paddock fencing marched for a long way along the concession road, before I came to a winding driveway that looked to be a quarter mile uphill. Eventually, the roof of the manor house became visible through reddening maples snaking up the hill. By the end, a circular driveway opened up, curling around a grassy mound filled with exotic-looking trees and bushes, smoke purple and red. I hadn't a clue what they were although they would be something I would expect to find at Cyn's house: big, colorful, and unique.

I swung around to park. My little Ford Escape was totally swallowed up by the sheer enormity of the driveway. I felt dwarfed by the three-story building looming over me. I hadn't really pictured where Bruno lived, but spread out before me, I wasn't surprised, for it was a little bit of the Old World here in the new. The gray stone edifice had chateau styling and proportions that rambled around to a four-car garage posing as a coach house. There was even an archway beside a portico entrance. Concrete balustrades and urns overflowing with branches and greenery framed the entrance.

I walked up several wide stone steps to two very large oak doors. I felt like Alice in Wonderland after she drank the shrinking potion. I pounded using a big iron knocker before I noticed an unobtrusive doorbell. I half expected a butler to formally answer on the other side. Several minutes later, it was not a butler but a very tall, buxom blonde, clad in a turquoise velour sweat suit, with the top unzipped enough to show me cleavage that looked manufactured. She would fit right in on the show "Desperate Housewives." Now that I saw her up close, for all her youthful face with its high Slavic cheekbones and shoulder-length mass of blonde hair, her face held a hardness I had only seen on faces years older than this twenty-nine-year-old. After brief introductions, she jerked her head and said brusquely, "C'mon in," with a faint accent.

I walked into a two-story circular foyer with a massive canopy of tier-upon-tier of crystals in the form of an antique chandelier overhead. Two wide staircases like swans' necks curved on either side of a central hall. A tall, luxuriant bouquet of fall flowers bloomed on a heavy, round table in the middle of the foyer. At any moment I expected a royal footman to appear and lead the way. Instead, with a wave of her hand, Tanya ushered me into a library-like room to the right. The large, cherry-paneled den had mullioned windows and downy looking, dark leather club chairs. I sank in, worrying I would become so comfortable I would fall asleep long before the interview finished. The comfort was decadent and the leather supple. I must have looked as if I had died and gone to heaven because she said, "Bruno loved these chairs and spent a lot of time here reading the paper. Do you want a drink or anything?"

I declined, but she left for several minutes and brought a tray of martinis anyway. "I hope you don't mind if I drink; it's been a rough few days." I could only imagine what she was going through.

I asked the usual pleasant questions to help her relax and talk about herself. For starters, I was interested in that accent. Far from European, her accent was French Canadian from some small town north of Montreal in the Laurentians. She wasn't *laine pur* however; those high cheekbones were courtesy of her Polish mother. She told me a weepy tale, "off the record" of course, about the sex scene being her only avenue of escape from the insular provincial atmosphere of rural Quebec. Although the scenery was idyllic, home life was demanding, siblings numerous, and money always tight. The economy in northern Quebec left much to be desired. Jobs were scarce and seasonal, and to Tanya, who felt like Oliver Twist, there was a steady parade of tourists that could afford skiing holidays, fancy lodges, slope-side chalets and expensive gourmet restaurants. The goodies of the world were all in front of her and all out of her reach. The story was a variation of a theme heard often—an escape to a world that then became another world one desperately wanted to escape. The whole experience had left her jaded, tough, and unable to go home.

Bruno had been manna from the heavens, opening a gate to a world she had been around, but which had been just out of reach, and one she was obviously going to have to be dragged away from kicking and screaming. "I felt like a somebody. Before, I was just a body with a person living inside who no one was interested in getting to know," she said.

I could see someone like Bruno falling hook, line, and sinker for this. He must have imagined himself a chivalrous knight in his castle rescuing a beautiful damsel in distress.

"So, tell me about Bruno. Do you have any idea why someone would want to kill him?" I always went for shock value. I always got a truer reaction and read on a person. My tactic was to disarm and then go in for the jugular. She was taken aback, and just as quickly recovered.

"Yes, I did know it was a homicide because Sheriff Armstrong called. He asked me the same thing. I didn't know Bruno's business associates, but he once told me that he didn't make this much money by being a nice guy." She shrugged.

I thought the same could be said for her. She didn't get all this in her life by being a nice girl, either.

"When did you report Bruno missing?" The Sheriff hadn't told me, but I think if she had reported it then Sheriff Armstrong would have known Saturday when I called. It had been something I had wondered about.

"I didn't. I had no idea he hadn't come home on Friday night." I looked at her quizzically. "He's a lot older than me, and he doesn't sleep that well. We decided to have separate rooms since it woke me up and drove me crazy when Bruno would walk around at four in the morning."

I could understand. As my parents aged, my mom had the same complaint about my dad. He would be in bed by nine and then wake by four or five in the morning. It drove her nuts too.

"Then you must have been doubly shocked by the call?"

"Stunned. I was sleeping and the police woke me up." *A hard night of loving will do that.* "I couldn't believe it when they told me it looked like suicide. I mean, we were planning to get married next spring. Bruno told me he had never been so happy with anyone."

I would probably say the same thing if I were screwing a twenty-nine-year-old.

"Then I guess when they told you it was murder, it made more sense."

"Yes and no. I mean, why?"

We spoke for a while about what Bruno meant to her and how unfortunate his death was before I dropped the bomb. "Well, luckily you have an alibi because of Nacho."

For a second, I was afraid she was going to fly out of her chair and strangle me. "What the hell are you talking about?"

Yikes I hadn't anticipated this. "Sorry, I didn't mean to offend you. It's just I was told that you and Nacho were together on Friday night."

"Who told you that?"

"I got it from the horse's mouth, pardon the pun. Nacho himself told me," I replied, trying to lighten up the mood but wincing myself at the bad joke.

"I have no idea why he lied like that. I know him because he coached my husband, but we did not have a sexual relationship. I certainly hope you will not repeat such a thing. It would ruin my reputation."

Was she kidding? "Tanya, I'm not judging you, but this is now a murder investigation, and I imagine everyone is under suspicion, including you and Nacho. You will be asked about where you were."

"I have already been asked, and I was here all night, as I told the police. I had nothing to gain and everything to lose with Bruno's death. I would say this interview has ended!" With that she rose and pulled herself up to her full five-foot-nine frame and gestured for me to leave.

I mumbled apologies. At the door, she was almost spitting. "If you print one word of what I have told you or of that lie, I will sue you and that stupid paper. Got it?"

I nodded. I believe I did. But I wasn't worried about me.

I remembered the name Nacho had given me of their accomplice in passion. Maybe an accomplice in a crime of passion? I turned and asked, "Does the name Monica Stanislaw mean anything to you?"

"Get out!" she screeched. The thud of the heavy door propelled me forward a few steps.

I had thought to come away with some clarity or at the very least some reassurance that I could leave my daughter in the hands of her favorite coach, a weak man guilty of an incredible lack of morals rather than a horrific crime. I was now not sure what to make about Nacho's alibi. Someone was lying, but I didn't know who or why.

Thirteen

When I got back to the office the Pit Bull was getting ready to call it a day. Just as well, too, as I was far too preoccupied and disturbed by the conversation with Tanya. She was right about one thing: she had everything to lose by Bruno's death. On the surface she would have been a fool to have been involved in Bruno's death, and a fool to be involved with Nacho and put her upcoming marriage to the golden goose in jeopardy. The problem was she just didn't strike me as a fool which meant the alternative was that Nacho was lying. I sat down with my head in my hands. A headache was imminent.

I was brought out of my speculation by the intrusive Pit Bull's face peering around the corner into my office. "Frank Malfaro called earlier. Call him back at his office before five-thirty." She walked in and plunked the number down on my desk. "This week's edition needs to go to press tonight," she warned, casting herself as some Angel of Doom. There was a certain amount of glee in her tone that implied I would screw up royally.

I hated to admit that I, too, was worried about this inaugural issue, especially given the town-shaking events the week had held. "Thanks for the reminder," I replied trying to keep the sarcasm out of my voice. I didn't want to incur more wrath.

I called Frank right away. Oddly, he asked if we could speak face to face at my office about his dad, and he wanted to have the conversation immediately.

When Frank arrived, I was surprised by how much he looked like a younger version of Bruno. I'd heard he had the same drive and ambition; however, with far more spit and polish. Frank had grown up affluent and therefore acquired a veneer of civility; any rough edges had been smoothed out thanks to private schools and country clubs.

He was wearing a crisp blue shirt, silk tie, pale yellow cashmere V-neck, and a buttery smooth black leather tailored jacket. His nails were manicured, and his graying hair was cut and styled. He looked like the last man you would ever find at a construction site, even though land development was his bread and butter. I could see where Marco got his stature and dark eyes. His manner was brusque but smooth, befitting a man used to getting his own way.

"I was looking forward to meeting you, Darcy, although nothing would have made me think it would be under such circumstances."

I detected genuine pain there. *Would a murderer respond like this?*

"Please, have a seat." I gestured towards a chair positioned in front of my desk. I was curious to hear what he had to say.

"My dad taught me everything I know about the business," he started, then paused and shook his head. "There was still more I wanted to learn from him. He was a self-made man and put so much effort into the business to make it successful."

"That must have been hard on the family."

He gestured with those well-groomed hands. "You're absolutely right. He didn't have much time for us. I would say, only in the last ten years did we approach anything resembling closeness, and that relationship was forged in the boardroom, not at home. His values of hard work and loyalty were forever drummed into me from the get-go. He had no time for laziness or backstabbing. He generously rewarded those around him who gave 110 percent and stood behind him, and he severely punished those who just took and betrayed him behind his back. The Italian way, he called it. He came over to America as a young man but never forgot his roots."

"It's kind of nice that you have boys so that you can pass on all this knowledge, as well as the business, which I think is also the Italian way. The boys are lucky."

"Marco is a work in progress," he replied, whatever that meant. "Perhaps my youngest son, Dom, will be the one to follow in Dad's and my footsteps. He was always interested in taking things apart and putting them back together. But you never know. You give them all you can, and one day you have no control. They have minds of their own, and you can't tell them anything." The parent in me knew well enough when to leave this discussion of someone's children alone. That would be deferred to another day when the murder had been wrapped up and all this was behind him.

"Why did you want to meet face to face?" I wasn't sure now where this conversation was going.

"I want you to understand that he was a hardworking man who did everything he could for his family, and I want you to be careful ... how you portray him." He gazed at me intently as if to see if his message was hitting home. I had to stop from squirming. "Malfaro Developments spends a lot on advertising in this paper, and we would like to see that continue. Morty and I, we had an understanding." I could have sworn he made a gesture with his thumb and finger that indicated *dinaro*, money. "One that benefited both of us." I think I was now getting his drift.

Actually, there wasn't much doubt about his message. Time to think fast without being offensive. "My mother taught me not to speak ill of the dead, and I intend to follow that advice," I said to assure him. Our paper was free to the public and relied solely on advertising revenue to exist. I hardly wanted our largest advertiser on my bad side in my first week and a trial week at that. I wasn't going to throw out my journalistic integrity either, so I added, "I was also raised to conduct myself with the utmost professional integrity. We will only print what can be verified as facts; we are not in the business of conjecture. Given that your father's death is now being considered a homicide, you understand it will be front page news, though."

"Can't be avoided. I understand," he said his eyes narrowing slightly as he pondered something.

Please don't offer me money.

Abruptly switching gears, he said, "For this edition, I'd like to double our ad space to capitalize on the increase in circulation we expect will happen due to the sensational headlines."

"I'll have to refer you to our Ad Department manager, Simon, whom I'm sure you know." Capitalizing on his father's death to help sell more houses—tacky. A murderer's ploy? "You'll have to talk to him about next week's edition though, as we are going to press tonight."

He stroked his chin thoughtfully. "With everything going on I forgot. One more thing: while I know you cannot exclude mention of my father's fiancée, Tanya, I would rather you keep mention of her to a minimum, if you know what I mean."

I didn't know exactly what he meant, but I could surmise that he wasn't exactly proud of his father's choice in women. "I won't be going into detail on her previous employment if that is what you are hinting at," I said. I had to keep on his good side while keeping off his payroll. In fact, I might put myself in harm's way if Frank was a prime suspect. Morty flashed through my mind as I rose to see Frank out.

"Fair enough. You seem to be a discreet woman." He rose and shook my hand.

After he left, I collected my thoughts. Had I been imagining what Frank was saying, or had Morty really been paid to keep certain things detrimental to the Malfaros out of the paper? Was this something I should share with the Sheriff? I made a mental note to ask Cyn about it. In the meantime, I knew I was in for a long night.

I called Kiera. I was thankful she was alone now. I told her the latest news about the homicide designation. She seemed more perplexed than upset. The fingerprinting really threw her. I reassured her that this was just police routine, and no one seriously suspected her. I reminded her that everyone who had been at the barn on Friday night was involved, no matter how farfetched the idea. Before I could ring off, she had a beef to air.

"Mom, I'm not six; I can handle my own problems. You didn't even give me a chance before you jumped all over Marco about chaperoning me. It was so embarrassing."

"I know, and I just thought of it that moment and didn't know when I'd get a chance to speak to him again. You mean the world to me, and it's my job to keep you safe no matter how much it irritates you. Suddenly the barn looked scarier to me. Remember that this may not be a permanent solution. It will do for now." We rung off, and I thought it was just as well that I would be late at the office.

I needed to polish off the article on Bruno while the last few conversations were fresh in my mind. What transpired over the next few hours was a portrait of a steely, hard-driven man who demolished any opposition by either buying them off or buying them out in his single-handed quest to be top of the game. Call it an escape from his childhood poverty or paranoia at being deposed from his top dog position, the man had difficulty relinquishing control. I could see too clearly that there were any numbers of toes that Bruno had stepped on in his climb, and the collateral damage had included friends, siblings, a long-suffering wife, and an estranged daughter who had left the area. I wondered if in the end it was worth it, when he sat in his lonely castle at four in the morning with his only companions being those he had bought. But much of this was not publishable, and only the sanitized version would actually make it into print.

Only in the last few years had Bruno begun to give back to the community, and that had been at the urging of his grandchildren, who had paid the price for the sins of their grandfather. If there was anything that Bruno had left behind, it was a legacy of ill will. I filed a cleaned-up and tarted-up version of Bruno Malfaro's bio for the edition. I looked forward to going home and putting my feet up with a glass of wine, but that had to wait as I still had to put the edition together so it could go to print tomorrow.

I pulled out the Weekly Dummy that Simon had already filled in. The dummy was a mock-up of how the space in the paper would be used. Normally the paper was about sixteen pages total. This week I could see twenty grids on the dummy. It looked as if others had had the same idea as Frank and beefed up their ads. Each page of the paper was represented by a grid on the dummy. Simon blocked out where the ads would go on the grid. Ads were priority. The empty space is what I had left to fill with articles. Using Adobe InDesign, I was quick to block out the ad spaces to match the dummy then pull in the articles and photos.

I started with the article on Bruno, front page news. I pulled up my email and retrieved an article from the Fall Fair Committee along with their photographs. The Pit Bull had emailed a calendar of events to me. As a community paper, a majority of the space was dedicated to upcoming events: library programs, church socials, and sports finals. Bruno's memorial service on Saturday was also listed. Given the change in circumstances, a memorial service seemed the route to go, while the real burial, whenever that happened, would be a family-only affair.

There were a few more articles I had written earlier about small local stories that I pulled in. Once I'd laid out the articles, I reviewed my work for graphic elements, larger headlines and articles on top, then ensured all had been edited correctly. A few hours later, I'd done it. My first edition was ready. Now for that glass of wine.

That lovely vision disintegrated with the text that came from Kiera. "Help. Get home quick. Grandma and Grandpa here." Will's parents had descended on her. Knowing them, they would be quite upset with everything going on.

On the drive home, I tried to foresee all the concerns that Will's parents would have. They had been upset that Kiera was hooked on riding—the very activity that had interfered with Will's life, causing him to leave the family business and us by pursuing his dream of being a professional rider. Now, here was their granddaughter following in their son's wayward footsteps. To them, I was aiding and abetting Kiera just as I had with Will. Little did they know, I had no influence on a grown man. He was going to ride because his parents had put the kibosh on it years ago. He had never let the childhood dream go. When his mid-life crisis hit, his adolescent dream was resurrected and his family paid the price. I thought I had all my arguments in a row.

I barely got in the door before the barrage began. First my ex-mother-in-law started in. "I didn't know your fancy new job was going to mean that Kiera was on her own to get dinner for herself."

Nice to see you too. "Matilde, you forget your granddaughter is growing up; she's seventeen and able to cook for herself. Right, Kiera?"

Kiera nodded. "I told Gram that already, Mom, and that you have been there for me for years."

"That's right. Kiera will be going off to school in another year and should know how to fend for herself and be independent. I did, and Will did."

That seemed to appease her but only for a moment. "Well, she won't graduate if she keeps skipping school!"

"What are you talking about?"

"I answered the phone when Kiera was in the bathroom, and it was the school. Because Kiera skipped a number of classes, you have to meet with the teacher, a Mrs. Payne." I didn't know who to chew out first. I looked at Kiera and she grimaced.

"You answered my phone?" I asked, somewhat dumbfounded that Will's mom still felt this house was her territory. "I have voice mail."

"I know, but I thought it was important when I saw it was the school." Apparently, the message that Will and I were divorced hadn't got through. "Anyway, you're to call a Mrs. Payne to tell her if you can make it after four tomorrow for a parent/teacher meeting."

Oh joy.

At this point I couldn't think of anything civil to say to my ex-mother-in-law that wouldn't make things worse, so I turned to Kiera. "And why was Mrs. Payne calling so late about tomorrow?"

"I forgot to tell you about it, so I guess that's why she's calling now. There were some other parent/teacher meetings tonight."

"You better come for that one, Kiera."

"But Mom, I have a lesson at four-thirty tomorrow," she pleaded.

Good going Kiera. Just add fuel to the fire.

"Actually, Kiera and Darcy, that's what we stopped over to talk about," piped up Iggy, my ex-father-in-law. "We are very concerned that Kiera is at a barn where a murder took place. That is no place for her. I never did like the fact that place was run by a playboy foreigner, and now my fears have come true."

"You're kidding me, right?" I could see Kiera was on the verge of blurting out something that involved four-letter words. "Kiera, hold that thought for a moment," I said, my eyes boring into her, hoping she would keep her trap shut.

"I'm not giving up the barn or Amigo or Nacho!" she said, stomping off. The door slammed, making us all jump.

"It's been an emotional week. I know you mean well. I also have concerns after what has just happened."

That defused Iggy a little. He nodded in agreement.

"Till now," I went on, "the barn has been a godsend to Kiera since Will left, and Nacho has been a large part of Kiera coping with that. I honestly don't think she would have adjusted well without that distraction and focus in her life. I've seen her other friends go through their parents divorcing, and they ended up failing or into drugs. Amigo has taught her responsibility, and Nacho has helped her feel good about herself."

"I know you think it's the riding that's our priority, but it's more that man, Nacho. How could something like this happen at his barn?" Iggy asked.

"I don't know how it did or why, but I'm in the business of finding out. It could have happened anywhere."

"I don't trust that man," added Matilde. "He's too good-looking and too foreign."

"That's a bit hypocritical, don't you think? After all, you emigrated from the Netherlands and my parents from Ireland."

"But we've been here longer than we lived in Holland. We built a business here and raised our kids here."

"And that is exactly what Nacho is trying to do here: build a life and a business. I thought you would be more sympathetic." I felt hypocritical myself, defending Nacho when I too had misgivings about Kiera being with someone I now distrusted. But I was the one to decide what to do about it.

"It's frivolous—horse showing. We're farmers in the agricultural business, providing food which is a necessity," added Iggy. Will's parents had bought land and market-gardened before they started a thriving business in retailing canned goods. Before long, they had built a successful food processing factory. The rest was history.

"Horse-showing is a passion with people, and it is a business. There is a market for it. It involves expensive prizes and expensive horses. My goodness, it is an Olympic sport! People build careers from it, such as breeding, training, and showing." I was getting myself worked up. When I get backed into a corner, I come out fighting. Normally, I would share their point of view, especially when it had come to their son and the sport, but to come into my house and tell me what to do, that I couldn't stand for. I was frothing for nothing. I would never change their minds.

"Well, we don't approve of him, and now with the murder, we think you should remove Kiera. It's obvious it is interfering with school. Maybe if you hadn't taken a job ... but our concern is with our granddaughter," Iggy continued.

I was speechless. They had always hinted they didn't agree with certain things but never so overtly demanded I do things their way. I bit my tongue before I started a full-scale family feud. With Will in Florida, I had to maintain a harmonious relationship with Kiera's grandparents.

"I appreciate your concern for Kiera, and I am glad you are involved in her life; however, now that she's older those decisions are up to her and me. I will call the school tomorrow. Kiera is doing well in everything, but this teacher and this class is not one of her favorites. So, you need to be patient." I kicked off my shoes so I wouldn't be tempted to fire them at their heads. "As for the barn, Kiera has already made arrangements to have someone with her at all times. If it's not me, then a responsible friend. We will give that a chance, but, as you have said, we may have to do something more drastic. However, that is a mutual decision, and we'll make that decision when we come to it."

I don't think they were happy, but they had said their piece as I had said mine. As soon as they were gone Kiera burst out of her room, hysterical. "My life is ruined! Don't take away Amigo and make me leave the barn. Mom, please, I love it there, and I love Amigo and Nacho. There's nothing else I want to do except ride."

"Calm down. We're not there yet. I meant it when I said we would try having someone with you at the barn. Don't worry tonight about Amigo and Nacho. Right now, we need to deal with Mrs. Payne so you don't lose your credit." How everything was going to be fine, I didn't really know. Things weren't looking good at the moment for staying at Maple Lane Stables. The last thing we needed were the Van Dykes on their high horses, and Mrs. Payne compromising

Kiera's graduation. As if on cue, my cellphone went off. I thought it was Lorne checking to see if the paper was a wrap. It was a text from the insistent Mrs. Payne reminding me yet again. But there was another text message that I must have missed earlier. This one was far more cryptic and far more sinister, one that made me finally go to the wine rack and grab that bottle of wine. "Keep your nose out of where it doesn't belong," it read.

FOURTEEN

As I walked up the stairs to the second floor of York Ridge High, I felt more and more as if I was a condemned woman. With each step I was more pissed and not sure exactly who to be pissed at, Mrs. Payne or Kiera. Why couldn't Kiera just play the game for once? After all, this course would be over in a few months and then I would no longer be on the hook for these parent/teacher summonses.

From down the hall, I caught sight of something for sore eyes—Sheriff Armstrong. I made a mental calculation whether to tell the Sheriff about the anonymous text I had received on my cellphone the night before. I hadn't told anyone for fear that somehow I would jeopardize my ability to gather information. I knew too, that Sheriff Armstrong would immediately forbid me from poking around. If I didn't, I was afraid we would never get to the bottom of things, and I would be living in fear a whole lot longer. Besides, after a few glasses of wine last night I had convinced myself that the phone text was not as threatening as I first thought. It meant progress. I was on to something.

"Sheriff, fancy meeting you here. I thought I was the lone parent of a delinquent."

He smiled. "I assume you were also summoned to a command performance." I nodded. "And it's Adam, Darcy." A little shiver went through me at the sound of my name on his lips, and his frank gaze suggested that perhaps we could be friends. *Or more?* Yikes, maybe I'd been alone too long. Best to play it a little cooler with a fellow parent and a source of information for my job.

"Okay, Adam ... I'm thinking this is going to be a long year, and it's barely started."

"I have to agree with you."

"What are you in for?" I asked.

"The emails about Andrew's, for lack of a better phrase, 'attention span' have been coming hot and heavy. And you?"

"Kiera's been skipping class. I thought by this age they would have these conversations with their teacher on their own. I don't know if I can stomach anymore classroom drama." Actually, I did know. I'd had it with hysterics over papers lost and last-minute runs to the copy store to print color copies, not to mention girlfriend squabbles and arguments over clothes and clubbing. I was ready for high school days to be over for Kiera, whether she was or not.

"I confess there hasn't been much drama for me. Boys, you know? I probably would have gone crazy if I had had to raise a girl on my own."

Single, that's good. "How long have you been a single parent?"

"Sara's been gone now about five years." *Gone? As in left?*

"That's a tough age to lose a parent," I commiserated.

"Sara was sick for about a year, so we had time to say good bye and sort of prepare for what was to come. Both Andrew and I were devastated but thankful at the end that she wasn't suffering anymore."

"So sorry," I mumbled. I meant it. Will and I didn't work out because he never grew up, but to lose someone permanently whom you loved and were happy with was unthinkably tragic.

"Bad things happen. Life moves on. The great thing about kids is how resilient they are. They're like dogs," he said, "at least boys are; they live in the moment. Didn't you find that?" Wait a minute. What does he know about my situation? He must have read my expression. "People talk," he said. "It's my job to listen. You're a very attractive woman, and it's a small town ... It's all good," he added with a sheepish expression, perhaps realizing he may be digging himself into a hole. I decided not to let him squirm; after all, he thought I was attractive.

"I guess good gossip is fine, but to answer your question, I'd say both yes and no. After my divorce, Kiera went through a real rough patch. What saved her were her horse, Amigo, and the stables. She threw herself into riding, and Nacho became a kind of father figure. Her dad was never around."

He pursed his lips and became Sheriff Armstrong again. "No comment."

Did he know something he wasn't telling me? "You don't trust Nacho. I can't imagine he had anything to do with Bruno's murder. It just doesn't make sense to do something like that on your own doorstep."

"But it was a homicide staged to look like a suicide," he said. "Crimes of passion ... Who knows what people are capable of when they're pushed?" I thought back to Nacho's angry words the day before Bruno's death and inwardly shuddered. He was right. I wondered if he put Tanya and Nacho together. Surely Nacho had told him by now.

"Do you have any other suspects in mind?"

"A few ..." Adam replied. He obviously wasn't going to share any more. "I forgot to mention I have a story you may want to cover for the paper. In two days, we have a chopper coming in to fly over the northeast part of the County for surveillance."

"What are they looking for?"

"This is completely confidential until I give the word."

"My lips are sealed," I said. "Pinky swear." He looked at me as if I'd lost my mind.

"Sorry, it's an in-joke with Kiera. We used to do it when she was little, and now we just use it for fun to keep secrets. I'm still new to espionage."

"Cute. Anyway, we got a tip that people have been concealing marijuana-growing operations in the middle of certain cornfields. Due to the height of the corn, we can't see the weed from the road."

"A drug bust—I'm in!" I said a little too enthusiastically. The community was quaint, but if it weren't for Bruno's murder, I would only be covering a Tree Planting Ceremony or local library programs.

"You can ride with me. I'll pick you up from home in the morning, day after next." This was exciting. Remember to tell no one what you are up to. I am counting on you, or I wouldn't have included you; this isn't the norm. Morty would never print anything detrimental to the community. Not printing it means to me that the practice is accepted, and worse, people are kept ignorant of what is going on in the community. Are you sure you're willing to publish the story?"

"Of course. You're right. Nothing changes if it isn't acknowledged. I want a safe community for our kids without the criminal element in it." It was curious that Morty hadn't covered drug busts with more vigor.

I almost hesitated to ask, but the worst he could say was no. "Can Cyn, my photographer, ride along too?" I asked. "The story wouldn't have as much impact without some great shots." Helicopters especially were first page material.

"Sure, have her meet us at your place but, again, emphasize the confidential nature of this operation. And Darcy, you and Kiera still need to stop in to be fingerprinted."

"Will do."

At that a student appeared around the corner, announcing it was my turn with the firing squad. Of course, Kiera was a no-show. I received a text that she had got a ride to the stable for her lesson. I still had to address that and soon. "Wish me luck with the Pit Bull the Second," I said. Doubt spread over his face. "A newspaper joke." I left and went in to face Payne, contender now for second place as the largest annoyance in my life. By the end of the interview, she was vying for first along with the Pit Bull and my ex-in-laws.

When I got home, I was still fuming from the interview with Mrs. Payne. I was just seething that Kiera, who had always done decently, if not well, was now receiving failing grades in senior year Data Management. I was thinking I could get Will to spring for a tutor. According to Mrs. Payne, she had given Kiera a failing grade to scare her rather than because those were her marks. She had included a late assignment for which she received zero even though there were so few marks so early in the year. What kind of logic was that? "Oh, you scared her all right," I had said, "to the point she wants to drop your course, which means she will be short a credit to graduate." Things went downhill fairly rapidly from there. There was no way I was going to have her kept back a year for one subject. It was time for her to be more independent at university or college.

When Kiera finally did return home, her head wasn't full of school; it was full of the horse show coming up in a few weeks. This was the last chance to accumulate enough points to maybe qualify for the National Horse Show in Harrisburg.

"Mom I'm so worried. A few more people are talking about leaving the barn. They're acting as if Nacho had something to do with Bruno's death. They're not going to arrest him, are they? Some people said it's only a matter of *when* not *if*."

This was the conversation I had been dreading. "They may have a point. I'd like to believe that Nacho had nothing to do with this, but I don't really know. My concern is with your safety, and I too, was thinking that one option is leaving the barn until this is resolved." I didn't have long to wait for the fireworks.

"What?" she erupted as she bounced off the bar stool. "Nacho could never do anything like that. I thought things were bad because we may not go to the Classic. Next year I'll be too old for Children's Hunters. I was so excited. Now you want us to leave! Nothing is ever going to work out! Besides, you said as long as Marco was there it would be okay." At that the tears started, and she stormed out of the room.

When she finally emerged, I tried to comfort her, but she was having none of it. "Stop Kiera. The barn may not be safe, and you have many more years to compete in horse shows. Besides, it may only be temporary until they arrest someone. You're worrying about things that haven't happened yet. I'm willing to give it a few more days with Marco, in case there is a break in the case, but after that we'll have to talk."

"Whatever."

"Hey, you haven't asked about Mrs. Payne," I said. "For once I am with you on this one!"

"I don't care," she said, glaring from a tear-stained face.

The next morning Kiera agreed to try a tutor before deciding to drop Data Management. Of course, this I knew was only part of a deal that she was formulating. I could tell by her acquiescence that she saw this as currency she could use to push for her way.

On the way to school, we stopped quickly at the police station to be fingerprinted. Odd though the experience was, it turned out to be not all that dramatic. By the time I arrived at the office I was feeling better and a little thrilled to see the first issue of my paper. Before I had even turned the first page, I was accosted by the Pit Bull. This was getting to be a nasty habit of hers.

"Ms. Dillon, I don't know what sort of other places you have worked, but I will not stand for this kind of behavior," she said, looking as if she had just swigged a mouthful of vinegar.

"What?" I had no idea what she was talking about.

She shoved a piece of paper into my hands. I unfolded it to reveal a short, type-written note in bold black ink and large font that said, "Back off Bitch!"

"Where did you find this?" I asked, my mind spinning.

"On my desk with the mail, where you clearly intended me to find it," the Pit Bull said, lifting her chin even higher as if she had a whiff of something offensive.

"With the mail?"

"Yes, you heard me. It was with the mail on my desk."

"Miss Pittman, I did not leave this for you, nor would I." I shuddered involuntarily as a cold shiver coursed through me. First my cellphone, now my office. I feared that whoever it was may find out where I live. My snooping had made Kiera vulnerable. She would be home alone numerous nights when I was out covering meetings and openings around the County. This was hitting way too close to home. "I have a feeling it was intended for me," I finally answered.

Confusion flashed across the Pit Bull's face. "For you?"

"Yes. I've been looking into things related to Bruno's murder. I must have hit a chord with someone." But who? I didn't think I was getting any closer to finding any answers to Bruno's murder. If I told the Sheriff, he'd tell me to back off too. I couldn't do that, as I didn't think they were anywhere close to solving this.

"I'll hold on to this," I said to the Pit Bull, trying my best to sound cool and calm. "If you can remember, please make a list for me of all the people who were in the office yesterday and today. And let me know immediately if we receive any more correspondence like this." I took the paper and somehow managed to walk confidently back to my office, and placed it in the top drawer of my desk. I put my head in my hands. For the first time, I thought I was in way over my head.

My cellphone rang, but I wasn't sure I was controlled enough to answer. I checked. It was my closest friend, Emily. It felt like years since we talked, but now everything seemed to take on a different time dimension, being either before Bruno's death or after Bruno's death. "Emily, I'm so happy to hear from you."

"Where have you been hiding, girl? I was getting worried about you. I thought maybe that little paper had swallowed you whole."

"Oh Emily, I'm sorry. There has been so much going on that I didn't get a chance to call. I don't know where to start."

"Just tell me that you and Kiera are okay because you're scaring me. I always worry when I don't hear from you."

It was hard to believe only a short time had passed since Emily had wished me good luck on the job. We'd been best friends since our first job together on a little art mag, straight out of university. We were so thrilled to have our names down as staff writers that it didn't matter that the job paid peanuts. We had a blast, but it didn't take long for reality to set in, when paying the rent was problematic with the pittance we received. We had had to find something at a bigger publication that paid more if we were to survive in publishing. Em pushed full bore into her career, never looking back. Now, in her forties, she was a dedicated career woman, at the top of her game as editor of a national entertainment magazine. She was constantly trying to get me to attend social engagements in the city, especially since my divorce. She couldn't fathom that I actually liked living in the country. There wasn't much I didn't tell her. She had been my "go-to" person for years, and right now I needed to spill my guts, omitting only the threats.

"My poor D, your paper is inadequately staffed to deal with huge news stories. Right now, I also think Kiera's attachment to Nacho is clouding your judgment."

"I'm worried about Kiera's feelings."

"Kiera will be fine. There are other barns and other coaches. Even if this operation shuts down, she will ride as always. If she goes away to college next year, she may change barns if she takes Amigo with her, or she may even decide to lease or sell Amigo. Don't forget she's changing. You don't know what down-the-road brings."

I knew she was right; maybe I just didn't want to hear that Kiera was growing up. I guess I had some growing pains of my own. I didn't think I could handle an emotional meltdown from Kiera if it was my decision to have her leave Nacho's. "You're right, of course, Em. I just don't want anything to change right now. Kiera has been in a good mental place."

"There's only so much you can control. So find out what you can about the murder and put it in somebody else's hands—just keep on his good side. That Sheriff sounds like a keeper—way more potential than Nacho, who has got himself in a fine mess. When Kiera graduates, I really want you to think about moving back and taking a job with my mag. We would be so fortunate to have you."

After I hung up I felt better. I hadn't told Em about the threats, since I knew she would come barreling upstate, insisting I quit a job that didn't pay enough to have my life threatened. If that was what the threats were about. I also knew as well-meaning as Em was, and however lucrative her job offer was, I could never muster enough interest to write about the latest Kardashian scandal. That, to me, defined frivolous. But the job suited Em and she did a fabulous job of increasing magazine sales in an increasingly digital world. Still, it was good to have an exit strategy, as my parents were fond of telling me. Mom checked with me every two weeks since they retired to Ireland, which reminded me: I had better call them before they worried and caught me in a weak moment.

In short order, the ever-efficient Pit Bull appeared with a typed list of people who had stopped in at the office yesterday and today. Among the FedEx guy, mailman, and various folks and high school students dropping off ads and photos, two visitors stood out: Frank Malfaro and some woman from the Environmental Defense League. This confirmed their inclusion in my top-ten hit list. My stainless-steel backbone snapped back into place. I was more determined than ever to do my job so everything in our lives would be back to normal. I just hoped I wasn't playing with fire.

FIFTEEN

My eyes scanned the rolling hills. Fields full of tall stalks of corn flashed past my window. High above the corn I caught sight of a hawk, wings spread wide, lazily tracing circles in the air. Oh to be as carefree as that hawk, I thought. I was then jolted back to attention when Kiera cried out.

"Mom! Watch out! A deer."

I turned my eyes back to the road ahead and slammed the brakes much harder than I should have. The car fishtailed, and I fought the steering wheel to straighten us out. I could feel my heartbeat in my throat. The deer was running at full speed on the right side of the road. Judging its trajectory, it would cross immediately in front of our car in a disastrous scenario if I didn't stop. I quickly checked my rearview mirror. Good—no one behind us. I didn't want to be rear-ended. I applied more pressure to the brakes, this time more controlled. The deer leaped out of the nearby ditch and onto the road. I held tighter to the wheel, my shoulders hunched up towards my ears, and braced for a possible impact. Hooves making contact with pavement, the deer skittered a bit, then regained its footing. Gaining momentum, it jumped past the front of our car and onward into the oncoming lane which, luckily, was empty, and then it disappeared into the bush.

I had been so preoccupied with slowing down that I only now

noticed a large black van bearing down the hill behind me. I picked up speed as quickly as I could. The driver of the van pulled around to pass without even slowing. All of a sudden, it dawned on me who it was when I saw the lettering on the side of the van that read "Environmental Defense League".

When we pulled into the parking lot for Bruno's memorial service, it looked as if there had been a sale on black vans and SUVs. Clive was stepping out of the same black van that had passed us and sauntered in ahead without even a word of greeting.

Once inside, Kiera was quick to part company to seek out Heather, which left me standing on my own in the large foyer of the Pleasant Valley Memorial Chapel. It was tastefully decorated, with white wainscoting three-quarters up the walls and a mint-green shade of paint on the upper quarter. I'd always called that color "Grandma green" as it was the same shade as the walls in my grandmother's living room in Ireland. Normally, it gave me warm feelings when I saw that color, but today I felt flat. I was not looking forward to the memorial service. I knew I had a job to do for the paper, but that did not stop me from feeling like I was an intruder. Kiera had more right to be here than I did. Her best friend was dating the grandson of the deceased. Who was I? *The one who found the body.*

Looking forward from the foyer, there was a grouping of stiff couches and straight-back chairs in front of a gas fireplace. Leading off from there were four doorways, each leading to different rooms in which to mourn and bid goodbye to the departed. Mounted on the walls outside the doorways to each room were television monitors. Three displayed the name and image of the chapel, while one outside the room directly at the end of the hall was displaying a slideshow, transitioning from image to image. Bruno's service was the only one today; a good thing I thought, judging by the size of the crowd already in attendance. The chapel would be filled to capacity. Luckily, the MacKenzies were able to open up the partitions in this room to accommodate more. I doubt the place had seen so many people in a while. My guess was that under normal circumstances they would have used Our Lady of Sorrows Catholic Church on King Road. Frank had told me they would be using it eventually for a private family service and the burial once the body was released.

I scanned the faces to see if there was anyone I recognized. Huddled just outside the room, Frank Malfaro was deep in conversation with a somber-looking gentleman, probably the Funeral Director, and most likely finalizing details. I had not yet had a chance to talk to Frank today. An opportunity was sure to present itself after the service when I offered him my condolences. Kiera was in a huddle with Heather and Marco and several other teens, watching the slide show on the monitor which was displaying pictures of Bruno over the years with his family. I shook my head. Even at a memorial service it was hard to get that group away from technology. Non-descript piano music drifted out of speakers in the ceiling, washing the crowd with calmness and tranquility. Everyone was talking in hushed tones until Tanya arrived.

The woman knew how to make an entrance. Teetering on tall pumps, she sashayed into the foyer, her cleavage leading the way. She had on a tight black blazer with a black lace bustier underneath which propelled her boobs forward as though she were serving them up on a tray. Hanging around her neck was a thick gold chain with a huge diamond-encrusted cross which rested just in between her breasts. Her skirt, also black, was tight and short to reveal long tanned legs, bare save for a gold ankle bracelet. Her hair was swept up in a loose bun, and a black netted veil hung over the top half of her face from a black sequin-encrusted fascinator, perched at an angle on the top of her head.

"What are you doing here?" Frank asked, breaking away from his conversation with the Funeral Director and storming towards Tanya.

"I have every right to be here," Tanya snipped, her head held high. "Bruno was going to be my husband. I've devoted my life to him."

"More like devoted your life to his money."

Tanya shot him a look and slapped him hard across the face. The Funeral Director deftly stepped in and pulled Frank aside, where he spoke to him in a subdued voice.

Cynthia waggled her fingers at me from the opposite side of the room, and I made a beeline for her.

"It's like an episode of Real Housewives," she said excitedly to me when I approached. "I'm waiting for the name-calling and hairpulling to start."

Cynthia was wearing a sleeveless V-neck little black dress—emphasis on little. At least all of her undergarments were covered, unlike Tanya's. I wasn't a prude, but there was a time and a place for bustiers, and in my opinion, the place was under your clothes!

"You like my LBD?" she asked, catching me appraising her looks.

I wasn't sure what to say and was thankful to be saved by noticing she had a distinguished older gentleman hanging off her arm.

"Who's this?" I asked, turning my attention to the man on her arm. "Are you going to introduce us?"

"David, darling, this is Darcy Dillon, the new editor of the Weekly," she said, extending her arms out like she was framing a potential prize for a contestant on the Price is Right.

I extended my hand and we shook hands. His grip was firm as he looked me directly in the eyes. "A pleasure," he said. He was older than Cynthia by about ten years at least, judging by the gray hair which had fully filled in at the temples. He was tall and well turned out in an expensive, dark pin-striped suit. Distinguished; I hadn't expected that. To be honest, I hadn't fully figured out Cynthia's type yet. I hadn't met her ex-husband. It was hard to imagine she had ever been married. Cynthia always struck me as a single gal, like those fashion crazed girls on Sex in the City—single and ready to mingle.

"So, you're the one dragging my girl to crime scenes," David said, looking serious.

"Just one," I said in my defense.

"Knock it off, Davey," Cynthia chided, playing with the lapels on his suit. "She's a hell of a lot more fun to work with than stuffy old Morty!"

"I see a business associate I need to say hello to," he said, pecking Cynthia on the cheek. "Nice to have met you," he said to me before turning to engage in conversation with a group behind us. Cynthia smacked him on the butt as he turned around, and he shot her a playful wink over his shoulder.

"You serious about him?"

"Who, Davey? No, no, bumped into him here; he used to work with Bruno. We've dated …," she trailed off. "What's going on with Tanya and Frank now?" she asked.

I looked over and saw that the Director was motioning them into a private room off the foyer.

"I'd like to be a fly on that wall," Cyn said.

"I might just do that. Cover me and let me know if anyone is coming?"

"I love it; we're going all top secret commando now," Cyn said, as we pushed our way over to the room Tanya and Frank had been ushered into.

I tried to look casual as I leaned one shoulder into the door jamb. With my right hand I slowly turned the door knob. I just needed it open enough to hear what they were saying. Cyn positioned herself so we looked like we might be in conversation. I could make out Tanya's voice.

"I have every right to be here. I was his fiancée."

"You weren't going to hold that title for much longer," Frank shot back.

"What do you mean?" Tanya spat.

"Just wait till we meet in the lawyer's office."

Cyn elbowed me. "What are they saying?"

"Something about the lawyer's office, might have something to do with the reading of the will?"

"The will? Have they read it yet?" she asked.

"No, sounds like it will be soon. Shhh, let me listen."

"Bring lots of Kleenex. You'll need them when your real losses sink in," Frank was saying.

Cyn elbowed me again.

"What?" I said turning to look at her. Cyn had a sheepish look on her face. The Funeral Director was glowering at me with his beady eyes.

"Can I help you?"

"Just looking for the washrooms," I lied, trying to act nonchalant.

"Over there," he said, pointing across the hall to the facilities which were very well-marked and obvious.

"Thanks," I said, as Cyn and I slunk off in that direction.

Standing in the washroom, Cyn asked, "Did you hear anything more?"

I scanned under the bathroom stalls. No feet. "Just that Tanya is most likely not going to get anything in the will."

"Oooh, I'll bet that blows all her plans," Cyn said as she reached into her purse and pulled out lipstick, which she applied generously to her lips.

Figuring that the coast was clear, we exited the bathroom and stood in the main gathering area. Bumping elbows with a person beside me, I said, "It's packed in here. It's like the entire town has turned out to show their respects."

The Funeral Director was now guiding people into the room so the memorial service could begin. I could hear his voice directing people and could feel the crowd around us moving in that direction.

"Shall we?" Cyn indicated the direction of the chapel, and I fell in step with her. The chapel was full; we were the last ones in the door. The Director shot us a look for holding up his carefully choreographed service, then quickly reverted back to his polished persona. Cyn and I ended up standing at the back of the room, as all seats were taken. It was a better vantage point to check out all of the mourners so I didn't complain. If things dragged on, there was an opportunity to duck out.

The organist struck up a mournful hymn, and the Director opened a door at the side of the chapel that led to a private room for family only. The entire family paraded in, following the Director, to the front rows of the chapel which were festooned with black bows on the ends. Frank and his wife, I assumed, a dark-haired woman somewhat thick around the middle, led the parade. Behind them in revered positions and aided by young, suited men was a contingent of short, chubby elderly women in shapeless black dresses, and several elderly gray-haired gentlemen, all of whom I took to be aunts, uncles and siblings. Then there were Frank's four children, Marco among them. Behind trailed the bulk of the cousins by the dozens, ranging from protesting babies to forty-something men and women. The women for the most part looked rich and sleek in black, tight designer dresses, designer hair and designer shoes. Even all the kids were gussied up: the girls in expensive, frilly frocks and small boys awkward in little suits or white shirts and dress pants, with slicked back hair. They filled the entire first five rows. Behind this impressive array sat several distinguished-looking businessmen and well-dressed women including the Mayor and several councilors. It was here that the notorious Tanya had staked her territory. Clive sat off to the side on his own.

Surveying the whole flock from a raised platform in front of an altar was an older robed priest, flanked by huge overflowing bouquets of flowers, and white-and-red carnation wreaths on frames. On an easel was a large, professional photo of Bruno from days gone by, looking fat, powerful, and indestructible.

The crowd hushed when the music stopped. The priest stood and proceeded to the lectern. Speeches from colleagues were interspersed with hymns sung by a young blonde woman, the priest's prayers, and mass rituals. Babies crying, kids shuffling and people coughing punctuated the ceremony. Frank delivered the eulogy and Marco recited a poem. No one cried.

I tried to keep my mind on the service, or at least to focus on the attendees, to help me put together an article on the proceedings. At a minimum, I should have searched the room for possible suspects to help clear Nacho. My mind flipped between flashbacks of the scene of Bruno's body hanging and vague terrors connected to the mysterious sender of the ominous message.

After the ceremony, the crowd spilled out into the main hallway. I leaned over and whispered to Cyn. "Have you learned anything more about Bruno from anyone?"

Looking over her shoulder she whispered, "I heard that Clive doesn't have an alibi." We locked eyes with raised eyebrows. No wonder Adam was looking at him as a suspect. "Apparently, all Clive wants is power and attention. Being Director of the League gives him both and allows him to grandstand. It makes up for him losing his bid to get elected to Council several years ago."

"I didn't realize he was gunning for Council, since he didn't run in my ward. Who gave you the scoop on him?"

"My darling Davey. He also pointed out a couple that farm some of Bruno's land. I thought we could talk to them."

"Sounds like a good idea. Where are they?" I turned to look at all of the people who had spilled back into the room.

Cyn scanned the crowd. "Over by the coffee urns, feeding on the free snacks like pigs at a trough." She grabbed my arm and steered me through the crowd towards the coffee station.

Cyn took a cup and started filling it at one of the urns. I did the same.

"So sad," Cyn said to the couple stuffing their faces with small sandwiches filled with egg and tuna salad. "Did you know Bruno well?"

Between bites of his sandwich the man said, "Yeah, well enough. We farm his fields."

The woman beside him, clutching a fist full of chocolate chip cookies, jumped in. "Owes us some money, he does. We planted four acres of corn on one parcel, and then he ups and tells us we can't farm it any more. Acted like we was deadbeats when we told him he needed to make up for our loss of time and money. Four whole acres!"

"Mandy!" The man shot a look at the woman next to him.

"What Joe? It's true. Don't think because he's dead I'm going to forget he owes us money for that corn. He threatened to rent the fields to someone else next year unless we went along with it. Not like he needed the money; he was just trying to show me how big and powerful he was."

"Did you farm a lot of his fields?"

"Made up over 50 percent of our crops. The man was threatening our livelihood."

"Mandy Bullen! Really, you've said enough," the man said, scooping up a small plate he had piled with brownies and other sweets. He grabbed her by the elbow and led her away.

I shot Cyn a glance. "Possible suspects?"

"Definitely possible, if you ask me," she said munching on a brownie.

I made a mental note to tell the Sheriff about them as soon as I could. They definitely had issues with Bruno. I just hoped they had more issues and opportunity than Nacho.

Sixteen

I wasn't going on a date. It didn't make sense that I felt like I did. Adam was picking me up to cover an article for the paper, I reminded myself. Cyn was coming along too, for God's sake. Still, I had butterflies, and paid careful attention picking my outfit. Jeans worked. I didn't want to look like I was trying too hard. I chose ones that fit me just right, not the Mom Jeans pulled out for painting projects and house cleaning. For a top, I picked a casual blouse in teal green, which Kiera had given me for Christmas, from the back of the closet. She and Cyn both knew something I didn't, because Cyn had also suggested this color would show off my bluish-green eyes and set off my auburn hair.

In the kitchen, a cereal bowl with a few remaining Cheerios disintegrating in the milk sat on the counter. Kiera was up. Voices were coming from the family room. I headed in that direction.

"Morning Sunshine," came an overly enthusiastic greeting from Cyn. I didn't know why I worried about my outfit. Next to Cyn, in her hot pink velour hoodie and formfitting track pants, I felt like a dandelion next to a hibiscus.

"Hey, Mom, I let Cyn in while you were in the shower. I didn't know you were going on a field trip."

"Thanks, hon." I wondered how much Cyn had told her.

"We've been talking more about how I could be a model. Cyn said she'd do my initial headshots for free. Isn't that great!"

"Of course, it will have to wait until I find a suitable studio to use. I'm really not set up to do Kiera justice. I'll need proper lighting and backgrounds," Cyn babbled.

"Yeah, great." I'd have to talk to Cyn about this later. I was having a hard enough time getting Kiera to focus on school with her riding. Modeling was the last thing I needed to add into the mix.

Kiera, sensing my censure, made a brave attempt to head it off. "Cyn said you should have been a model too, and probably still could for .. . you know … middle-aged women. She said I got my great looks and stature from you." She cocked her head and smiled her most charming smile.

Mercifully, we were interrupted by a loud knock. Adam was ready to take us on our drug-busting adventures.

Kiera headed past us on her way out the door to catch the school bus, backpack slung over her shoulder, one zipper half open, books hanging out. "Don't forget I am going over to Lana's house today after school, to work on the school float for the Fall Fair. Can you come by and pick up me and Heather later?" she asked.

"Sure. What time?"

"About eleven."

"On a school night? Really."

"Mom?" Kiera cut me a look.

I dropped the subject; I didn't want to have this discussion in front of an audience. "Fine. I'll pick you up then," I said, shaking my head in disgust at myself for agreeing.

Adam caught my tone. "I got similar treatment from Andrew this morning. Don't let it faze you. They're getting all excited about Fall Fair. Andrew had me digging crap out of the garage for the scarecrow contest."

"Thanks for reminding me! I almost forgot," I said, turning to speak to Cyn in the other room. "Cyn, did I tell you we need to cover a scarecrow contest in town on Friday?"

"Nope, but Pit Bull put it on my calendar already so you're all set," Cyn said, waving her new iPhone 4S in my direction, emphasizing I should buy something more sophisticated. She went back to typing something on her screen. She'd been distracted by it since I came down.

Adam appraised the kitchen as we entered. "You've done a lot with the place."

I remembered he mentioned his uncle used to own my house many years ago. "The old farmhouse had character but needed modern amenities, like stainless steel, granite, and open-concept living. Do you like the addition?"

"It's great. I always thought the place could be a real gem with the right work. I'd say you've improved it in a big way. I love how the kitchen opens out onto the living room now. It's great to see the yard. They used to build the windows small to not lose so much heat. When Uncle Jack lived here you couldn't see the fields at all. If you're going to live in the country, you want to see it. Your addition definitely maximizes the view," he said, looking directly at me.

I wasn't sure if he was talking about the fields or me. Caught off guard, I blushed like a schoolgirl. How desperate have I become, I thought, analyzing every word and finding meanings where there may be none. For the first time, I could imagine having another man in my life, instead of just my fantasies.

"So, we'd better get going if we are going to catch some criminals," I said abruptly. I gave Cyn a "let's get going" signal when she looked up from her phone, and we all headed out. Once we were all belted into Adam's Ford Explorer, I asked, "What are we expecting to find today?"

"I expect that we'll find marijuana concealed in the middle of a cornfield if the tip proves to be authentic. Since we're into fall and the corn is almost ready to be harvested, the stalks will be dried out. From the air, the marijuana will stand out as green patches in fields of beige. Earlier in the season we use infrared to spot grow-ops. Both marijuana and potato plants show up red. Then we need to check exactly which crop it is. In this case, it won't be required because of the season."

"Did they say which fields?"

"Yes and no. We have a relatively broad sector we're focusing on today." We pulled onto a gravel sideroad.

"Where are we going?"

"Since we don't have a local airstrip, we are staging things from a local farm. The owner is an amateur pilot and has his own private runway."

"Cool. Who is the local James Bond?" Cyn chimed in from the back seat, finally looking up from her phone. "I'd like a man with his own plane and airport on speed dial."

Both Adam and I chuckled.

"His name is George Mason. We're lucky he offered to help out."

"Cyn, what have you been doing all morning on your phone?" My curiosity was killing me.

"Talking with my tweet peeps," Cyn said. "We've been having a bit of a debate."

"A debate?" My eyebrows raised.

"High-waist pants—dead trend or fashion comeback," Cyn said with excitement. "I'm totally pro comeback."

"Right," I said, noticing the smirk on Adam's face. *I should have known.*

We drove for a bit in silence when Cyn piped up. "Did you hear that the reading of Bruno's will is today? I'm dying to know if Trashy Tanya got the booty or the boot!"

I laughed out loud. I couldn't help it. "I'm sure she will get what she deserves," I said, then realized I sounded catty. I blushed as I snuck a look at Adam to see his reaction. His eyes were still on the road.

We turned into a driveway on the right-hand side. Beside it stretched a long pathway of mowed grass with some dirt tracks. A white-and-red windsock flew from a pole nearby. A blue-and-white Cessna was parked inside an open barn. An old man in beige work overalls and a rumpled blue plaid shirt waved at us. Adam pulled over to park.

"James Bond, I presume," I whispered over my shoulder at Cyn. In response, she cuffed me on the shoulder. We piled out.

"Hey, Sheriff. Copter isn't here yet. Expect it will be shortly. Who are these lovely ladies?" he said, directing his attention towards Cyn and me.

Adam introduced us, but the loud drone of whipping blades interrupted us as a small black helicopter approached the field and positioned itself for landing. I found myself ducking even though it was more than a hundred feet away. After a few minutes the blades slowed to a stop and the pilot, wearing a headset with large pale green earphones, climbed out of the cockpit. More introductions took place. The pilot, Ned Bane, was from a narcotics division in a county south of us. The copter had a multitude of uses including being a spotter for forest fires.

"So, how does this work?" I needed details for my article, and I was also curious.

"Ned and I will be connected via radio. When he spots something suspicious from the air, he will radio us the coordinates, and we will drive to the location for a visual identification. As I mentioned, potatoes or weed." He made a balance gesture with his hands.

"Can I go in the helicopter?" Cyn sounded like some kid asking to go on a ride at the fair. "That way I could get some aerial shots," she added, patting her camera bag, slung low at her hip. I could see her setting her sights on the pilot already.

"That okay with you, Ned?"

"Absolutely," he said, eyes twinkling.

"It's not, of course, entirely routine to bring civilians along," said Adam, "but I'm desperate for a deterrent that I hope an article will provide. All I need you girls to do is sign some release and confidentiality forms, and then we're in business."

Paperwork complete, Ned gestured towards Cyn. "Come with me and I'll strap you in." It sounded so *Fifty Shades of Gray*, the way he said it. I hoped they would concentrate on the mission at hand and keep their eyes on the ground instead of each other.

That left me to ride with Adam. I had no intentions of getting into a helicopter. I'd heard they drop like stones if the engine cuts out, and that was enough to keep me on the ground. Besides, riding with Adam gave me an opportunity to talk more about Bruno's murder investigation, or, at a minimum, find out who were top of the list as solid suspects. As we got into Adam's Explorer he handed me a map. "You can help navigate."

I went to wave to Cyn and caught a full rear-end view of pink buttocks emblazoned with "Juicy" in a large jaunty script spelled out in rhinestones. The word grew even larger as she crouched low to enter the chopper. Adam's eyes followed mine. Except for the half smile, he didn't comment one way or the other. Instead, he really surprised me when he said, "You look nice today. I like that color on you."

"Thank you." I was flustered though pleased. "I'm happy to see Cyn actually has her camera out and has attached her zoom lens." There was hope that she'd do more than flirt. "So, do we chase them?"

"No, we'll let them scout on ahead. If they spot something, Ned will radio us the location. Then we can drive over to check things out."

"So now we wait?"

"Exactly," he said, fiddling with the dials on his dash-mounted radio.

I'd fantasized being alone with Adam, but now that it was happening, I didn't know what to say. I was starting to like him and wondered if those feelings were mutual. My schoolgirl thoughts were interrupted by a crackling sound from the radio followed by Ned's voice.

"Grid section one clear."

"Roger that."

"What does that mean?" I asked.

He leaned closer to me and took hold of the map he handed to me. He smelled good in a manly way, a mixture of shampoo and shaving lotion.

He flipped the map over and showed me a series of grid lines drawn across it. "To make the search more systematic, we divided each part of the county into a grid so we don't waste time going over areas twice or miss sections entirely. Ned has just covered this section here." He pointed to one of the boxes.

Instead of the next few hours spent in pithy conversation full of sexual tension, what transpired was awkward conversation and stolen glances broken by the occasional "all clear" report from Ned. I wasn't being myself. Although there was an attraction, it was forbidden fruit. I couldn't act on it even I wanted to, or Kiera would freak. Plus, the Sheriff was a vital source of information I needed, and I couldn't afford to screw up my professional life, not while I was still getting established at the paper.

I tried outlining articles to distract myself, although my efforts were half-hearted. Concentrating was tough. Just as I was plucking up courage to ask Adam for more information about their suspect list, Ned's voice burst over the radio. "We have a visual in grid six."

I closed my notebook and flattened out the map on my lap to scan it. "Here," Adam said, reaching across me and pointing. The hunt was on.

While I appreciated having Adam near, I put on my editor's hat and scanned the map. "Grid six looks a little close to home," I said. He just nodded and reversed out of the driveway.

Once on the road he grabbed the receiver and said, "On our way. Can you give me crossroads or further coordinates in the grid?"

"Closest you can get by road looks to be Beaver Creek Road and Seven Oaks Trail."

"Roger."

We drove down country lanes, where horses frolicked in the Indian summer sun or grazed lazily in large grassy paddocks punctuated by rustic rail fences. In one field, a horse under an old apple tree munched on the ripe apples littering the grass and roadway. It looked inviting. I was getting hungry—I hadn't eaten since breakfast. I made a mental note to bring snacks the next time I went on a drug bust, which felt more like country drive than a takedown.

Adam pulled off to the side of the road and discussed location with Ned. Then he turned to me. "We'll have to hike in from here. It's not dangerous. If anyone had been there, they would have been scared off by the chopper. You okay with that?"

"Absolutely!" I said, full of exhilaration, my editor's hat firmly in place. Finally, some action. I reminded myself again that this was a real live drug bust.

We slogged through a culvert and up into the field of corn stalks. The stalks were over my head even though I measure five-foot-seven, so I focused on following Adam, who was ahead of me. I appreciated how he held the stalks so they wouldn't smack me in the face. Even in pursuit of a criminal he had time to be a gentleman. The ground was uneven, and I concentrated on my footing. Turning an ankle would be easy and guarantee I wouldn't be invited for a return engagement. I was glad Cyn was in the helicopter. Three-inch heels and cornfields are a lethal combo.

The beat of the helicopter blades pounded ahead of us. The strong breeze signaled we were getting close. Adam stopped and warned me. "Now Ned has radioed that there is no one at the site, but as a precaution, if we see anyone, hit the ground and don't come up until I tell you. Technically, this is pretty routine. We're not here busting the growers or dealers, more their operation. We may never know who's responsible." That was a sobering thought.

The dry cornstalks rustled and sometimes cracked as we moved them aside. Startled bugs leaped out at me, and I ducked through a black cloud of no-see-ums, brushing them from my hair. Ahead, Adam forged on. Finally, we broke through into a pocket of green plants that were shorter than the corn and bending in the wind from the chopper. We'd found it—the grow-op. I glanced at Adam; he had a look of triumph, with his wide smile and gleaming eyes. I was more than a little relieved that no one was around.

I turned around, trying to get my bearings as I shielded my eyes from the dust particles. Since the marijuana plants were shorter than the corn, I could see further into the distance. Something up ahead looked familiar. I moved forward for a better look. I had to squint. Some of the plants had been cut down in the patch up ahead. I moved there to try to see further. Adam was busy talking on his radio behind me. Twinges of unease coiled around me as I viewed our location. I hadn't expected this to be grid six. I was sure I had checked in the car earlier. Still, I'd never come in from Beaver Creek Road because it ran in back. Flying dust assaulted my eyes; I could feel a headache coming on as I recognized our location. As much as I wanted to, there was no denying the fact anymore. In the distance was the back of Nacho's barn.

We were in the field past the outer paddock. I was on the verge of losing it. My world was falling apart, and I didn't know what to do. My heart raced. My head killed me. My breathing increased. Adam must have known all along where we were. Was this part of his investigation into Bruno's death?

Could Nacho have known about this? Was this his patch? Had Bruno found this, or was this the real reason for their argument?

Thoughts tumbled about in my aching head like they were in a dryer. I cursed myself for not talking to Adam when I had the chance. My mind continued to whirl as fast the helicopter blades. All I knew was I needed answers, and I wanted the truth from Nacho before I went mad.

At that thought, I stumbled forward. Cornstalks slammed me; dust swirled in my mouth and eyes. I spit out bugs as I thrashed my way blindly through the field. Half running, I tripped as my foot caught on something. I fell hard to the ground. Adam must have seen me fall, as I could hear him calling my name in the distance. "Darcy, are you all right?"

I was lying face down in the dirt. My body was jarred, and the wind knocked out of me. My head still pounded. I pulled my hands back even with my shoulders to push myself up. Immediately, I felt something sticky. Yuck, bug slime, I thought, as I looked at my hands. They were covered in something red. Blood? I didn't think I had fallen that hard. Then I saw it.

I tried to scream. Nothing came out but a gasp of air as revulsion choked my vocal cords. I became the silent scream painting—a freaked out caricature gasping as waves of nausea tried their best to drown me. I heaved myself off the dirt, desperate to flee. I scrambled backwards only to bump into something. Hysteria enveloped me as I thrashed to get away from the hands holding me.

"Darcy, stop; it's me, Adam. What's wrong?" Tension hardened his voice.

I slumped against him and sobbed. I couldn't speak. I could only point with my blood-smeared hand towards the body lying face down in the field, the back of the head split wide, like a pumpkin spilling forth its seeds.

SEVENTEEN

Adam stepped in front of me to have a look. I peeked over his shoulder. I didn't want to look again, but I needed to know who it was. The body was male, with dark hair curling about the ears, while the forearms were tanned and muscular. Could it be Nacho? I looked away, ducking back behind Adam. Nausea washed over me, along with a slick cold sweat. I was going to be sick. I pulled my hand up to my mouth … my hands, my hands were covered with blood and … I didn't want to think about what else. I frantically tried wiping them off on the dried leaves of the cornstalk next to me. I doubled over, my mind reeling. I hiccupped, holding back the reaction.

Adam turned around and reached out to support me. "Whoa, hang on. You've had a shock. It'll be better if you sit down." He pushed down some of the plants to form a soft spot and laid his coat down for me to sit. "Don't look at the body. I'll radio for help."

Adam rose as I tried to pull myself together. I hiccupped again. I heard flies buzzing, lots of flies. Then it dawned on me why they were buzzing. I couldn't hold it in. My stomach heaved. I leaned over and threw up. Adam wasn't going to want his jacket back.

"You okay?" Adam asked when he returned.

"No, not at all." I was afraid, but I had to ask. "Do you know who it is?"

"No, there's no ID on the body. Ned's landing the chopper. I've called this in. They'll be sending reinforcements."

By reinforcements, I hoped he meant vodka. "Could it be Nacho?" I asked again, trying not to whimper.

"I don't think so," he said, and stepped back to the body. He bent down and with gloved hands carefully lifted the face out of the dirt. It was pale white like the underside of a fish belly. I looked away. After what felt like an eternity, Adam finally said "No. It's not Nacho."

I took a ragged breath. But who was it? Why in this field, so close to Nacho's barn? So many questions raced through my mind.

Someone walked through the corn behind us, and I turned to look. I had lost track of time with all the commotion. The crime scene techs along with Robin, the Deputy Sheriff, had arrived. Like the flies, they buzzed around the body. Adam came over to check on me. When he noticed I had been sick, he grabbed an evidence bag from the tech guys and stuffed his jacket in there. "Not for evidence," he said. "Don't worry about it; it's washable."

"I am so sorry. Let me take it home and wash it."

"I won't hear of it. In my line of work, it goes with the territory," he assured me. Other than my dad, I didn't know they grew men this way anymore.

Of course, as here I was again, at the wrong place at the wrong time, Adam had to take an official statement from me. I didn't have much to say. He had been with me until just minutes before I literally stumbled upon the body.

"How did he die? I mean, it's obvious he has a head injury." *Putting it mildly.*

"We think someone hit him in the head with a machete or something similar."

"A machete? That's pretty specific. How did you figure that out so quickly?" Somehow, focusing on the facts, doing my job as a reporter, helped me be more detached.

"Much as I hate to admit that I am not a genius, it wasn't too difficult. While securing the area we found a machete a few feet from the body. He must have been using it to cut down the marijuana plants."

"So, are you saying that the machete was the murder weapon?" I was trying to piece it together, ridding myself of the cobwebs of horror that had slowed my brain.

"Not exactly. We believe the machete matches the wound pattern. However, until it's examined, we can't confirm it was the exact one that killed him."

With my head pounding it took a minute to clue in to what he'd said. "Was there a second machete?"

"Maybe; it is at least one of our working theories right now, but there are numerous other scenarios we're also following."

"Let me see if I follow this. There were two people out in the field cutting down the marijuana plants with machetes, and then one killed the other by splitting his head open."

"You're quick, Darcy."

"Can I print this?"

"Absolutely not! That is only one theory and an early one at that. This is all supposition without tangible evidence and without interviews. There are any number of scenarios depending on the motive, and all are confidential."

I hung my head.

He sighed. "Look. You don't go to press till the end of the week, so give me a few days to look into this. It depends on how much information we want to make public. I'll let you know what you can print. And don't go do any digging on your own right now, okay?"

I shrugged, hoping I didn't have to agree.

He was being cautious. Maybe he had a plan and some suspect in mind already. When I went on this bust, I had agreed to print the news of a drug find, and now, unfortunately, I was probably obligated to give the location near Nacho's barn. Of course, it depended on what the Sheriff gave me to report whether there was a way to protect Nacho.

More rustling came from the cornfield behind us. Probably Ned or Cyn coming to see what was going on. I was wrong. It was Nacho. When he saw me sitting on the ground, he rushed to my side.

"Darcy, are you okay?" he asked, bending down to my level. He touched my hand. I didn't draw mine away, but I was conflicted. I could see a suspicious look on Adam's face.

"I'll be okay. Do you know anything about this?" I asked, accusation hardening my tone.

"I don't know what you mean by 'this.' I saw the helicopter, then all of the police lights, from the barn. The horses were spooked, and I was concerned about what was going on, especially after Bruno. I thought maybe they found something."

"We found something all right—a dead body," Adam cut in. "Is this your property?"

"What? Huh, uh, no … well yes," Nacho said.

"Which is it? Yes or no?" Adam snapped abruptly.

"This field … it's part of the property owned by Bruno … I mean Malfaro Developments."

"You plant this crop?"

"What?" Nacho said, looking confused. "I'm an equestrian, not a farmer," he said, standing straight at his full height. "I don't know what crop you're referring to … corn?"

"Hardly." Adam made a sweeping gesture toward the weed patch.

Nacho's eyes grew big. "I see. This field is part of the property, but it is farmed by someone else on a lease basis. I only lease the barn and paddocks."

"Do you know who farms it?"

"No, I definitely do not. No one ventures beyond the paddocks at all. You'll have to contact Malfaro Developments," Nacho said.

He was starting to sound defensive. I stood up, thinking perhaps I should calm the situation. I went to smooth my clothes with my hand, remembered it was covered in blood and pulled it back.

Adam and Nacho stopped talking, although both were rooted to their spot, nostrils flaring. Any minute they might paw the ground. Adam looked from Nacho to me. Was he also thinking that Nacho was involved in drugs and now another murder? It was all becoming overwhelming.

He looked behind him and beckoned the Deputy over. "Robin, have Detective Baker take Mr. Rodrigo into the station for questioning. I'll be there shortly. First, I'm going to drop Darcy home." All my worst nightmares and then some were coming true.

I didn't speak to Adam for most of the ride. His look definitely didn't invite conversation, and I wasn't sure I was feeling strong enough at the moment to hear his latest theory. First Bruno and now this doper. Did he think they were connected? Obviously he did, and connected to Nacho. First, we had to stop at George Mason's farm to pick up Cyn before we went home. I thought I had better say something before we got there. "I'm having a difficult time thinking Nacho is involved with this latest murder."

"I don't know that he isn't," he said, looking over at me, "nor do you. What I do know is that I have two dead bodies in just under a week found on a property that your friend is associated with."

I crossed my arms and stared out the window at the fields passing by. Two small Shetland ponies stood in a field watching us pass.

When we picked up Cyn, initially she was full of questions. I told her what we had found and that Adam had sent Nacho in for questioning. The drive home became uncomfortably quiet; even Cyn was subdued for once, squirming occasionally in the back seat. The morning and all its excitement seemed a million hours ago. Adam was in his Sheriff's role. More than curious, he asked point blank whether there was anything I wanted to share from my snooping that might be of interest. He implied I was obligated to reveal what I knew. I resented the implication that I was covering up something. He didn't know I was heartbroken that I had to break more bad news to Kiera.

What I couldn't wipe out of my mind was the look in Nacho's eyes. He looked as if everything he had devoted his life to was now crashing around his ears in a matter of days. He seemed utterly bewildered that there was a weed grow-op on his farm, let alone a murder victim. At this point, there was still no positive ID on the body. Adam had had to phone in extra investigators to help with the grow-op investigation and now the new murder investigation. He, too, looked as if the weight of the world was resting on his shoulders. York Ridge had never seen this much action in decades.

I knew I needed to spend a few quiet minutes to clean up and clear my mind. When we pulled into my driveway, though, relief didn't come. As we neared the parking area, something seemed off about my car, but I didn't get a chance to register what, until Cyn screamed, "Oh my God, Darcy, look at your car … your tires!" We all jumped out of the car at the same time. I looked at my car which slumped forlornly into the ground. All four tires had been slashed.

EIGHTEEN

Adam looked beyond concerned. "Darcy, is there something you're not telling me? Is there some connection between these murders and your tires?" He must have realized I was near the end of my rope, as he backed off and didn't push it. Cyn put her arm around me and glared at Adam. I was fighting tears.

Cyn said, "Let's get inside where you can relax. I'm sure the Sheriff will make arrangements for your car." She gave him a pointed look.

She came in with me. "What am I going to do?" I sniffled. "There's Kiera to pick up tonight and work tomorrow."

Cyn took charge. "Don't worry about that stuff. I'll drive you to pick up Kiera tonight and come get you tomorrow. For now, go get cleaned up and you'll feel better."

Once I emerged from the bathroom, having washed my face and hands, I felt somewhat more composed. Cyn had made tea for us, which struck me odd since I didn't think Cyn would drink tea, let alone make it. By this time, Adam had come in and told me the tire slashing was called in, and the tow truck was on its way.

"That was a pretty big knife someone used to slash those tires." He shook his head. "I don't have much time, Darcy. I need to get back to the scene, but can you think of any reason someone would do this?" He had his notebook and pencil out, as well as his camera, making this official and on the record. My fears had been realized. Whoever was threatening me was now on my doorstep. I had to decide whether to tell him now about the other threats. What was there to lose? It was obvious someone was out to scare me, and maybe more!

I told him of the cellphone threat and the note, and that I thought they were connected to Bruno's murder since there was nothing else going on that would illicit threats. "I just don't know what I did or what I know, but someone doesn't want me snooping."

"You mean besides me. I don't want you snooping. It's dangerous, especially when we're talking murder … or murders." Was there some connection he wasn't telling me? Something in the way he said 'murders' triggered another thought so that I just blurted out, "Is this what happened to Morty? Did he get too close …?" I hiccupped. Cyn's eyes widened with a dawning horror, and she pushed my tea towards me.

"We haven't put all the pieces together on Morty's death, but again, I definitely don't want you snooping."

I was now afraid to ask or even say anything after his emphasis on snooping. The only common connection at the moment was the most obvious—Nacho.

"Darcy?"

I realized I must have been lost in thought. He was waiting for me to comply.

"Thanks, I understand," I said. I didn't lie, but I had no intention to stop investigating, and with all the more conviction. I had never thought I could somehow be in the line of fire. I trembled at the realization.

"Good. Stop in at the office with the note tomorrow. I'll send a patrol car around the area and call a security company in the morning. Talk soon." He hesitated at the door a moment, then gave me the shyest of smiles, and then he was gone, almost making me forget about the tires.

"Okay, girl, while we have a few hours before we pick up Kiera, let's do some brainstorming here," said Cyn. "This here badass murderer is getting on my nerves at the moment. Nobody threatens my boss when she's just doing her job. And I really wouldn't want to see that gorgeous South American hunk get fought over in prison if he didn't do anything. And Darcy ..." she paused, "this time you have to come clean and trust me."

"I'm sorry about not telling anyone. I just didn't want to worry anybody. There was already enough going on. I thought maybe it was just a kook, or I hoped it was, I should say."

"Okay, no more secrets. So what's this about Morty?"

"I don't know really. The Sheriff only said they were investigating his death, and it may or may not amount to anything. I just wondered if his death and Bruno's were in some way connected. Or maybe I'm just paranoid, and it's all a coincidence."

"I don't believe in coincidence. We have some work to do. First, let's get you a grownup drink instead of that granny drink. Where's your liquor cabinet?"

Cyn pulled out a bottle of vodka, shook her head, and put it back in the cabinet. A smile crossed her lips as she pulled out a bottle of Patron followed by triple sec. She then busied herself juicing some fresh limes from my fridge. "Let's start with Mr. Obvious—Nacho. Does he have a motive?" She dumped ice into a metal cocktail shaker, followed by a very healthy splash of the tequila.

"Yes, there are a couple. One, Bruno was going to cancel Nacho's lease and sell the property soon, causing a massive disruption for Nacho's business. They fought about it the night before Bruno's murder. People saw Nacho steaming, including yours truly."

"I could see Nacho maybe suing but not committing murder over something like that," she said, pouring the triple sec and lime juice into the shaker. "Besides, I think Nacho's like the Pied Piper. People would follow him anywhere." She vigorously shook the metal container, ice and liquid colliding noisily against its sides. Her comment made sense and gave me some hope. "And the other one?"

"He was carrying on with Tanya, and according to him, he was with her the night of the murder. But … she won't back up his alibi," I said.

Cyn salted the rim of a of wide-mouth glass and strained the drink into it, then passed it over to me. "That's disappointing to hear. I thought he was classier." *Me too.*

I sampled my drink. Taking a sip was like a mini holiday in Mexico. "Mmmm, good."

She smiled and sipped her tea. "I was going to make a Cosmo, but it's just too 'Sex in the City'. I figured a margarita would take the edge off." She looked thoughtful, and then said, "No one is going to commit murder for Tarty Tanya, let alone a hunk like Nacho. She was a roll in the hay, simply convenient. And, of course, she's not going to back him up."

I interrupted; the margarita was definitely taking the edge off. "Yes, the family already hate her, and it would give them ammunition to cut her out of everything. Would someone think they planned it together so they could get Bruno's money and be together?"

"Only a fool. If Tanya needed someone to bump Bruno off, she would have picked a stooge, not Nacho. Could be that she did hire someone. Maybe the dead guy in the field was hired to kill Bruno, and now he's been killed to shut him up? Maybe that's the connection between the two murders."

"I don't know because she would have to hire someone else to bump off the hitman. Tanya could still be another suspect. Nacho could be insurance in case she is accused. We'll wait to see who that guy is, although it may simply be a drug deal gone bad. Not bad at trying to connect the dots, Cyn. I can see a career as a crime reporter, or a bartender, for you," I said, taking another sip.

"Been there, done that." I took it to mean bartending. "Now I'd prefer to open my own photography studio."

I thought we should leave the model talk to another day when I was more up for it. "When the smoke clears on this stuff, we'll have that conversation," I said. "Back to crime solving. So, what's Tanya's motive? She seemed to have it all."

"Girly, we have to get you out more!" She threw up her hands. "Duh, hello, she's twenty-something and Bruno was like sixty-nine. He could have been her grandfather. I'm betting she has a pretty healthy libido. Crap, even Nacho may be too old for her!"

"You're right. It's been a while since I've had a relationship, and a while since I've been twenty-something." I took another drink.

"You know what they say, 'use it or lose it.' When this is over, we're going out on the town." I took an even bigger drink. This was a bit too close to my private life or lack of private life.

"You're on. Anyway, she claims she was at home, and he claims he was with her but at another location."

"Okay, would either of them send nasty notes or slash tires?"

"What? Nacho?"

"I'm just saying … this is what cops do, isn't it?"

"I guess, but I don't see either one doing this kind of stunt." I clutched my drink.

"Okay then. I think our third suspects are those horribly gauche tenant farmers, Mandy and Joe Something. Remember them at the memorial? She was a real piece of work, and she didn't look as if she worried much about what people thought. And I think it is the field they were leasing where the pot was being grown."

"It's a distinct possibility. Bruno crapped on them. But we need to confirm they were the ones farming that field, and those were the four acres they were complaining about. Could be when they found out the land they were leasing was being sold they became murderous."

"Or maybe they planted the weed. It's a better cash crop than corn. Bruno could have found out and threatened them. I think we should go and pay them a visit, and see where they were last Friday and this weekend. We need to confirm it is the land where they planted the corn that they had to abandon," said Cyn. "I have no doubt she'd love to be interviewed."

"I think Adam will likely find out faster than us if they are the tenants. If they are, I'm sure he'll be interviewing them after he's finished with Nacho. I'm not sure anyone had them on the radar screen till now."

"Who else? The family?"

"You mean Frank?" I asked skeptically. "I thought about him, but he was getting the business anyway, and they all had money."

"Darcy, for people like that there's never enough money. Maybe they wanted it sooner and didn't want to wait for old Bruno to croak. Could be they were afraid once Tanya got her hooks in him, he'd leave it all to her. Frank and Tanya sure hated each other."

"True, but it sounded as if she wasn't getting anything, according to Frank. He seemed to know that, though maybe she didn't. Nacho told me she had a slew of lovers. Maybe one of them flipped out or wanted her to be a wealthy widow?" I added.

"Bruno wasn't stupid. It could be he already knew. He had a lot of eyes working for him."

"I wanted to talk with both Frank and Tanya again anyway. Maybe tomorrow would be good. Could the weed patch have been Frank's? It was Malfaro property, after all," I said, although I wasn't sure of the motive.

"I doubt it though a little grass might loosen Frank up. Anyway, there's still a cast of thousands. What about the tree huggers?"

"Watch it! I belong to the Yorkdale County Trail Society. Part of it goes through the rear of my property. I also want to preserve the planet for Kiera and my grandchildren. But the YCTS are no fans of the Environmental Defense League—way too radical for them."

"No offense meant. We should look at the Environmental Defense League, then. I heard the same thing; they're radical to the point of being cult-like scary."

"Exactly," I said. "Remember the Birkenstock chick at the Marsh opening? She is the second-in-command at the League. She and the head honcho, Clive Carruthers, are over-the-top scary when it comes to environmental stuff. I did a little research on them already. They've been out on ice flows protesting the seal hunt and on missions with Greenpeace. Clive has almost got cult leader status with his members."

"I shot some video of Clive at a rally a year or so ago. He was half-crazed, and he got the crowd half-crazed," Cyn added with a grimace.

"I hadn't really included them as suspects because I didn't think they were capable of something like murder," I said. "I didn't like the vibe I got from him at the photo shoot or the memorial for Bruno. I don't think he is quite what he pretends to be, but I have nothing but a gut feeling to go on."

"Maybe, maybe not, but he could goad some of the looney tunes they attract to step over the line. That crowd mentality can be frightening."

"Yeah, I wish people could be more responsible when they speak since they have no control over what they're unleashing." Maybe tire slashing, I thought. I also remembered that someone from the Environmental Defense League had visited the Weekly office during the time the nasty note had been delivered.

"At any rate, they should be on the list to be investigated, if nothing else. They have always been at loggerheads with Malfaro Developments over their monster house developments on agricultural land, and land that we all thought was protected legislatively," waxed Cyn, to my surprise. She had never struck me as a nature conservationist.

"My guess is they also toke weed. No one would think twice

about them traipsing about the fields. It's a perfect cover. Maybe the dead guy was cutting down their weed."

"That's good, Darcy. If you've already committed one murder, then I guess the second isn't as difficult. I would say motive and means moves them to the top of the list."

"This brings us to the town councillors. Who of them could be bought, and who of them had something to gain from Bruno's death?" I asked.

"Armida Caughlin hated Bruno. She represented most of the farmers in the district," commented Cyn. "We'd need to find if she had an alibi and if she was connected to corpse number two. I bet Sheriff Armstrong never even interviewed any of these people."

She could be right. So far, he seemed to be fixed on Nacho, with Clive a distant second.

"And those in Bruno's pocket?" We didn't get any farther with that line of thinking before the phone ringing interrupted us. Thinking it was Kiera, I answered, but to my eternal dismay it was my adolescent ex, Will Van Dyke, or Van Dick, as I thought of him. Thank heavens I'd had a few swigs of tequila.

"Will, how are you?"

"It's Willem now, remember?" Oh yes, I remembered. Will had recreated himself as snooty European horse royalty by going by his full name. How typical and pompous of him.

"I didn't forget, Will," I answered.

"So like you. I didn't call to argue over things that aren't your business. My parents called and told me what's going on, and I want Kiera away from murder scenes and criminals!" He was practically shouting. How did he know already? We had just got back from the barn.

"What are you talking about?" I asked just to be sure.

"As if you don't know, Ms. Smarty Editor. Bruno Malfaro's murder at the barn ... where Kiera rides," he said, enunciating every word as if I was some imbecile.

So, *that* murder. I actually considered myself lucky at the moment. I couldn't imagine him if he knew about today's events. "Your parents are overreacting as usual. Trust me, I will be the first to make sure she's safe and nothing happens to her." *I just had to figure out how.*

"This isn't up for discussion. If you don't get her out of that barn and away from that murdering playboy, I'll bring her down to Florida, and she can finish her final year of high school away from that terrible influence!"

"Over my dead body." I was so mad I was spitting words. "Like you care. You abandoned her two years ago to go be a teenager yourself!"

"I'm not arguing with some hysterical, bitter ex. Just do it!"

"Excuse me! You think you can just pick up the phone and order me around? You pompous ass!" He slammed the phone down. I stood there, so angry I was shaking.

Cyn came and wrapped her arms around me, and the tears finally came. She sat me down and refreshed my drink. After I'd calmed down, I told her about Will's threats. "Kiera would jump at the chance to go to Florida and ride. That would be the end of graduation. All these girls already fantasize about being on the Olympic Equestrian team. She doesn't need Will's encouragement, as so few ever make it. She needs a Plan B, a profession."

"But you have custody," right?"

"Joint custody. I don't have the resources that his parents have, since Van Dyke Foods has made the family a fortune in the last twenty-five years. I couldn't fight them. Anyway, Kiera will be eighteen soon and can do what she likes, and Wellington is Nirvana to a rider. In the modeling world it would be the equivalent of being invited to take part in a Versace or maybe Armani runway show in Milan or Paris, somewhere wonderful," I blubbered, and drank all the more. "And if this goes on any longer the stables may go under, or maybe Nacho really is the bad guy."

"Darcy, dry your tears. We're going to get to the bottom of these murders!"

I started blubbering all over again, "Oh my God, Cyn. Will doesn't know about the second murder and weed at the barn. I'm toast!"

"Then we better get started first thing in the morning. We'll split up. I'll take the tenant farmers, and you take Tanya, and maybe Frank, depending on what you find. Then we'll regroup at lunch. Speaking of Kiera, isn't it about time we picked the girls up?" I had lost track of time with all the drama and sifting through possible suspects.

It was about eleven when we rolled into Lana's. The tow truck had come and hauled off the Escape before we had to leave, thankfully. I texted Kiera that we were outside and got a misspelled weird message back that put all my Mother spidey senses on high alert. Other parents were waiting outside, and the kids rolling out seemed a bit too loud and a bit too wobbly. We could hear rap and hip hop music blaring from the backyard. It was deafening.

Finally, Kiera and Heather drifted down the driveway giggling like a couple of goons. It took a few shouts before they realized we were in Cyn's car. Looking at their eyes, it looked as if their brains had taken a vacation on some distant planet. They didn't really even notice I wasn't driving. Cyn and I both got a good whiff when they entered, and they reeked of weed. I instantly sobered. I rolled my eyes and felt as if I was wound so tight I might levitate like that helicopter. But before I could erupt, Cyn grabbed my arm. She shook her head at me and asked the girls, "So how was the float making?" Just wait till we get home, I thought.

Nineteen

Before we got home, Cyn said, "Once I drop Darcy and Kiera off, I'll take you home, Heather. It's late, and school's tomorrow so I want everyone to go right to bed," she said, looking at me. "We all need our beauty sleep. We have a big week ahead of us."

The girls giggled like morons. "Do you have anything to eat?" they both asked.

"At home," I said through clenched teeth as I practically bit off my tongue. As if everything wasn't bad enough, what if Will ever found out Kiera had been smoking weed!

Before I got out of the car Cyn grabbed me, and warned me as soon as Kiera exited. "Darcy, be like Scarlett O'Hara in *Gone with the Wind*." I must have looked puzzled. She continued, "Worry about this tomorrow."

Both Kiera and I took Cynthia's advice.

The next morning, I felt like Gumby. Nothing worked—a result of tossing and turning much of the night, rummaging through events in my mind, rehearsing speeches to give Kiera and Will. I sat at the computer trying to distract myself. Kiera came downstairs with a look that suggested she was wondering when I would take aim and fire.

"Sorry, Mom; things got nuts. Lana's parents went out, and it turned into a party. Everybody was smoking and drinking. I don't do it very often, and I try to be honest with you and tell you what I'm doing. I don't want to lie to you."

That got me. I looked at her, realizing she really was maturing, enough to accept responsibility. "I know and I appreciate that but be careful. I don't want you to have a criminal record, and you don't want people seeing you do illegal things. Besides, it's bad for your health!"

"Thanks Mom ... for caring, I mean." She gave me a hug and a smile. I was glad she didn't retort that it was now legal in a few states. "By the way, where's the car?"

"Uh, at the shop. I had some car problems last night, but I'm picking it up this morning." I know I should have told her the rest of the story about the night before. Some of it she would hear at school. I wanted to protect her a while longer. I wasn't sure how to do that, and I didn't want her worrying about me. It worked both ways for us. This morning I had my work cut out for me.

"What are you doing?" she asked, looking over my shoulder at the computer screen.

"Adding to the Facebook fan page I set up for the paper. Time to bring the Weekly into this century."

"Huh," she grunted, unimpressed. "Mom, don't forget to pick up those things for Heather and my scarecrow. We've only got a few nights to work on it for Friday. I left you a list on the counter," she said, grabbing her backpack and heading towards the door to catch the school bus.

"What are you doing again for the contest?"

"Zorro on his horse with a bloody sword," she answered gaily. A shiver ran through me, and I was back in the weed patch. "Marco's idea. It's brilliant."

"Speaking of Marco reminds me that your dad called." She gave me a quizzical look. "Before I tell you what he said, I need you to promise me you won't go all drama queen."

"What is it?" she spit out ominously. This wasn't looking good.

"He's worried about you after what happened at the barn, and wants you to leave the barn." By now she was glowering. "Before you start, he has a point … "

"You said we wouldn't leave. You said you were fine as long as Marco was there. You're a liar."

I held up my hand. "Hold on here. This is a discussion, not an opportunity for name-calling. That isn't helpful. I did promise we would try that and so far, so good. Unfortunately, Nacho is under a great deal of suspicion. Besides, if he is innocent, then it is someone else that has access to that barn, and I agree with him that I don't want you in harm's way."

"Whatever," she answered, but this time it wasn't flippant. She wasn't even looking at me but had assumed her game face.

"Well, I am giving you a head's up. I'm sure your dad and Grandpa and Grandma aren't going to wait much longer before insisting you move barns."

⤳

Cyn picked me up. For her, she was dressed in her best business attire—skin-tight killer black leather. It was like having Catwoman as a partner. "Darcy, you need to put on your crime-fighting clothes." She was right. In my conservative jacket and black dress pants, I looked as if I was off to fight with books at the local library. "We should be Women in Black, and not like those skanks at Bruno's funeral."

I laughed. "Okay, next time for sure."

At the garage, Wayne, my mechanic was very sympathetic. "Those were some huge slashes, Darcy. Someone had it in for you, I'd say. Insurance, though, should cover part of this."

Cyn, of course, smelling testosterone, couldn't wait in the car.

She draped herself over the counter, causing Wayne to have some trouble with his paperwork. "Do you have business cards, Wayne?" she purred. "I just may be in need of your services one day."

How could anyone make an ordinary request sound so suggestive? Wayne blushed and started adding up the charges all over again. If I was lucky, he would slip in a discount.

In the parking lot, we agreed to rendezvous for lunch at The Blackbird. Cyn was off to visit Mandy and Joe, the tenant farmers, and take photos. We chose to do an article on the impact of these crimes on the locals and their reaction to big-city trouble in the middle of our small community. It gave everyone a chance to spout their two cents and Cyn and I an excuse to investigate. I was off to the Malfaro Mansion to interview—more like interrogate—Tanya about the outcome of the will reading. After my rapid retreat last time, I was sure I would never be granted another audience. When she agreed, I guessed that she now saw this as a chance to get some good PR for herself, or maybe get back at Frank.

Past the gate and driving up the long driveway, with just the roofline of turrets and gables spreading across the horizon, I couldn't imagine what Tanya was going to do if she had to give all this up. It would be heartbreaking.

Today, when she opened the door, although she had on a Victoria's Secret tangerine hoodie and sweats, the energy and the defiance were missing. She led me through a wide hallway, tiled in white Carrera marble. Huge three by four-foot oil paintings in ornate, gilded frames, looking as if from the 18th century, decorated the walls. The hall opened up to a huge, hotel-sized kitchen where an elegant island easily twelve feet long, topped with more white marble, dominated the room, not an easy feat with twenty-foot ceilings and a wall of floor-to-ceiling windows. The cupboards were cherry with ornately decorated cornices and a French provincial hood over a large Garland restaurant-style stove. The rest of the appliances were recessed and stainless. It was hard to think of Tanya cooking in here. She was making us both a coffee with her Tassimo coffee machine.

I took in the view. Just beyond the wall of windows was an infinity pool. To the right of that was a tennis court with a smattering of leaves already blanketing the clay surface. "Did you and Bruno play tennis?"

"No, he just put it there because it looked good. Bruno was all about show. Besides, he never had time. He was always working."

She handed me a frothy latte in a beautiful mug, although I was more interested in drinking in the view. In the far distance, red-tinged maples and fifty-foot hemlocks ringed a meandering natural lake. "Thank you. That's so beautiful—your own lake."

"Yeah, ironic though," she commented sadly. "Lake Tanya. Of course, now it will be renamed."

Uh oh, doesn't sound good.

"What happened at the will reading yesterday?"

"Frank gave me three weeks to get out! Bruno, the SOB, left me nothing. Well, he did leave me my car, my clothes, and the engagement ring but no cash and not the house." The house with its fifty acres had to be worth at least ten mill or more, I thought. "We had a prenup with different conditions both pre-marriage and post-marriage. In fact, Bruno had gone in to change his will about a week before his death. Stupid me, I thought at the time I was maybe getting more. Money was one topic you really didn't talk about with Bruno. He kept his cards very close to his chest."

Yikes, I almost felt sorry for her. What's worse than never having anything is having it on some massive, over-the-top scale like this and going back to nothing, and with odds that you will never in your life have anything ever approaching this again. "Ouch, did you ever find out how or why Bruno changed his will?" *Did he know about Nacho? Was he getting ready to turf her out anyway? Maybe she brought the subject up and there was a fight?*

"No, we never talked about it. He just threw the comment out there one day as he was going out the door. I thought of appealing the will, but I don't have money for lawyers, and Frank has really deep pockets and a real hate-on for me. He offered me $100,000 to just get lost and leave quietly. I may try to get more than that from him. He just wants me to shut up and disappear fast!"

"Because?"

"I'm an embarrassment to them. Bruno was too. He was too old-country, not classy enough. I guess that's what happens when your kids have it easy and never have to get their hands dirty. Frank just buys someone to do his dirty work for him."

I thought back to my interview with Frank who, in his cashmere and leather, definitely never had to get his hands dirty. It seemed at that moment that Frank may have had more motive than I thought. I hadn't realized Tanya was seen as such a threat or that Frank was cut from the same cloth as Bruno. How naïve of me.

"What kind of dirty work?" I asked hesitantly, wondering just how dirty things got.

"Let's just say I have to be very careful. If I push too hard, Frank has ways to make me disappear … for good!"

"We're talking violence here?" I asked as goose bumps began to form. I was thinking back to the threats I received that I never connected to Frank, and wondered.

"Oh yeah. The only difference is Bruno did his own, while Frank has his goons. None of this is on the record, or I'll be toast. I just want someone to know what's going on."

"As insurance?" I asked, realizing I was now in the precarious position of not only being used as a pawn, but with someone who could well be a murderer. "So, you're going to tell Frank that I know how lethal he is, in case something happens to you?"

"You catch on quick."

As if I don't already have a target on my back.

"It probably won't come to that if he's feeling generous. As I said, he likes to keep a low profile. I'm counting on the fact that they don't need any more bad publicity. Bad for sales and that's all they care about." She sighed, and for the first time I saw the vulnerability.

"And did Bruno ever hurt you?" I asked gently. In for a penny, as they say.

She nodded. "At times." She became quiet as if reflecting. I wasn't sure if I saw fear or resignation. I guess luxury has its price. That is, if she was on the level.

"Is this what you're to keep quiet about?" I asked, seeing more now of her own self-destructive behavior.

"Among other things."

"Don't tell me, then I don't have to lie." Again, she nodded. I was too scared to know more. I thought I should concentrate on what I really came for.

"So, are you going to tell me what you were really doing the night Bruno died?" Maybe I was pushing my luck after last time, when she had thrown me out for the same line of questioning.

"What have I got to lose now, really? I was with someone I shouldn't have been with."

"Nacho?"

"Hey, no names. You're a newspaper woman, and I haven't yet collected on my just deserts. Be kind to me in any articles, and I may tell."

"Tell the Sheriff, you mean? Someone's livelihood may depend on it, and maybe their life."

"Yes, of course the Sheriff. I'll call Frank today and try a counteroffer. Just don't do any numbers on me in the paper so I live to collect." A chill coursed through me.

"I never had any intention on doing anything like that. We're not a tabloid, and I would never intentionally use the paper to hurt anyone. You should know that I'm very concerned that an innocent person could be implicated because you, for your own reasons, have not told everything." Lied was more like it, but as Mom said, 'You catch more bees with honey than vinegar.' "And one more thing before you leave town. Do you go by "*tastygirl*" in your email?"

She nodded, but suspicion narrowed her eyes. I knew it. Her antennae were starting to emerge.

"Talking hypothetically, if you got an email from your husband's riding coach that said he had taken care of Bruno, what would you think?"

I saw her visibly relax. "That's easy, hypothetically speaking of course. Bruno, being the demanding person he was, always had some question or something he needed for Dante. I think he loved that horse more than me or his family. If it wasn't some ointment for Dante's leg, or acupuncture, or the dentist to look at his teeth, then it was a question about enough bedding or grain. It was always something. He could never just go to the barn and ride. He pampered that horse like a baby."

"Thank you so much for that, Tanya." She even smiled a little.

I left feeling a little more hopeful that Nacho may be that much closer to having his name cleared over Bruno's murder. I was relieved the email was not as incriminating as it sounded, and I could just imagine how Nacho had taken care of Tanya. I didn't need a video. Still, I was quite shaken up about the revelations of Malfaro brutality. Tanya obviously hadn't yet heard about the latest death. I thought better that I don't tell her, as she was already nervous. I did wonder though if there was some connection now with the Malfaros. I was feeling a bit vulnerable myself, just being there. I made a quick exit. I had just enough time to go into town and pick up Kiera's supplies, and stop in at the Sheriff's office before I met Cyn.

On my way in I gave a quick call to Adam to see if he was going to be there. He picked up on the first ring. We exchanged pleasantries, and I let him know I had picked up my car. Before I could ask about

Nacho's questioning, he told me news that changed the day. "We have an ID on the body."

"Great, that was fast."

"A missing person report was made Sunday over in Chormley, by the guy's live-in girlfriend. His name was Carl Hanover, twenty-one years old, small-time drug dealer with several convictions for possession and trafficking. No violent crimes, still on probation."

"And the girlfriend's name?"

"Candace Swartz. One of the detectives from Central Drug Enforcement is interviewing her this morning."

"Any leads on the killer?" I asked as I mentally traced the route to Chormley in my head.

"No, but it looks as if two people were harvesting the crop, and something went wrong, and one turned on the other. I don't think it was premeditated because no one would leave such a valuable crop unharvested. Cause of death was a head wound from a machete. The boys spent last night combing the area for the murder weapon. The machete we found only had the vic's prints on it."

"Thanks for the info. I also wanted to tell you that I talked to Tanya, and she now admits she was with someone. I still think it is Nacho, but she said she may be ready to confirm that soon."

"So, nothing's changed; you're still fishing and nosing around."

Oops. "Fishing for news if that's what you mean. That's my job."

"Anyway, nothing's official until she calls me and goes on record. I've known lots of people to change their minds ... for one reason or another."

I felt somewhat wary after this remark, thinking back to my conversation with Tanya, wondering just how much Adam knew about the Malfaros. Probably a lot more than me.

"Anyway, if she does corroborate Nacho's story, then we may have to pursue the angle that both Nacho and Tanya were in cahoots."

"Okay, whatever you say. So, this Carl dude lived in Chormley?"

"If you're thinking of going out there, then please think again; it's a rough area," he said, as I was in the process of Googling Carl's address on my GPS. *Damn.* I wasn't used to men being tuned into my psyche. Obviously, the Sheriff got me, but at the moment that didn't seem like a good thing.

"Who said I was going out there? I just need the facts straight for when we go to print with the details."

"Sure. Drop off that threatening note sometime today … and Darcy, watch your back."

It was just before noon when I rolled up to The Blackbird Café. I parked the car as close to the window as I could. There seemed to be a lot more parked cars on the street than usual. I was still spooked and didn't want to take any chances. Maybe the Blackbird could keep an eye on it while I grabbed lunch.

I opened the door and scanned to see if Cyn had made it. The place was crowded to bursting. The mishmash of tables often made three a crowd at The Blackbird. Today qualified as amusement park level. I heard Cyn call my name from a table tucked into the back. I threaded my way through the table and chair obstacle course, when a head popped up as I tried to slide by the counter.

"Hey, Ham Sandwich," Amelia called loudly in greeting. I rolled my eyes. Sheesh. Was it my imagination or did everyone have to turn and look?

"Cyn, does your friend not know the meaning of subtle?" I whispered as I slid into a chair next to her.

"Don't worry about her, it's just her way. She grows on you."

"Why such a full house today?"

"The TV news crews are circling. The second murder in a week in our very conservative, wealthy town has brought them running. Mandy and Joe told me there were crews tramping around all morning, trying to corner anyone they could for an interview."

I thought I had better check my iPhone for messages, as something similar had happened with Bruno's death, and the big dailies and the big networks wanted information. I had to think Nacho might be going ballistic at the barn if they were pestering him. Unfortunately, Kiera had a lesson scheduled for tonight, and whether I wanted to or not, I had to deal with this.

We decided we had better keep our voices low and be discreet. Cyn quietly got out her shots of Mandy and Joe, who could well have been the poster couple for one of Whistler's paintings. "I'm surprised you didn't add a pitchfork for a prop."

She laughed. "They were a little stiff—hardly professional models. But boy, did they have a lot to say about Bruno, and none of it was nice. They did confirm they were renting that land and that is the exact same section of the field they were told to stop farming, the exact same four acres. Some guy from Malfaro Development called and told them they would no longer be able to work that four-acre patch. They were pretty pissed because they had just planted their corn. They did get reimbursed for the rent, but not for the corn and all their hard work. Someone left an envelope with cash for a rent rebate and a note on Malfaro Development stationary."

"Did they know who?"

"They never knew. Bruno didn't deal with them directly."

"So let me get this straight. Someone who claimed to represent Malfaro Developments paid them to not farm that section."

"You don't think it was …" Cyn didn't get a chance to finish.

"Hey, Ham Sandwich, what are you ordering?" shouted Amelia, and I felt my sphincter muscles tighten. You'd think I'd be lost in this crowd. I looked to Cyn for help. She whispered a suggestion.

"Café Americano and a brie and raspberry panini, please." I felt as if I were nine years old and needed help from my mom to order.

"How do you take your coffee?"

"Sweetener and milk."

"Don't do chemicals here," came the gruff reply.

Was there no end to the humiliation? Did someone just giggle?
"Sugar's fine."

"Cane?"

What? I stared back dumbfounded.

"Cane sugar?" she repeated as if I had the IQ of the chair I was sitting on.

"Sure," I croaked.

It was all downhill from there. I got my panini and hated every bite, while cane sugar had a long way to go before it gave me my sweetener fix, but I finished both. Who knew what punishment awaited those who didn't comply? I was already on someone's hit list. I didn't want to add Amelia to the mix.

According to Cyn, Joe and Mandy were extremely distressed that no one had ever harvested the corn. Cyn and I deduced that it was probably the drug dealer disguised as a Malfaro employee who had called so they could anonymously use the land. I told her I'd fill her in on my news in the car, as it was a bit too public in the Café. We sat in the car after I escaped, thankfully without too much notice from Amelia. I filled Cyn in on the interview with Tanya and the Sheriff's findings about Carl Hanover, the dead guy, who could have been the one who called Mandy and Joe, and his girlfriend Candace.

"So, what's next Sherlock?" asked Cyn.

"A change of plan is in order. I'm going to pass on interviewing Frank at the moment, but I think a visit to Candace to check out what she knows would be helpful."

"All right. Count me in. No way are you going over there alone." That was the same sentiment I had about Kiera and the barn.

"We might need to stop to get armor," she added.

"Very funny, Cyn."

"Do you see me laughing, Ham Sandwich?"

TWENTY

"Crap," I muttered. "Kiera asked me to pick up some craft supplies for her and Heather. They are making a scarecrow for the Fall Fair contest. I haven't gotten around to it."

"Oh, that's the thing I have to shoot photos of tomorrow. The old folks' home in town is putting together an entry, and each grade of the elementary school is preparing one too. Sounds like fun," replied Cyn.

"It's just that, now we know the murder victim from the field had a girlfriend, I wanted to go talk to her right away."

"So, we'll get the supplies on the way."

"Great," I said, handing Cyn the list of supplies Kiera had given me earlier.

"Eight yards of black felt!" Cyn said reading from the list.

"She said they're doing Zorro; I can only imagine that the felt is for the horse."

"Points for creativity, also style points for ditching you with the bill for the felt," Cyn said teasingly.

I grimaced. Cyn was right, I was stuck with the bill, and it wasn't going to be cheap— typical teenager. Kiera was going to have a rude awakening when she moved out on her own.

As we hopped into my car, I couldn't help but check the tires.

While I may have been a blubbering mess about everything yesterday, today was a new day. Today, I wanted vengeance. I wasn't going to be a victim; whoever was perpetrating these crimes had brought it to my doorstep. Big Mistake!

We managed to snag some corn stalks out of a field en route so we had one item checked off on the scarecrow supplies list. The dead guy's girlfriend lived in Chormley, by Beakmans Lake, in a trailer park.

When we arrived, neither the trailer nor the park were what I had expected. I knew this wasn't the best part of the county, and I guess I had a picture in my mind of what a drug dealer's place would look like. What I saw did not match at all. It was a trailer in a trailer park, but the park was near the lake, down a lane with a tidy row of trailers. Outside of trailer # 34 they had constructed what looked like a permanent deck with a pergola and planter boxes. Bright yellow chrysanthemums sprouted gaily out of the planters around the deck. No leaves littered the deck, and on each corner was a Tiki torch. Two newly varnished Adirondack chairs sat on the deck surveying the rest of the park. This was a home. I knocked on the door.

A young woman answered, her light brown hair pulled back in a ponytail. Her eyes were red and puffy, and her mascara had run in streaks down her face. She barely held the door open, and her eyes seemed to scan the distance behind me.

"Candace?" I asked, and she nodded uncertainly. "I'm so sorry to disturb you. I'm Darcy Dillon, the editor of the Yorkdale Weekly. I wanted to get some background on Carl Hanover for an article I'm writing. I want to make sure people understand who he was as a person."

"Will you really put information about the good things about him in the article? You won't just label him as a drug dealer?"

"I want the truth, whatever that truth is."

She sniffed and wiped her nose with the back of her hand. "And who's that?" she said, indicating Cyn at the base of the deck stairs.

"That's Cynthia, the paper's photographer. We won't take any pictures that you are not comfortable with," I added, hoping to reassure her. Cyn nodded and smiled.

It seemed to work, as she indicated that we should come in, but not before she took another nervous glance behind us. The inside of the trailer was small but well kept. I saw several tissue boxes on the kitchen table, tissues wadded up beside them. She sat down at a clean arborite table. Cyn and I sat on the couch opposite.

"He was a good guy," Candace started. "He fell in with a bad crowd for a while, but he was starting to turn things around." She started worrying at the skin around her thumbnail. She was more than just grief-stricken. She was anxious about something.

"Had the two of you been together long?"

"We'd dated in high school, then drifted apart when he dropped out. We'd just gotten back together again. I'm not a fool. Off the record?" I nodded. "I know he was dealing drugs, but I swear he was trying to put that behind him."

"How was he trying to put it behind him?"

"He had enrolled in night school courses. He was going to get his high school diploma. And talking about going to a trade school, apprenticing, that sort of thing."

"What sort of trade?"

"Construction. He built the deck out front. He was a good carpenter." Candace reached for a tissue and blew her nose.

"Do you know why he was out in the field chopping down marijuana Sunday night?"

"That guy, he called and told Carl to meet him. Carl told me he was going to go and finally tell him once and for all that he was out of the business. He told me the guy was really bad news. If only he had stayed home ..." she trailed off, in tears.

"Did you know who he was meeting? Like a name?" *Could it really be that simple?*

"No. I only knew him by the nickname that Carl called him," Candace said.

"What was that?"

"Dirt Devil. I'm sorry. I wish I knew more. I just hope he leaves me alone and lets me get on with my life."

"Has he threatened you?" I asked with concern.

"No. It's just that Carl said he was losing his grip. Even Carl was kind of afraid of him and what he was capable of," Candace said, biting her nails.

"Do you have a picture of Carl that we could print?" Cyn asked.

"Yeah ... sure, let me get it for you," Candace said, and went to the back of the trailer.

I turned to Cyn. "Dirt Devil?" I whispered. She shrugged.

When Candace returned with the picture she was frowning, as if she was fighting internal demons.

"Is there anything else you wanted to add?" I asked, uncertain if that would relieve her of her burden.

"It's my fault he's dead!" she wailed, and burst into tears.

I didn't know what to do so I stood and rubbed her on the back. Her breathing slowed, and she straightened up to reach for more tissues. "Why do you think it's your fault?" I asked, now she was more in control.

"I called the police." She stopped and cradled her head with her hands. We waited. "I called in an anonymous tip that they were growing weed. I just wanted to end it once and for all. I didn't know Carl was going to go out there again," she blurted, then squeezed her eyes tight. Cyn and I exchanged a look. One piece of the puzzle dropped into place—the anonymous tip. I would have to tell the Sheriff this new information.

She took a huge breath and continued. "I think maybe the guy knew the police were on to the grow-op and maybe blamed Carl. I don't know."

"You were doing the right thing," I tried to reassure her. "Whoever Carl was working with is clearly unstable. You were looking out for him."

"You think so?"

"Absolutely," I said with conviction. The corners of her mouth curved up slightly.

After Candace had regained her composure, we thanked her for the picture, and I promised to write a complete profile of who Carl was, and not just focus on the fact he had been a drug dealer. Cyn asked if she could take a picture of the deck out front. Candace agreed since she felt it would help with the positive spin on his life. She just asked that we not be specific about the location. She wasn't keen to be found by anyone.

I turned around to say goodbye and was moved by the frightened eyes of a very sweet, vulnerable young woman only a few years older than my own daughter. "Good luck and take care of yourself." I meant it, and I wondered if Carl really appreciated how fortunate he had been to have found her.

Back on the road I spotted two old, dark brown, corduroy couches put out for the trash. I pulled over.

"You aren't seriously going to put those dreadful-looking things in your house?" Cyn looked at me with horror.

"No, give me some credit. I'm thinking Zorro could ride a brown horse instead of a black one."

"Sweet."

"And free," I said, grinning.

I hopped out of the car and opened the hatch. I was pretty sure I had a box cutter somewhere in the back. I pulled it out and set to work pulling the covers off the couches. Cyn pitched in and helped. This was going to save me a fortune. I was pumped. I turned to Cyn. "What else is on the list?"

"Buttons, old clothes, red paint, black cowboy hat, a sword … geez, these kids aren't messing around."

"Kiera's very competitive. If she's in it, it's to win it."

"She must get that from you. I don't see you letting these bad guys back you off."

I guess she was right. I'd worked so hard to have stability in my life since the divorce, and these deaths were threatening that. Besides, I still couldn't get Candace out of my mind, and it angered me to think of the senseless murder of her boyfriend. It sucked, as Kiera would say. Whoever was behind these murders didn't have a chance.

༄

"I love it!" Cyn exclaimed as she popped out of the dressing room in a '60's mod mini skirt. "Here, snap a picture of me in it." She handed me her iPhone. We had found a small second-hand store on our way back from Candace's place. We had both agreed it would be the perfect spot to find an outfit for Kiera's scarecrow.

"You're not seriously going to tweet this outfit, are you?" I asked with eyebrows raised. We'd gotten a little sidetracked from our purpose.

"What? It's retro chic," she said, posing. "Reduce, reuse, recycle," she added as I snapped. "Oh, wait, hand me the phone. That's the perfect caption!" I handed the phone back to her as I shook my head. I couldn't believe two hundred thousand people followed her, for fashion advice of all things. I wouldn't be caught dead in that outfit.

"Can we focus on an outfit for the Zorro scarecrow?" I suggested, though I had been enjoying myself. It had almost made me forget about the murders and the threats.

"Oh please, we can pull that together in no time. What about this outfit?" She held up a floor-length strapless ball gown in hot pink. "Neon colors could be making a comeback." I smiled and shook my head as she disappeared back into the change room.

Rummaging through racks of men's clothing, I found a bolero

jacket at a decent price that would work for the scarecrow. It was very Zorro-like. I then looked for a white shirt, all the better to show off the blood from his sword. I could only imagine that was what Kiera and Heather were going to use the red paint for. I found a kid's plastic sword; it would have to do. I still needed a black wide-brimmed hat. With a swish of fabric and a loud "ta-da," Cyn made yet another appearance.

"Of course, I wouldn't tease my hair up like '80's big hair. I'd update it with sleek hair and a smoky eye," she said, admiring her neon self in the full-length mirror, her hands on her hips. In response I held up my finds for the scarecrow, to which she gave me two thumbs up. She handed me her iPhone yet again, and I obliged by taking another photo before she ducked into the change room again. I paid for my purchases while I waited for the fashion goddess to emerge. She ended up buying the neon pink gown, which surprised me. I never thought she'd buy anything that covered up her legs. Still, perhaps they couldn't hold a candle to Double D neon tits.

As we bundled our packages into the back of the car, I remembered that I hadn't called Adam to tell him about our discussion with Candace. He'd want to know that she was the one behind the anonymous tip. I pulled my cellphone out of my purse and dialed his number. I was doing that a lot lately.

"Adam."

"Darcy, what's up? I don't have much time, and I'm in the middle of something."

"No worries, I'll be quick. I was just out interviewing Candace, Carl's girlfriend, and I wanted to let you know that she admitted to me that she was the one who called in the anonymous tip on the marijuana field."

"What did … did she say anything else?" he asked.

"She said Carl was trying to get out of the business, set his life straight. Adam, she seemed really spooked. I think she is afraid that whoever killed Carl may also be looking for her."

"We'll have to talk more about your interview later, see if it yields any clues. I've been called out to investigate another homicide," he said. I paused to digest that, thankful it wasn't mine, given all the threats. Still, I was shocked. Before I could ask a thing, he rang off and I was left hanging.

TWENTY-ONE

To say I was distracted was an understatement. In my mind I juggled the turn of events, my own emotions, and the comments of Candace. Kiera was beyond shaken up when I walked in the door.

"Why didn't you tell me!" she cried. "You were there for heaven's sake!" Kiera had picked up a distorted version of the drug bust and murder from the rumors and innuendoes going around at school. No one had the correct story. Her version was like "broken telephone." People had spun tall tales of Nacho being some South American drug lord who was involved in producing illegal crops and now involved in murders because of some turf wars. Me, I was arranging and rearranging the puzzle pieces in my head, thinking I was close enough to touch the answer but not able to put all the pieces in the right order. There were still some pieces missing.

"I'm sorry I didn't tell you, but if you calm down, I will tell you exactly what happened blow by blow," I said firmly. After minor teenage harrumphing, like a summer storm, she blew herself out. So I told her, all the time thinking how sheltered I had been at the same age, and I had grown up in the city. The irony was we were here, where we thought she would be safe from all of this.

At any rate, I told her that for today her lesson would go on because I had made her a promise; however, today I was part of the package. Tomorrow was another story; one I would have to take day by day. We proceeded to the barn as usual, even though it was anything but business as usual. From the fallout of the divorce, I learned that what helped us both was to keep up a routine rather than descend into chaos. To do otherwise suggested that the rug was being pulled out from under us. I didn't want to let some murderer or murderers control our lives.

In my heart of hearts, I believed Nacho was someone caught at the wrong place at the wrong time. That could happen to any of us. It certainly did to me. However, the cautious side of me arrived at a compromise Kiera and I could live with. Amigo would stay at the farm till the end of the month, and she would ride in the parade, but only resume riding and lessons when Nacho was no longer a suspect. Then she would resume our current arrangement and always be accompanied by Marco or me until the murderer was apprehended.

I ran out to the car before we went because I had forgotten the scarecrow stuff, and right now it was a great distraction. "Thank you, Mom; this stuff is awesome. Heather and I are going to win for sure. I just need to find a hat."

The beauty of normal life. Besides, my "distract and conquer" strategy worked almost every time.

As we drove, I tried to have a teenager think with her head and not her heart about all the disturbing events from the last few days. Although, who was I to talk? "Firstly, let's do some math, and look at things to see what adds up or doesn't add up. Have you ever known Nacho to do drugs?"

She didn't need time to even think about that one. "Oh my God, of course not. He's a first-class athlete. He takes care of his body. You should see how careful he is about the food he eats—no junk food allowed at the barn. And he works out, besides riding several hours every day. He always says that both we and our horses have to be in top physical condition to compete."

"That's what I figured. I mean, look at you. You are so lean and muscular, and you do this part-time whereas this is his full-time job."

"He would never do drugs, ever. If anyone came to the barn stoned, I'm pretty sure he would kick them out."

"And the other night when you were …" I didn't finish.

She whipped her head around, her voice raising an octave. "You wouldn't tell him, would you, Mom? I would never come to the barn stoned."

"No, I just wondered where you got it, so I guess not at the barn?"

"Of course not. Marco had it; he knows a guy. Anyway, it's not something I do—buy weed." She shook her head in disgust.

"Was the guy's name Carl?"

"I don't know, Mom. I mean, it's not like I make a habit of this."

"That's a good thing," I said, glad she hadn't followed in my own youthful missteps, which were far more wanton than hers, but not info she needed to know. Best that she keeps on thinking I'm a goody two shoes.

As we pulled into the driveway, both of us tensed a little, especially Kiera, unsure of what to expect. Thankfully, life seemed to be normal. The horses were all out in the paddocks grazing. Nacho's car was there. There was no yellow crime scene tape swathing the barn. Since the murder scene and pot patch were out beyond the paddocks buried in the cornfield, we couldn't see them from here. Nacho was just coming out of the tack room when we entered and seemed happy to see us. He shouted a hello. Suspect or not, he still cut a fine figure in his tight riding pants and tall boots as he strode out the door. *Be still my middle-aged heart.*

He told Kiera to tack up, as they could start a little earlier today. Unfortunately, the other two girls in her class were no-shows. Other than the emptiness of the place, everything seemed routine and no ghosts, ghouls or bodies were lying about the premises. She obviously realized just how preposterous the school stories were. Her face visibly relaxed. I had no other strategy under the circumstances, other than what we discussed in the car. Being here would give me a chance to have a word with Nacho about our decision. Before I got a chance to ask, Kiera threw another wrench in the works.

"Sorry, Mom, I forgot to tell you that Grandma and Grandpa Van Dyke called. They want you to call them back." I closed my eyes and sought inner peace.

"Okay, dear," I said, calling on my inner Zen. I needed a plan and fast. "You got a second?" I asked Nacho.

"Anything for you and Kiera, Darcy," he said with a smile. I was glad to see that, at least his good nature had returned, although I wondered whether it was just a front at the moment.

Back in the tack room, I was again off guard by the sheer physicality of him, in such a small space. It was overwhelming to the point that I had difficulty remembering what we were discussing. I decided I was far better when we met in wide open spaces, where he didn't fill up the room so much. "So, how did it go with the Sheriff?" I asked.

"Hard to tell." He threw his hands up. "I was told not to leave town, but that info is not for public knowledge. I'm hoping they find the SOB who's doing this soon. It might affect me being able to take Kiera out of town to the Fall Classic. I know she will ... how does she say it? 'Freak'."

So, he was still a suspect. Kiera wasn't the only one who was going to freak. He was going to freak because I hadn't come up with anything better than keeping Kiera away, until his name was cleared.

"I haven't said anything about that restriction," he continued. "I don't want to alarm anyone. And I don't want any more clients defecting."

My stomach muscles tightened, and I tried not to react. "Do you remember seeing anything strange going on, or have any clues that might help the cops?" I said, grasping at straws.

"I wish, or I would have gladly given the information. I'm so focused on the horses and clients that I don't pay much attention to what goes on out back. I didn't even realize that couple weren't farming back there anymore. That's how much attention I give to things not immediately related to the barn and horses."

He sat down and took over the couch. He pulled off his baseball cap and revealed a head of lush, tempting hair. "To tell you the truth, if this goes on much longer with shit happening right under my nose and me under suspicion, I'll be ruined." He wove his fingers through his hair. "I can't believe all that has happened. It makes what Bruno was planning to do look like a picnic." He dropped his hands and gave his head a slow shake. The brave façade was now totally gone. The whole reality of his precarious situation seemed to have sunk in.

"I'm so sorry to have to do this ... I'm not comfortable with Kiera here neither, nor is Kiera's dad."

His face crumpled even more. "I understand. I don't blame people for leaving. They're not used to this kind of trouble and neither am I. It's scary ... distracting. It's hard to plan. Even Rena is anxious about coming to work for fear of what she might find," he said, pushing his hair off his brow.

I told him that maybe Tanya was close to corroborating his story although that did little to cheer him up. It was obvious he didn't put much faith in her word. "At this point, I'm not even sure that would help. She herself is under suspicion."

I didn't know what to say. Somehow words seemed inadequate. "I was hoping there would be a break in the case by now, before I had to pull Kiera out. By the way, do you know of anyone called 'Dirt Devil'?"

"Like the vacuum." He smiled. First one today.

"Exactly," I said, wondering how that image fit in with drug dealing. Coke snorting? Shoveling? What?

"Sorry, no I don't, but it's a nickname I would have remembered."

The next half hour was a pleasant reprieve for Kiera. Amigo, in all his muscular magnificence, easily leaped over three foot three jumps with varying oxers, showing off in the September afternoon. I sat in an Adirondack chair, warmed by the sun, relishing the fringe of umber and yellow trees, watching my daughter fly around the sand ring as if in heaven. For one moment, life was good.

The ride back was better than the ride to the barn. For the moment we were both mellow, thinking about Amigo and an otherwise beautiful fall day.

"Have you ..." she started.

I put up my hand. I knew what she was going to say about calling her grandparents. "No, I don't intend to spoil the moment. Your grandparents will want answers." I expected flak as usual, but for once I think she got it. She just nodded. "I had to tell Nacho that you wouldn't be coming back until he was no longer a suspect." I felt her body tense beside me.

"He told me, Mom. He told me he can't leave town for the horse show. As much as I wanted to go to the State competition, I just wanted to continue my lessons with Amigo at Maple Lane. This just sucks. My whole program will be out of whack if we move. All those years of work to hit the top of the Children's Hunters will be for nothing. Once I hit eighteen, I won't qualify any more. And I don't even know who could replace Nacho as coach."

"I understand, honey, but I don't have another plan."

"Maybe a miracle will happen," she replied quietly.

"In the meantime, we should research other barns, just in case we're short on miracles." The rest of the ride home was quiet.

Balancing a slice of delivery pizza in one hand, I read an incoming text from Adam. "I'll stop by about eight. Important." That just gave me time to have a quick shower and look presentable. The day already felt twenty-four hours long, and I thought I could fool my body into thinking it was the start. After I cleaned up from dinner, I picked up papers and things that had been left haphazardly from the morning. I hadn't yet adjusted to working outside the house, and the flotsam and jetsam of a very hectic week was accumulating in the corners, and adrift in the mudroom.

"Mom, why the big tidy and fold? Is someone coming?" Kiera asked suspiciously.

"Sheriff Armstrong," I answered as casually as I could.

"Because?"

I could tell her only interest was whether it was professional or personal. She would die if I ever hooked up with a classmate's parent. Relieved it was business, she bounced up the stairs, carting her scarecrow treasures.

I had just flung on the least dirty clothes I could find. Laundry was another casualty of my new job. Sleek stretchy jeans and a fine turquoise sweater freshened up my appearance and my mood. I had just got them on when the doorbell rang. I realized I was actually looking forward to seeing him and then chastised myself for being so unprofessional. I think I may have even blushed when I opened the door. Adam looked incredibly rugged in the five o'clock shadow that was just forming. We exchanged some awkward pleasantries as he apologized over again for bothering me at home.

"I would have waited till morning and seen you at your office if it wasn't so important," he offered.

"Nonsense, I appreciate you coming over right away if you know anything. I'd like to help you solve these murders, and fast," I added. Also, I far preferred seeing him here rather than under the telescopic eye of the Pit Bull. "There are lots of ears at the office."

"I really don't want you involved," he said. He must have seen my hurt look. "Not because I don't think you are smart and capable." I relaxed. "I don't want you hurt, Darcy. I am quite concerned by the boldness of these attacks against you. There's a murderer out there, and I don't want you in the line of fire."

"I can take care of myself," I said, straightening. I wasn't sure though I believed that anymore. Out of habit, the hackles in my back would go up when anyone suggested I was helpless.

"Darcy, it's obvious you are more than capable, but there's a lunatic loose cannon out there," he pleaded. "It's my job to protect you." It really was a Knight in Shining Armor come to rescue me. As independent as I am, it was my fantasy—a guy who had my back. Too bad it was in such a professional capacity. "And I really don't want any harm to come to you." Was I reading more into this? Well, I was going to. I wanted a strong male ally in my corner, too. And I wanted to be cared for again.

I was mollified, and I still had my dignity. "Sorry. Would you like a coffee, drink?"

"Coffee sounds great," he said as I ushered him into the kitchen and family room. I bustled around the kitchen while the coffee brewed. He made himself at home on a barstool at the kitchen counter, as I put out sugar, milk, and store-bought brownies. I saw him admiring the large oil painting of green fields and lovely Georgian stone home hanging over my fireplace.

"That's a painting of my parents' farm in Ireland."

"The real thing must be breathtaking since this painting is stunning. What a beautiful historic home."

"Actually, the house is new, but County Limerick has strict building codes. My parents inherited that farm when Granddad passed away, but the house was too small and old to use so they built this one new, in an eighteenth-century manner. When my parents retired, they moved back to Ireland. Now my dad is a gentleman farmer raising Black Angus cattle. Sometimes life comes full circle."

Before I got too far into my reverie of my family's past, I was brought back to Earth. Adam brought out his recorder and his notebook.

"I'd love to hear more, but I'm afraid this isn't just a social call.

Sorry to do this. Would you mind telling me again from the start about your interview with Candi?"

I drew a blank.

"Candi … Candace Swartz," he said again."

The realization dawned. I took a seat beside him, fixing my own coffee so it resembled more Häagen Dazs than coffee.

"I didn't realize she goes by Candi." I proceeded to tell him the details of our visit. I took great care to get the details very correct since his recorder and his notebook made this official business on the record.

"You don't mind, do you?" he said as he gratefully sipped his coffee and munched on a brownie.

"No, I'm just so glad to be of help and glad someone cares about Candace, umm, Candi."

I told him as much as I could, and several times we went over the same ground about Candi's mood, and her fears, especially of the guy called "Dirt Devil", and the reason for them. He also made a point of asking if I saw any suspicious people or cars hanging around on the way in or out of the trailer park. "I didn't, but Candace, Candi, was sure spooked. She kept looking out beyond us and looked out the window with every outside noise. Both Cyn and I noticed how jumpy she was. Remember, she was the one who called and left the anonymous tip. Well, it made her paranoid. It was sad since she is such a sweetheart, and she really loved Carl."

"What was the exact time of your visit?"

"I would say about two-thirty to three in the afternoon."

"Is that a guess or do you know?"

I was a little puzzled by his insistence. "I know we left about three because I looked at my watch. I had to get some stuff for Kiera from the store to work on her scarecrow. I wanted to get it before I went home and took her to her riding lesson for four-thirty. Why? Has someone threatened her too?"

He looked at me strangely. "Darcy, do you remember when I couldn't talk to you earlier today?" I nodded not liking the sound of this or the pity in his eyes. "I'm sorry to have to tell you this. The homicide that I was investigating today, when you called, was Candi's."

TWENTY-TWO

"What the hell? No!" I shrieked.

Adam turned off his recorder when I started to sob, thankfully, and sob I did—for Candace and Carl and all the promise of those young lives cut short and wasted. What monster could do such a thing? It took me a moment to realize Adam had his hand on my arm, and as I regained control, I instinctively pulled my arm away.

"Mom? Are you okay?" asked Kiera from the stairs. I hadn't seen her slip downstairs.

"Yes, dear, sorry. Adam, uh, Sheriff Armstrong told me about the death of someone that I had just met … not someone you know. Not to worry. I was just shocked."

She looked a little dubious. "You sure? Is everything okay at the barn and with Nacho?"

Adam spoke up to relieve her mind. "This has nothing to do with the barn. Don't you worry about Nacho. Everything will be fine."

I didn't know if he meant it, but coming from him it seemed to have credibility in her eyes. He, of course, realized this. "Thank you," I said in a small voice.

"I have a teenager at home," he said after Kiera left. "According to Andrew, I know nothing; however, he listens to everyone else."

Boy, could I relate to that. It's a wonder I ever got this far in life, being such an idiot, at least in my daughter's eyes.

I was still shaken but wanted to know all the details about Candace's murder. More and more, I was realizing just how different news reporting was from magazine articles. If I wanted to be a good newspaper woman then I had to deal with gory stuff. I just never anticipated that in York Ridge I would be dealing with murder, or be so physically and emotionally involved.

"It looks as if it happened just after three. Someone threw a Molotov cocktail into the trailer, and with the propane stove and furnace, it was toast in minutes." I felt faint and thought I might fall off the stool for a second. I was horrified thinking of that poor girl and what she must have gone through. "You okay?" I nodded, but I was anything but okay. "Sorry, it would have been quick at least," he continued. "She wouldn't even have known what hit her. Between the blast and the smoke, death would have been instantaneous. The cause of death still hasn't been released."

"How do you know the explosion wasn't an accident?"

"We have an eyewitness and evidence."

"And … I need details Adam. For my own sanity," I added.

His eyes softened. "Okay, off the record. The neighbor across the lane in the trailer park called it in. She was looking out over the lane while she was washing dishes, and she saw something come flying out of the window of a dark-colored SUV into Candi's trailer. The vehicle took off at breakneck speed. At the same time there was the explosion and fire."

I needed a moment to rein in my emotions. "Adam, if there is anything I can do to help, I will. I won't print anything until you tell me to. Look, I really liked Candace, and I was proud of her for making a life for herself and Carl. I admired her for trying to save him. It completely breaks my heart that this happened to such a young, hopeful person." I continued even though I knew the steam generator inside me was going into overdrive. "I want the SOB that did this caught and made to suffer. Okay?" By now my blood pressure was off the scale.

"You're supposed to be objective, you know?"

"Give me a break. I'm not used to this violence. I mean, I wrote about real estate, home design, market trends, and stuff like that."

"And you're a passionate human being, too," he said, with what I thought was a nod of approval.

"Your point?" Thank heavens he didn't tell me to calm down, or I think I might have done something I'd regret.

"Darcy, that's a good thing. It means you're not calloused and you care. I like that."

"Oh." I was surprised and could feel my cheeks flush. "Thanks, but why on Earth would anyone do that to Candi? It was so senseless and so horrific. The poor girl did nothing."

"You're absolutely right, so that leaves us thinking the motive had something to do with Carl and his death."

"You mean, she was killed because she knew something?"

"Looks that way. It could be not *what* she knew, but *who*. The other motives such as robbery have more or less been eliminated. Perhaps the killer or killers thought there was something there that might incriminate them. We are assuming that Candi's and Carl's deaths are in some way linked. It may be the same killer, although the MO is different."

The wheels started turning for me. "Are you thinking the killer is the dealer that Carl was working with? The guy that scared Candi? That 'Dirt Devil'?"

"That's certainly a lead we will follow up on. That's why your information is so important to us. Other than the killer, Cyn and you were the last people to see Candi alive," he said, with a look that meant business.

I sat up straight. "You're not saying I'm a suspect? I mean, Cyn was with me. She took a photo of the deck as we left. It probably showed Candace in the photo. I mean, they're time stamped," I rattled on, realizing just how easy it was to be in Nacho's position, and how scary, too.

"Hold on before you jump to conclusions," he said, raising his palms in the air. "No one is accusing you of anything; however, I would like to see all the photos that Cyn took inside and outside the trailer. Maybe there was a car or vehicle parked nearby?"

Did this mean I was off the hook? I guess no one in the world of police business is above suspicion. Then a more terrifying thought struck. "You mean, the murderer was watching us and waiting for us to leave?" The implication made my voice catch and my words sounded strangled even to me. I coughed.

"That could well be the case. Anything out of place come to mind?"

I relived the movie of our visit to Candace in my head. All I had noticed was how charming and neat the trailer was, and that it was so different from what I thought it would be. I still couldn't wrap my mind around the idea that she was gone, and we had been there only minutes before. Then an even more horrific thought popped up. "Adam, did we interrupt something, or were we being followed?"

"That's the question. Do you recall seeing any car behind you?"

"No, but it never occurred to me to look. Could I have led the killer to Candace's?" I closed my eyes as if that could abolish the thought, too horrible to bear, as was the notion that someone might have been watching me. All of a sudden, I felt vulnerable. I hated the feeling. "How could I have been so stupid as to go to her house? I wasn't thinking, and I should have been, after my tires. How careless of me!" I was waiting for him to tell me 'I told you so.'"

"No, I don't think it had anything to do with what you did. Detective Baker had already been to interview Candi in the morning. It wasn't as if she was hiding. Nor could she identify anyone, according to you. In fact, you got more out of her than Baker. To ease your mind, I think someone had already targeted her. You being there probably didn't make any difference."

"You sure?" I asked, seeking comfort.

"Yeah, I'm sure. She was already a target when Carl decided to bolt. She would have been perceived as a loose end who needed to be silenced."

"I guess by trying to save Carl, she condemned herself."

"Probably." He sighed. "Happens all the time with good women. They try to rescue a guy and end up dragged down with him."

So, there was a cynical side to him after all. I wondered if he saw me as someone who rescued men like Nacho. I hoped he realized my motive was much more selfish—it was to keep my daughter happy. "I guess we don't choose who we love."

He looked at me intensely for a second. "But we can choose to walk away."

I knew there was a history to that remark and hoped one day I would solve that enigma, unless it was a message for me. At any rate, the mood only lasted a second before he was back on track with his recorder.

"Did she mention receiving any threatening phone calls?"

"No, just that Carl thought the dealer was an out-of-control lunatic. That was why she made the call with the anonymous tip about the marijuana patch. She wanted the guy to be out of business or caught. Anything to get Carl away from him, and fast. Maybe the killer figured this out and was vengeful?" I paused and added, "I'm just thinking out loud here."

"That's one possibility."

"I appreciate you being so open with me. I hadn't expected police cooperation; then again, I wasn't expecting much to happen here."

"You'd be surprised," he said, and turned off the recorder. "It just doesn't always make the papers."

I looked at him quizzically, although I thought I already knew the answer.

"People in high places," he said by way of explanation. "By the way, if you are filing this story, when are you filing it?"

"Of course, I'm reporting it. I'll probably do the article on it tonight and then put it in Thursday afternoon for the Friday edition. I'll check with you first, in case there is something you don't want revealed that might hinder your investigation."

"Thanks. That gives me a day-and-a-half. I haven't told the TV crews or big dailies as much as I've told you. The phone has been ringing off the hook at the office. They're driving us crazy and now, of course, with the drugs, we have a state task force member involved. I appreciate you holding off on a few details before you do put the edition to bed. Check with me first. I may have some further news."

I wondered what Adam was up to. "So, I'm getting a scoop?"

"I'll know more in a day. I can't say more at the moment. Anyway, thanks for the coffee and brownies. Keep the doors locked."

Adam left. The kitchen felt empty as I sat taking in the overload of information.

I looked out the window into the dark. Our country place was heaven during the day, but in the dark, the sheer isolation now made me feel creepy. The thought that someone may be out there lurking about in the trees or on the lonely country road had me, for the first time ever, closing all the curtains. I knew I'd never sleep tonight so I decided, while everything was fresh in my mind, that I would write the articles on the drug bust, Carl's bio, and as much as I could on Candace. I'd have to do some more research on her tomorrow. In the meantime, I would phone Cyn and get her to forward the photos to Adam and me. I knew she would be just as shocked and dismayed by Candace's death. We had both commented on the ride back on how impressed we were with her.

I had just hung up from Cyn when the phone rang again. The worried voice of my pal Emily came on the line.

"What the hell is going on up there? Another murder! It's all over the TV. By my count, that's three in the last week and a half. I never hear news from York Ridge, and suddenly you take over as editor, then all I hear is murder and mayhem."

"Em, you're right. The place has turned into the Wild West. First Bruno, then this kid Carl, and now his girlfriend, Candi."

"And you seem to be in the middle of it? How did that happen?"

"Wrong place, wrong time, or if you're the editor, right place, right time."

"Well, thank heavens you didn't discover the third victim."

"No, but I was just informed I was the last person to see her alive!"

"Darcy, good grief, get out of there and down here to the city where it's safe. In all my days as an editor, I have never been involved in any crimes, let alone murders. This is all way too close to home, girl."

"This is not the norm in the county, and especially not York Ridge, as you know. Anyway, I think the Sheriff thinks, at least two of the murders are the work of one lunatic, rather than random murders. He just needs to find the culprit."

"You're pretty good at analyzing. Do you have a theory on whodunit?"

"The list of suspects just keeps getting longer with each murder. For Bruno's murder, there's Frank Malfaro, Bruno's son; then Nacho, unfortunately. There's Tits Tanya, Bruno's girlfriend, who was sleeping with Nacho; Mandy and Joe Bullen, the Malfaro's tenant farmers; Clive Carruthers, a local hippie environmentalist; and then assorted rival developers and Council members. All have motives and from what we've been able to glean, many don't have solid alibis," I recapped.

"And your money is on?"

"For Bruno, I was thinking Frank, although the Sheriff is thinking Nacho, maybe Clive? The jury is still out on that one."

"And the other two?"

"For Carl and Candi, the most likely candidate is some doper called 'Dirt Devil', whoever he may be. I don't see much of a link between their murders and Bruno's death, but the cops are working on that. For me, the other suspects seem unlikely to be responsible for these other two deaths. Candace, the latest victim, was insanely afraid of this Dirt Devil guy and thought he was responsible for Carl's death. I know how that feels because I've been getting threats as well."

After recounting the menacing note, phone call, and slashed tires, Emily was horrified. "I hope that bloody paper is paying you *mucho* bucks for putting yourself in harm's way to get a story for them!"

Actually, the only big bucks I'd be seeing lived in the woods. "Are you kidding me? I've had to fight to get my news in the paper. Ads rule. They are always telling me it is a community paper and to put as many town kids and town celebrities in the paper as I can. The way they carry on, you'd think I didn't know what I was doing. Damn, a little more than a week on the job, and already I'm ranting. I thought I was made of stronger stuff."

"But what a week. Pack it in now, D, or start packin'—I mean, a gun. You weren't destined to play with these local yokels, more like local locos. Come down and play with the big boys where you belong and collect the big bucks without being terrified."

At this weak moment, she didn't know just how tempting that sounded, but how could she see that it wasn't only Kiera's riding that kept me here? I loved the country house and thrived on the fresh air and the small-town pace.

"The money and autonomy are tempting but the traffic, the pollution, and the noise, ugh. I really do like country life. Besides, I've never been a quitter. The paper is a challenge, and I think I am the one to change their old school ways." I would rather chew glass than admit defeat.

"I know you. You just don't want them all saying you couldn't cut it. I get it, but don't be foolish and put yourself in danger to prove a point." She was right, of course. "Keep me in the loop," she ended. I promised.

Kiera went to bed, and all was quiet while I wrote my quite riveting stories of the bust and Carl's murder. One could be factual without being dull. I had a little more trouble being unbiased when it came to Candace. The memory of her cozy trailer and her sweet face were just too fresh. I decided to call it a night and work on it again in the morning.

Unfortunately, sleep didn't come. Every night noise had me peeking through the curtains, turning on the light, and checking the doors and windows. How had I been so oblivious to the sinister sounds of the night before? I wish our Golden Lab, Bailey, was still alive to be an early warning system and bring some measure of comfort. Perhaps it was time for Kiera and me to think of getting another dog. I made a mental note to mention this to her soon. The sensation that someone was watching me was hard to shake. The Sheriff and his boys had better make an arrest soon if I was ever going to sleep again.

TWENTY-THREE

Walking into the Yorkdale Weekly Offices, I noticed that the Pit Bull had built what I can only describe, as a monument to Morty. The bottle of antacids now had a prominent position on her back file cabinet. Raised on a mini platform, the bottle was flanked by two flower vases, each with fresh cut flowers. I was mid eye roll when the Pit Bull and her perpetual scowl came bustling to her desk from the back office, hot coffee in hand.

"Nice of you to put in an appearance," she snarled.

I took the high road and threw a comment over my shoulder as I headed to my office. "It's nice to have fresh flowers in the office. They really brighten the place up." It was the only honest thing I could think to say that was a compliment. Her skirt and blouse were so a decade ago, and her hair. No one should get me started on the gray perm. I giggled to myself. I think Cyn was starting to rub off on me. I hoped it didn't extend to micro minis and five-inch heels next.

I sat at my desk and pulled up my email. I needed to check if we had any local submissions I should try to work into this week's edition. I was so glad I had worked on my articles the night before. It would make it easier to put the edition to bed tomorrow morning for publication on Friday. Tomorrow night I had the Council meeting to cover so it was going to be a busy day. Despite all of the excitement this last week, I felt like I was starting to get a feel for the rhythm of a weekly publication. Simon, our ad guy, passed by my open door and stopped in his tracks giving me a dark look. My hackles already rose before he said a word.

"Darcy, what we are running here is a feel-good paper: local interest stories, pictures of children helping plant trees or cuddle puppies. Is it correct that I heard you are going to be putting another murder on the front pages again this week?" he asked, horrified, his smattering of freckles disappearing as he visibly reddened.

"This is a local interest story, Simon. Locals have been murdered. People are already gossiping about it and want to know the facts. Who he was, who did it, why … it's news," I said matter-of-factly. *It's not a no-news newspaper!*

"You do realize that our biggest advertisers are housing development corporations," he said, staring at me, his close-set eyes looking even beadier. I waited for him to finish his point.

"And …" I prompted.

"And you are making Yorkdale County sound like a horrible place to live. This community is the ideal country setting. An idyllic life with fresh air, clean water, meandering paths … and now murder and drug busts!" he spat, his pinched face even sharper than ever. For a minute he sounded as if he was on the Malfaro payroll.

"I'm not the one murdering people," I said defensively. "I'm just covering the stories that are happening right here in our community. Besides, papers will be flying off the racks; everyone wants to know what's going on. I would think increased readership would make advertisers such as the Malfaros very happy." I made a point of naming names. Simon responded with a sniff of that pointy nose and narrowing of his eyes. He was too devious to be baited.

"Can't you at least bury it to page six? Run a cover story about the local high school team's basketball star or something."

"Absolutely not!" I stabbed the keys on the keyboard. Simon

stormed down the hall. This was a relationship I was going to have to work on. I had barely written a sentence when Simon came back, marching right into my office.

"Here are the ad dummies for this week's edition. Be sure to fit in your articles accordingly," he said, with a mirthless grin as he tossed them at my desk and walked out.

I knew in an instant as I looked over the dummies what he had done. Advertising space gets marked out first, then I have to fit in my stories. In the dummy, he had marked out a full half-page ad on the first page, along with a quarter-inch sidebar ad down the side. The weasel had squeezed me into a box, literally, and it was a pretty small one once I accounted for a headline. I was going to have to feed most of the article on Carl onto other pages. I scanned through the rest and found he had blocked off pages two through five entirely for ads. He was relegating the majority of my article to page six, just where he wanted it. I still didn't have much information on Candace so that would be lost in the back pages.

I jumped up from my desk and stormed over to Simon's office, where he was sitting, a smug look on his face. "What the hell is this?"

"Fall Feature advertising. You can't stock up on shovels and snowblowers early enough. You never know when Old Man Winter is going to rear his unsightly head."

"You've got to be kidding me. I'll be talking to Lorne about this," I said, by way of warning.

"Go ahead. Advertising drives this paper, not articles. Oh, and don't forget that the Events pages are going to be quite full this week—you need to fit in all the Fall Fair."

I walked down the narrow corridor towards the back where Lorne had his office. On the frosted glass window of his door, his name was stenciled in gold paint. Beneath his name in large letters was his title: Publisher. I knocked.

I heard a muffled, "Come in." I flew in, propelled by adrenalin.

"Lorne, have you seen the ad dummies for this week's edition?" I asked, waving the pages in front of him.

"Simon's done a bang-up job selling this week, hasn't he?" Lorne sounded like a proud father.

What? "So, you've seen them?"

"Yes, I can't believe he was able to get a feature in so early in the season. It's likely we'll be able to run it more times before the snow hits. Genius," he said, a delighted smile playing about his lips.

"So, you are okay with the lack of space for headline news, like the murder of that drug dealer?" I felt the fizzle going out of me.

"Look, for Bruno it made sense to make it front page news. He was a big advertiser of ours, a figure in the community. Who cares about the death of a low-life drug dealer?"

Was he serious? I couldn't believe he could be so callous. The first conversation I had with Cyn and Adam came back to me. Now, I knew part of the reason for the lack of coverage of grow ops. "I care. His name was Carl Hanover. He was a young man with a whole life ahead of him. He had people who cared about him … and one of those people who cared also ended up dead, and she was innocent!" I was sure I was speaking to deaf ears. "I also care about living in a safe community, and I think burying things we don't want to acknowledge just means people think they can get away with them. Better to have them out in the open, so we can all be part of the solution."

He looked at me thoughtfully for a moment. "Very eloquent, Darcy; however, we are not a social agency. We are a business and advertising runs this paper. You knew that when you signed up. I'm not saying you can't run the article. You can even run it as the lead headline. But I will not compromise on the ad space for this," Lorne said, shaking a finger, making his point very clear.

"Understood." Disappointment flooded in to replace indignation as I backed out of his office. I couldn't risk losing my job, not while I was still on trial. I wasn't going to be winning any Pulitzer Prizes for journalism working here. I knew that. So why was I so perturbed? Lorne had put me in my place, that was clear. I felt small enough that I figured I may as well get a coffee from The Blackbird. There was nothing Amelia could say or do that would make me feel any worse. Shoulders slumped, I headed towards the front of the office.

The Pit Bull intercepted me.

"Ms. Dillon, I have received a bill for the setup of an iPhone account in your name. Surely, you do not think the paper will be paying for this expense?" She glared at me, almost defiant.

Not now. "Miss Pittman, I am often out of the office, and people need a way to get a hold of me. Plus, the resolution on the phones is good enough that, should Cynthia not be able to accompany me, I can take pictures with it to enhance the articles."

"Morty never had a cellphone," she countered.

I had to bite my tongue. Morty was a dinosaur who probably used a letter press to put out each edition. I'd bet he waited for the news to come to him. I was just starting to formulate my next retort when I spotted something out of the corner of my eye. An object was flying at the front window of the office. "Get down!" I yelled, just as the object made impact with the front glass. I crouched with my hands tight over my head. Shards of glass rained down on me; one caught the top of my hand, giving me a nasty gash.

Standing up, I quickly checked to see if everyone was all right. Then I looked out the window to see if I could spot anyone suspicious. Whoever had done this had not stuck around to see if they had hit their target.

The Pit Bull's flowers lay scattered among the shattered glass on the floor. She gingerly crawled out from under her desk where she had taken cover and made a beeline for the antacid bottle, to ensure it was okay. Looking through the debris on the floor, I found a large rock. It was wrapped in paper, secured with rough twine. I pulled the twine off the rock, releasing the sheet of paper. Blood was dripping from the cut on my hand. On the paper, in bold black script, were the words, "You're next."

TWENTY-FOUR

I peered out the windshield into the darkness to see if I could see the moon; even it was hiding. Country roads are charming during the day, but at night they take on a whole new character. Gravel crunched under the wheels; large tree branches loomed over the road. The odd bump startled me as the car hit a rock or broken branch from a nearby tree. On nights like this I yearned for a well-lit, paved city street. Of course, the rock from yesterday, the latest in a series of threats, had unnerved me even further. I was glad Cyn was with me tonight.

I'd finished editing this week's edition of the paper earlier in the day. It had been a challenge to work with the space Simon had left me, but I was proud of the end result. Tonight, we were headed to the Town Council meeting to cover it for next week's edition. The Council met every two weeks; this was going to be our first time to cover one together. Over a ridge in the road, my headlights highlighted a yellow-and-black sign with the silhouette of a deer on it. *Great, deer crossing*. My hands tightened on the wheel.

"You okay?" Cyn asked, looking over at me.

"I guess I'm a little spooked."

"No shit, Sherlock! Whoever is behind all of these murders has it in for you. I'd be concerned if you *weren't* afraid," Cyn said, pulling down the visor in front of her to look in the mirror. She pulled lipstick out of her purse and began applying it. "Hmm."

"What?"

"Has that black vehicle—maybe a truck—been behind us very long?"

I looked in the rearview mirror. "I hadn't noticed. Do you think it's following us?"

"I'm sure I'm just being silly; your paranoia is rubbing off on me." She put the cap on her lipstick and slipped it into her purse. She kept her visor down and kept glancing in the mirror. Normally, I would have thought she just loved her reflection, but tonight was different. I was sure she was keeping an eye on the truck behind us.

I turned a corner, glanced in the rearview mirror, and saw that the truck followed. I was getting more and more uneasy when suddenly the truck was practically right on our bumper. I increased my speed, but the tires lost traction on the gravel. The truck behind us sped up too. Cyn turned and looked behind, and then sent a worried look my way. I sped up even more but had difficulty controlling the Escape. Still the truck kept right on our bumper. Way too tight. The headlights lit up the back of Cyn's hair. "This guy's a lunatic. I can't go any faster on this gravel."

"He's trying to run us off the road!" Cyn screamed. Suddenly the truck hit our back bumper. My head lurched forward with the impact. "We're gonna die!" yelled Cyn. I gripped the wheel in a death grip as I searched the darkness ahead for a road to turn on to. No luck. My head lurched forward as the truck hit us again. I felt something wet run down the side of my head. *Yikes, I must be bleeding.* My hands hurt as I clenched the wheel. My stomach tied itself in knots. I tried to beat down the fear and hysteria. My heart raced. Cyn started shrieking.

What happened next felt like slow motion. The truck hit us hard for a third time, and our SUV lost traction. We careened into the ditch and started to roll. I heard the sickening thud of metal against the ground, and screaming, lots of screaming. Cyn wasn't the only one screaming. Side windows broke and shattered when they hit rocks and branches on the ground. My purse flew into the back. I got knocked in the head by something as it achieved liftoff. The car went into a spin cycle. I don't even know how many times it rolled. We thumped to a stop. I was just glad that we finally stopped. We were upside down, resting on the roof of the car. Both Cyn and I were hanging from our seatbelts.

"My nose!" Cyn screamed, with her hand up to her face. "I think I broke my nose."

I had to catch my breath before I could even assess myself. "Take your hand away so I can see," I finally managed. She pulled her hand back to reveal her nose. It was difficult to see in the dark. It didn't seem to be out of shape. I don't know about broken.

"I'm ruined. I'll never model again," Cyn whimpered. *Oh please.*

"I'm sure it will be fine. Once we get out of here, we can get some ice on it. Worst case, you could see a plastic surgeon."

She started carrying on again. "Shh," I said. I heard her sharp intake of breath as she figured out why I was listening. I had no doubt the truck driver was the person who made the threats. I couldn't recall hearing whether the truck kept going. What if he was out there waiting to see if he needed to finish us off? We spent several minutes like that, just listening, our ears straining. Other than Cyn's stifled sniffing and my heavy breathing, I didn't hear anything but the wind rustling through weeds, and the odd night bird. Nothing foreign. I was just about to turn my attention to how to get us out of this predicament when suddenly Cyn screamed, "Oh my God!"

I panicked. My body tensed. "What? Are you all right? Did you hear something?"

"Look how fabulous my tits look upside down."

I was about to tell her off for scaring the hell out of me when the absurdity of it hit me. I laughed, and then stopped abruptly. It hurt. I think I broke a rib. I reached around and gingerly touched my side. I took in a breath of air quickly, surprised at the intensity of the pain. Yup, broken rib. I reached up to steady myself with a hand on the ceiling of the car, brushing away broken glass shards as I did so. I felt my head and found it was wet. I must still be bleeding. Hanging upside down wasn't helping any of these injuries. Once I braced myself, I reached down to release my seat belt. No luck. It was jammed.

"Cyn, try your seat belt; mine is locked." She struggled with the release button with the same results. I had a box cutter in the back, and I tried to twist around to reach for it. The effort was futile. Even if I could reach, it may not be there. Everything in the car that wasn't nailed down had been tossed. "Looks like your tits are going to keep looking fabulous for a while. We're stuck like this until someone comes to help us. Can you reach your cellphone?"

"No, my purse went flying when we rolled. I can't find it," Cyn said, patting her hands around her to feel for her possessions.

"Same problem here." I wondered why I hadn't gotten one of those fancy vehicles with OnStar. *Next time.* Before I could think further, loose gravel rolled down the embankment. I froze.

"What was that noise?" Cyn whispered to me. "Do you think someone's back to …?"

"Shush." I put my finger to my lips to signal her to be quiet. I didn't think anyone would return. I thought any finishing off would have happened right after the accident. After a few minutes I whispered, "I think it was just gravel settling. I'm sure whoever it was is long gone."

I had no idea how much time had passed. The face on my watch had broken in the crash. Cyn never wore a watch, believing it looked too chunky, detracting from her wrists. We had both gotten over the initial adrenaline boost of the crash. Now shock started to set in. My teeth chattered, and Cyn shivered beside me. Someone had to find us soon.

"Who do you think it was?" I finally asked.

"Some evil bastard from hell." Even in the dark, I saw a scowl on her face.

"Do you think it was Frank?" I asked, remembering my conversation with Tanya about how I was her insurance policy. *What was my insurance policy?*

"Frank or one of his goons. I could totally see that."

"I don't see Frank having a nickname like Dirt Devil. His hands were manicured, for God's sake."

"Back to the theory of a goon doing his ... dirty work," Cyn said, barely getting the last words out as she shook uncontrollably. We needed help soon. I'm no doctor but I thought that if the shock didn't kill us, the build-up of blood in our brains certainly could—except mine was draining away. My feet were numb and tingling from the loss of circulation.

We grew silent as we heard a vehicle on the road nearby. I panicked for the fortieth time. I tried to think rationally that the vehicle could be a good thing. But the feeling of helplessness from being upside was overpowering. We were hanging ducks. I heard someone sliding down the embankment. Gravel skittered down the hill, dislodged by feet. I started to hyperventilate Then I heard a familiar voice. Relief overcame me.

"Darcy? Cyn? Are you two all right?" Adam yelled.

"We're here," Cyn and I yelled in unison.

Adam tried to open my door, but it was jammed. He opened the hatch in the back and climbed in.

"Thank God, the Cavalry," Cyn said as he made his way through the overturned car to the front.

"Are you two hurt?" he asked with concern.

"Cyn is worried about her nose. I think I broke a rib and cut my head, and I feel lightheaded from blood loss."

"I'm enjoying the blood rush," Cyn said. I knew she was kidding; she was still enjoying the way her tits looked.

"Our seatbelts are jammed."

Adam reached out to support me by wrapping an arm around my torso, then pulled out a knife and cut the belt. I fell into his arms, and he helped me turn myself upright. He helped me out the back hatch, then turned his attention to Cyn.

Once we were both out of the vehicle, Adam half-carried us one at a time up the embankment. When we were safely seated in Adam's Explorer and covered in blankets, I asked, "How did you know it was us, and how did you find us?"

"Kiera called me. She was freaking out because Lorne called your house when you missed the Council meeting. Since you had told her you were headed there, she panicked and called me when you didn't pick up your cell."

"I didn't hear my cell. It's back there somewhere."

"I checked all the possible routes from your house. What happened?" Adam continued.

"Someone freakin' ran us off the road!" Cyn exclaimed.

"Did you see who it was? Can you describe the vehicle?" The words tumbled out. For a moment Adam became unglued. I hadn't seen him like this. Usually, he was so composed.

"It was a black pickup truck, or at least a dark-colored truck or SUV-type vehicle," I provided. "It was so dark; it was hard to tell."

"Did you see the driver?"

"No. Too dark."

"Could you figure out the make of the vehicle?"

"No." *As if.* I never paid attention to those details.

"Okay," Adam said, clearly frustrated as he ran both of his hands over his chin. "I'll call it in and have the tech team come out and try to get tire tracks. I just wish we had something to go on." *Me too.*

"I'm afraid your car might be a write-off, but you can call your insurance company. When we're done, they can tow it. In the meantime, I'm going to take you both to the hospital to get checked out, once the team gets here. I'll have an officer wait and take both of you home after, unless they want to keep you overnight."

Damn. Just what I didn't need. Now I may be looking for a new car—well, new *used* car.

I must have looked pathetic. Adam pulled the blanket tighter around me and put some kind of cloth on my head. "Hold this against your head, Darcy." I gazed up into his blue eyes; I saw concern there, and maybe something else. "I want you to stay home for the next few days while we try to find out who is behind this."

I pulled back. "I can't do that. I have to get another car, and I have the Fall Fair to cover for the paper. It kicks off tomorrow night."

"Darcy, your life is being threatened. You are injured, for heaven's sake!" He released his grip on the blanket around me, gesturing in the air with his hands. Then he rested the palms of his hands on his forehead and laced his fingers together.

"I'll keep an eye on her," Cyn said.

"I can see I'm getting nowhere with you two," he said, pursing his lips.

"We'll be fine," I said firmly. "Anyway, you're not the only one worried. If you can grab my purse for me, I need to call Kiera to thank her and tell her we're fine. Hopefully my phone still works."

"Be careful, both of you. You're lucky I wasn't dealing with two more homicides tonight." Of course, he was talking about us.

TWENTY-FIVE

After a taped rib and stitches in my head, I got that lift home from the hospital. After many reassurances to Kiera that I was fine, the night took its toll. I fell into a deep sleep only to be tormented by dead bodies like zombies coming after me. It was like being trapped in an episode of that show, *The Walking Dead*. I couldn't even toss and turn, as I was curled up in the only comfortable position I could find. Even morning didn't bring relief as I moved from my nightmares to the nightmare of my reality.

Still, with the paper put to bed, I decided to take both Adam's and the doctor's advice and take it easy most of the day. After all, I was working the night shift by going to the corn roast and kickoff for the Fall Fair tonight, a Friday night. Then I was covering the parade and scarecrow judging contest tomorrow. I did call my insurance company and arrange for a rental car for later in the day. I was sure the SUV was a write-off.

Kiera had wanted to stay home and help out. She had never seen me incapacitated and beat up. She was scared. That bothered me; I wanted her to feel safe. Again, I wondered if the job was worth it. I told her to go to school because I would probably need her to drive me in the evening. My instinct was that she was safer there.

First thing in the morning, I phoned to get a security system installed which was something I should have done a long time before, such as when Will left. I had mistakenly thought I was invincible. I ran the idea of another puppy by Kiera, and she was ecstatic. Once show season was over, we would go searching, but this time she had to take over much of the responsibility for walking and feeding. For all our succession of pets, we had started off with a great deal of enthusiasm and promises, only to deteriorate to me doing all the legwork. Thinking about all this spun me in a positive direction and made me feel proactive. Before the day was out, Adam called. Nacho called. Lorne called, and Cyn called. I felt like I had won the Miss Popularity contest and was quite drunk with the attention.

By the time early evening came I was feeling more myself, although my body was sore. Kiera drove us to town where she was to meet Heather to finish their scarecrow, which we had jammed, in pieces, into the back of the rental Jeep. I was to catch up to Cyn, who was racing around getting shots of all and sundry.

Main Street was quite transformed. Scarecrows sprouted like dandelions on lawns and porches of the old homes. Cornstalks and cornucopias decorated the restaurants now occupying the old granary and feed mill, while hay bales were strategically placed as benches. Fall Fair banners fluttered from replica lampposts like moths in the breeze. Groups of kids and clusters of adults were already gathering, although it was still half an hour to kickoff. There was a wonderful air of expectation and excitement in the normally laid-back town of York Ridge.

We pulled up to Heather's aunt's Victorian house where an excited Heather eagerly awaited the jigsaw puzzle of Zorro parts to spew from the Jeep. The girls were going to place it in a prominent position on her aunt's lawn for maximum impact. We arranged to meet in the fairgrounds later that evening.

I took the Jeep and parked on the street, then made my way over to the fairgrounds along with the meandering crowds. In the soccer field, huge pots of water were on boil on propane burners, ready to cook the corn. Huge commercial BBQs were set up to grill burgers, hot dogs, and ribs. The smell made me hungry, and I looked forward to indulging in the last corn of the season. Even Amelia and The Blackbird had a booth here in the field, where her counter had various urns of coffee and lattes, along with her vegetarian options. *Oh yum, sprout Paninis.*

Above the crowd I heard, "Hey, Ham Sandwich, are you going to go wild and try an espresso tonight?"

I had a good idea of where she could put her espresso. As always, Amelia was saved from me running over her with my broomstick by Cyn. She was in her glory, snapping shots and shooting the breeze with the big frogs in our small pond. I heard her call out. I couldn't wait to see what Cyn thought would be appropriate attire for a Fall Fair. As always, she didn't disappoint. I welcomed the distraction from fuming over Amelia and thinking of ways to drive her back to the city one urn at a time.

Cyn was a vision from head to toe for perhaps a film called "Cyn Does the Fall Fair." A snug red plaid shirt opened to there was tucked into skin-tight blue jean leggings. I didn't know cowboy boots came with so high a heel, and she had her dark, thick mane reined in with a bandana. Lucky she didn't wear her Daisy Dukes, or the whole thing would have been X-rated.

"How's the nose?" With all the make-up, I wasn't sure what was going on there.

"I'll live. Not eligible for a nose job yet. Nice hat, by the way."

"I borrowed Kiera's cowboy hat to cover the gash on my head. They had to shave a little patch of hair for the stitches, but I covered it with bangs."

"How about the rest of you?" she continued.

"I'm fine as long as someone doesn't ask me to slow dance and grabs me around the waist. But not much chance here."

"Other than with Adam, any slow dance would be grounds for assault."

I chuckled. "Oh, and don't make me laugh." I winced. "So, I see it's all the usual suspects," I said, scanning the crowd.

"You mean the usual unusual. From walking around, I'd say the whole gang is here."

"Surely not that tasty morsel, Tanya?"

"No, word is she took the money and ran. Maybe after the last murder she decided to play it safe."

"You have to be kidding me." Cyn shook her head. "I wonder if she ever 'fessed up to the cops about being with Nacho."

"I wonder if Adam even knows she's gone. Amelia told me that it was quite sudden. Not that anyone would have thrown a going-away party."

"Other than the Malfaro victory party that they'd got rid of her so easy."

Speaking of Malfaros, there was dapper Frank in his designer country-gentleman getup of wide-brimmed cowboy hat and tan ultra-suede blazer, walking alongside his frumpy wife. He strutted like some peacock, sure and cocky. He got a glimpse of me and made a quick U-turn. From his stride, I could guess all guns were blazing.

"Uh oh," said Cyn. *Uh oh was right.*

He wasted no time on pleasantries. "Ms. Dillon, I never want to see the words drugs and Malfaro Developments again in the same sentence!"

"Frank, at the very least, a news article covers the basic five w's: who, what, when, where, why, or how. Those are facts I can't leave out."

"Ms. Dillon, I am warning you to be choosy about what you decide to print."

"Frank, I'm just the messenger. You don't want to shoot the messenger because you don't like the message. Besides, now that you're at the helm, I'm sure you'll be keeping a close eye on exactly what goes on with your properties, so that a situation like this never arises again."

"If I had my way, I'd get rid of those wretched stables and farm. I told my dad to dump them a long time ago."

This was news indeed. "Does that mean you're selling, and do you have a buyer?" I wondered if he knew what his dad had been up to.

"No comment." In two strides he was back with the little woman.

"Uh, wow," said Cyn. "You were wonderful."

"Tanya warned me. I wonder if there's a chance now that Nacho can buy the stables. I just didn't get the 'if I had my way' comment. After all, I thought he was now the Emperor."

"You're right. Why doesn't he just sell them?"

"From watching that, and after what Tanya told me of the charming Frank, I could well see him as the most wanted." Cyn agreed.

We continued to stroll around the fairgrounds. Politicians glad-handed, the high school band played, and we dutifully took photos of kids, animals, and fairgoers. We got quotes from everyone for the paper, all the while on the lookout for those on our hit list.

"I don't know," Cyn said. "What about that wacko in the environmental club booth over there?" I looked around. "There, by Amelia, manning his booth and selling his book like some prophet. I'm not knocking the cause because I believe in it, but why do eco things like that attract such a lot of weirdoes?"

There was Clive with his long, stringy hair, looking like some time-warp hippie with his long-skirted girlfriend, forcing pamphlets on anyone within spitting range. "Fanatics glom onto bandwagons like that. I think it has to do with attaching themselves to some just cause. Then they do anything in the name of the cause. I mean, fanatical religious causes attract the same scary people. They often do more harm than good because they scare reasonable people away."

She looked at me funny. "Okay, let's get you to the podium."

"I guess I got carried away," I said. "Anyway, the Sheriff thinks Clive is all about power, and he drives a black van. Food for thought?"

"But is he capable of murder? And if so, why?"

"Dope and development?" I pondered.

"Could be." She shrugged. "He doesn't want development on his acres of weed."

"Wait a minute. You may be onto something. Clive grows weed? Do you think ... Oh no, shoot me now! There's Kiera's Data Management teacher. Quick ..." I pulled Cyn down another corridor of booths. "I will get such an earful and there'll be no 'saved by the bell' here." Just then I heard my name and froze. I wondered if Cyn could tell from the look on my face that door number two was no better.

Turning, I forced a smile on my face. "Iggy, Matilde, how are you both?" We were in front of the Van Dyke Foods booth with its designer shelves filled with jars of gourmet jams, pickles, relishes, and dips. "I didn't think you'd be here at the booth yourselves. I thought Hailey and Josh might be here." Usually, Kiera's older cousins, who were being groomed for the family business, made the round of the fall fairs.

"Since we're not in the store any more, this gives us a chance to talk to our old customers and maybe see what other products they are asking for," Iggy replied. He eyed Cyn as if she had just dropped in from some R-rated movie.

"Good thinking. This is Cynthia Davis, the paper's photographer," I quickly said, before they started haranguing me about not calling. Cyn, on cue, asked them to pose for a photo with their booth, which pleased them no end.

I was poised, waiting for the attack, when Matilde surprised the heck out of me. "How are you, Darcy? Kiera told us about your accident when we called the other night." I would have to remember to thank her for keeping the outlaws at bay.

"A sore rib and head, but 90 percent for the rest. Thanks for asking."

"She also told us you had made arrangements for her about the barn. Thank you. When you get a few minutes after the weekend, give us a call. We need to talk."

I hate that phrase. I nodded. "Will do," I said. *When hell freezes over.* "Cyn and I better keep going since we have a fair to cover."

When we had moved off, Cyn wanted to know what that was all about. For once she was quite comforting rather than flippant when I told her about my ex and his meddling family. "Well, there's a sight for sore eyes and noses," she said. I followed her gaze to the back of a tall, lean man. I almost didn't recognize Nacho in jeans and a white button-down shirt; I was so used to seeing him in his riding clothes. "How do I look? Is my nose noticeable?"

I felt a little twinge of unfounded jealously. "I don't think he'll even notice your nose," I said, and I meant it. Really, he would be too mesmerized by the cleavage.

Cyn came up behind him and in her sultry voice said, "Hello there, cowboy."

He whipped around, completely startled. He relaxed when he saw me beside her. He had the opposite effect on me. In spite of my misgivings, I could still admire the breathtaking view.

"Cyn, Darcy, great to see you."

"I almost didn't recognize you in your civilian clothes. Cyn spotted you," I said. He smiled at her with a little mischievous grin that I didn't like. Player alert. "I'm glad to see you here," I continued.

"I'm glad to be here doing something normal. Besides, I have nothing to hide." With his accent it sounded like "no ting to hide" which was completely charming.

"That's the spirit." It put my mind at ease somewhat. If he were guilty, there's no way he'd be walking around here, would he? Let alone flirting.

By this time, the hunger pains in my stomach were overpowering the pain in my ribs. "Cyn, I don't know about you, but I am going to do some serious damage to some cobs of corn."

"I ate at Amelia's." Since no one else was game for corn, I left her talking to Nacho, making that two of us now who had noses out of joint.

The corn more than made up for my jealous twinges as I chewed my way through several buttery cobs. I was trying to surreptitiously pick corn out of my teeth while wiping my chin when Adam moseyed up beside me. Damn, he looked good in a uniform. My timing just sucked tonight. No wonder Cyn didn't eat corn when out—smart girl.

"You missed a spot," said Adam, grabbing a napkin and wiping the bottom of my chin while eyeing my hat. *Aren't I just the sexiest?* Corn stuck in my teeth, butter running down my chin, and stitches in my head. I felt all of eight years old. I couldn't even think of anything clever to say. It was almost as bad as someone walking in when you were in the washroom. "Out keeping the peace tonight, Sheriff?"

"That, and the boys and I are hoping to pick up any information we can on the murders, particularly anything that might link them together. I can't see that it's a coincidence that three people have died suspiciously in the same town, but I have nothing to go on." Adam went on to make a few polite inquiries as to my ribs and Cyn's nose. Then I remembered Tanya.

"This may help, and maybe you know already, but rumor has it that Tanya has taken off, and in a hurry."

"What? She didn't!" he said, as an Arctic storm front gathered in those ice blue eyes. He was definitely pissed. "Son of a gun, I told her not to leave town! Damn it all. Now she's got herself in worse trouble and has just made my job all the harder. Any idea where she went?"

"I'm hearing this third-hand, but I do know she was scared of Frank when I talked to her. She looked as if she was ready to bolt. Do you really consider her a suspect?"

"Well, she still has no one to vouch for her whereabouts the night of Bruno's murder. And if she was lying in her statement, then she is also in trouble. She could potentially have some vital information. After all, she did live with Bruno." He was lost in thought for a moment. "Is there anything else I haven't heard?" he replied somewhat icily.

"I don't know, but I do have a question and it's one that has been bugging me. Nacho said he didn't know who was farming the land behind the paddocks. And he didn't know the Bullens. So, did you ever discover who called Mandy and Joe?"

"Another mystery. It was a question that bugged me too. It was news to Malfaro Developments that the Bullens were told they couldn't lease those four acres. They couldn't corroborate their story."

"Which means the Bullens could be lying?" I asked hopefully.

"I don't think they are; however, they never saved the envelope or stationery so there is nothing to back up their story."

"Wow."

"Wow is right. I have a cast of a thousand suspects and no answers. So, if you hear anything else no matter how trivial, I'd appreciate hearing it. You have my cell?" I nodded. "Well, any other Fall Fair I could socialize more, but I best be off and catch some bad guys." I could relate to that feeling. "And Darcy, I'm no farther along figuring out who's threatening you either, so keep an eye out, and try to keep out of trouble." He gave an intense stare to back up his words.

That did it. Even the Sheriff was paranoid about me. As if I could relax and enjoy the Fair now. In one fell swoop, my wonderful memories of taking Kiera here as a child were swept away by the thought that there really could be a live monster in our midst.

Suddenly, the night felt cool in spite of the crowds, and the warm fuzzies I had felt were rapidly being replaced by tentacles of fear. I didn't see Cyn so I thought I would go back to the car to drop off my notes and see if the girls had finished their scarecrow. Really, I just wanted to reassure myself that Kiera was all right.

Dusk was setting in, and crews were lighting fires in oil drums that lined the streets for warmth. A larger bonfire was set alight in the middle of the fairgrounds. All the competitors were finished setting up their scarecrows and had wandered back to the food stands. By the time I got to the car, Main Street was almost deserted. The faces of the scarecrows that had looked so cheerful and welcoming took on a menacing air as darkness descended. Reflections of the bonfire flames licked at their faces as they stared out ghoulishly. Absentmindedly, I rubbed the bandage on the back of my hand where the glass from the Yorkdale Weekly office window had torn it open. I quickly walked to the car and stashed my notebook.

Adam's words rung in my ears. I shivered. I needed to get back to the crowd of people on the fairgrounds. Safety in numbers and all that, but anyone among them could be a murderer. Were they desperate and deranged enough to act in public? I thought that my investigations would have uncovered answers, but all I had were questions. A branch snapped behind me and I jumped. Looking over my shoulder, I picked up my pace. I didn't see anyone, but that did little to reassure me. I hadn't seen my attacker before.

I passed the old Victorian house where Heather and Kiera's Zorro and his brown stallion reared in front of me. Perhaps it was my state of mind, but Zorro and his horse were terrifying. There was no sign of the girls, but they'd done an awesome job. The judges would either love it for their creativity and scale or hate it for pushing the boundaries of the family-friendly competition. Suddenly, a dark figure rose up from behind the haunches of the model horse. My heart lurched. A small scream escaped from me.

"Boo!" he said, stepping out into the light from the nearby bonfires.

"Marco," I said, relieved. "You scared me." I had to stop seeing ghouls and goblins everywhere.

"Sorry, I was just making sure the base was secure for Heather. What are you doing out here alone?"

"Putting my notes in the car. I was just heading back. Where are the girls?"

"Somewhere in the fairgrounds. Let me walk you back."

"Thank you, that's very kind. I also want to thank you for looking out for Kiera at the barn."

"No worries. I have to be there anyway for Dante, and I wouldn't want anything to happen to her."

"I didn't think you would have come to the barn after what happened, but I so appreciate it."

"It's my way to commemorate my grandfather's memory, by grooming and exercising Dante. If I don't, my dad will just sell Dante, and that's not fair to the horse."

"That's considerate of you. It has bought me some time while keeping Kiera safe. After all, you don't look like someone easily intimidated."

"I'm not. Any more news on the murder investigations? You are looking into that, right?"

"Yes, I am, but at this point it's anyone's guess. The suspect list just keeps growing."

"In that case, I guess we all need to be careful." He said it so seriously that shivers went up my spine. *Get a grip.*

TWENTY-SIX

There is something wonderful about small town parades. I never liked parades when I lived in New York. There the floats had been immaculately done, and in many cases the decorations were over-the-top, one-of-a-kind creations, but I felt disconnected from it all. However, in a small-town parade, I knew people on every float. I could see the craftsmanship, or lack of it, in each entry. In York Ridge there were no professional float designers, and I liked that. Each float was an original with character.

Cyn and I arrived early morning and positioned ourselves on Main Street in front of the Yorkdale Weekly Office, so we had a good view of all of the floats. Cyn was on a mission for a knockout picture for the next edition and had brought along all manner of camera equipment for the occasion. The street was lined with the scarecrows erected last night. On this sunny Saturday they looked jovial, having morphed from their sinister appearance of last night. I was anxious to see the school float Kiera and Heather had helped construct. Most of the builders had been drunk or high during its construction. Heather was riding on the school float, while Kiera chose to ride Amigo, along with Nacho and the other boarders from Maple Lane Stables. He was doing his best PR work to promote his training facility and shore up his reputation, given recent events.

Little children jostled for seats on the curb, anxious for ringside seats to be in the best position for the floats that threw candies and small trinkets. Parents with strollers stood back from them, ever watchful. Neighbors yelled greetings to each other across the street, while dogs barked and pulled their owners along, eager to greet the next person and sniff the next scent.

Adam and his team would be on alert and patrolling for trouble. I hadn't seen Adam yet, but I did see that Amelia had her Tofu Dog barbeque set up in front of The Blackbird. I would, of course, do my best to avoid it. I didn't need to add Amelia, or tofu, to my day. And what a beautiful fall day it was. The leaves on all the century trees on the sweeping lawns in front of the historic brick mansions on Main Street looked as if someone had brushstroked them red and gold. Looking at the wholesome scene, I couldn't believe that three murders had taken place here in the last two weeks. Life really does go on.

I jumped with a start at the wail of a vintage County fire engine, then shook my head at how unnerved I was getting. Traditionally, all County parades were led by one of the historic fire engines, sirens blaring for all to hear. The children chattered and squirmed with anticipation. The excitement was palpable, like a wave through the crowd.

I jotted a few notes as fall-themed floats pulled by tractors and monstrous pickups lumbered by. I needed the details for my article and the photo captions Cyn and I would create later. It was hard to focus, as my mind wandered back to last night. I was sure the murderer had been among the crowd at the kickoff corn roast, but who could it be? Could it be the same person for all three crimes? Was I next? Maybe I had dug too deep into things. Cyn nudged me to pay attention. "The High School float is next. Should be a doozy."

"More like a boozy."

I wasn't far off the mark. The theme was 'Growing our Future'.

When I thought about what the high school might do for their float, I imagined earnest-looking students sitting at desks and some on risers in cap and gown, waving diplomas, or dressed to depict scientists involved in future research. The teens had gone for a more literal translation and had dressed several cheer leaders in green leotards that left little to the imagination. Their fresh faces peeked out of flower petals. The girls shimmied and sashayed to music as they rose and descended from crudely constructed large clay-colored flowerpots. The guys on the float were dressed in large sacks with the word "fertilizer" stenciled across the front. The writhing and contorting reminded me of a Lady Gaga video. I was embarrassed for Heather, who was the third pot from the front. I was thankful that Kiera was riding her horse instead. If I'd been one of them, I would have saved all the booze and weed to take just before the parade. I would have needed it just to get on the float.

"Gotta get me one of those green leotards," Cyn said appreciatively. "I could see a lot of uses for that." *Of course, she would.*

The school float was followed by several loud diesel-powered tractors flying banners with the theme written across them. George from the airstrip was driving one. "Hey, it's James Bond on his tractor," I remarked to Cyn. "Remember him?" I got a scorching look.

The last in the tractor line had a "Farms Feed People" banner and I knew the Environmental Defense League members were definitely in attendance. I looked around for Clive Carruthers but could not see him. That made me nervous. I looked over my shoulders every few minutes as people jostled by our position on the sidewalk. The Pit Bull was stationed behind us in the doorway to the office, handing out the latest edition of the paper. As an ugly reminder of the week's events, the front window of the office was still covered by a sheet of plywood. We had not been able to replace it in time for the parade.

I turned my attention back to the street when I heard the familiar clip clop of hooves on concrete. Nacho led the way, looking spellbinding in his polished boots, white Grand Prix pants, dark blue riding jacket, and black helmet. Behind him were six riders. My heart sank. In other years he'd had as many as twelve. Where was the support?

"Kiera!" I yelled out as they passed and waved my hands wildly so she would spot me. She looked over and nodded with that annoyed look that instantly communicated I'd embarrassed her. I didn't care. She looked so beautiful, and I was so proud of her. "Cyn," I said over my shoulder, "make sure you get a good shot of Kiera for me."

"Already shot about a dozen of both of them," Cyn said with a winning smile and a wink.

As the last of the floats passed by, the people took to the streets behind them. From experience, I knew that everyone would follow the parade route, then turn into the fair grounds for the rest of the festivities. I helped Cyn pick up her equipment and we followed.

Later, as day turned to dusk, I settled Cyn into a good viewing position in the stands to take photos of the upcoming evening events. I wandered down into the safety of the midway crowd. Even though I was on edge, I still had a job to do. I was working on getting more quotes from attendees to include in my article. The rides in the midway flashed with dazzling, colored lights. Kids screamed with excitement. Someone shouted in a deep smoker's voice, "Hey lady, wanna try your luck?" I turned abruptly. A carny was holding out three rings for me to toss. I waved him off. The midway smelled sickly sweet. The aroma of grease from tiny donuts being fried wafted by, as I watched a food vendor deftly twirl pink cotton candy onto a paper cone for a young couple. Kiera used to love cotton candy. I hated the stickiness but loved the delight in her eyes when she tore small bits of candy clouds and let them melt in her mouth. An announcement blared over the PA system. I stopped in my tracks. Had I heard correctly? I cocked my head to hear better and caught the tail end of the announcement. Heart thumping, I replayed it in my head.

"… in the second heat of the ATV race, Green Machine, Farmer's Folly, and Dirt Devil!"

I was sure of it. I was sure I heard "Dirt Devil." What to do? I turned around, wildly scanning the crowd, my eyes darting everywhere. The rides spun faster. The music pounded. Pulling myself together, I yanked out my cellphone, intent on calling Adam. I couldn't get a signal. I ran around frantically, holding my phone in the air, hoping for more bars. No luck. I was going to have to figure out who he was alone. I prayed that Adam or Cyn had heard the announcement and were already acting. There was no time to search for Adam or fight through the stands to get Cyn. All I knew was I couldn't let him slip through my fingers. I couldn't live another minute of my life in jeopardy.

My heart pounded as I jostled through the thick molasses crowd towards the track. Droves of teens and young people roaming in packs slowed me down as I pushed onward. An elbow in the ribs almost made me double over. I winced from pain but shoved my way on. I pushed forward with my hands out in front of me. Panic made me aggressive.

"Pardon me; excuse me," I said. I pushed this way and that, looking for the path of least resistance. I saw the bright lights of the track ahead of me. I was close.

I'd manoeuvred myself into the front of the bleachers, flashing my press card as leverage. I found a position close to the fence on the outside edge of the track to the side of the stands. The announcer had said Dirt Devil was racing in the second heat. I heard the revving of the ATV engines. I didn't think the first heat had started. I was sure I would have heard the roar of them round the track, even when stuck in the crowds. This close, the noise from the revving deafened me. If I called out, no one would hear me. I calmed myself with the thought that hundreds of people surrounded me. Who would be fool enough to pull anything? Once more I grabbed my cellphone, praying for a signal. I threw it back into my purse in frustration. Then with a shot of a starter pistol, and a jump of my heart, the first heat was on. I tried to maintain my position close to the fence while I shimmied closer to the starting line. I needed to see the second heat racers now. An excited and oblivious crowd focused on the first race pushed back. I soldiered on, enduring blow after painful blow to the ribs.

I was close. I could see several ATVs off to the side, waiting their turn for the next race. I scanned the drivers. I didn't recognize anyone. All were clad in head-to-toe tight outfits, with helmets on their heads. One entrant, who had been leaning down to fix something on his machine, popped up and reached to get his helmet. I was stunned. Adam had been on the right track. Clive Carruthers was stuffing his long stringy locks into his helmet, readying himself for the second heat. I thought about it. Of course, the name made sense. I should have figured it out. Clive was all about the Earth and getting his hands dirty.

I fumbled my phone as I frantically punched numbers. The crowd erupted when the first racers crossed the finish line. More cheering swelled the stands as the results were announced. Still no signal. I was sweating. I didn't want to leave to find Adam. I couldn't think clearly what to do. Hordes of people, officials, and the first heat entrants pulling into the exit area blocked the view. Over the PA the announcer boomed, "In the second heat, Dirt Devil is a scratch; he will be replaced by Hell on Wheels." What? What happened? Was there a mechanical problem? I scanned the area to see if he was still there. I had to find him.

"Looking for me?" said a menacing male voice behind me.

I turned my head slightly and glimpsed a helmet-clad man looking down at me through his smoked visor. I couldn't see his face, but it had to be Dirt Devil. I felt the tip of something sharp pushed into the small of my back. "Walk," he commanded. "Open your mouth and you're dead meat."

TWENTY-SEVEN

My mind stopped. Panic overcame me. I sweated more while my heart raced. My breathing fast and gasping, I tried to focus. I knew one thing: I wasn't rational. I was jelly. Should I run, scream, fall down, what? Hardly, I could barely walk, let alone make a decision. I put one foot in front of the other, prompted by what felt like a knife in my back. Dirt Devil grabbed my elbow to steer me. I was like some slow computer that took forever to compute. I was processing instead of acting.

The crowd and the swirl of humanity jostled us. Dark shapes flitted; feet were tripped over, and everywhere was relentless noise. People cheered; kids yelled; loudspeakers blared as the sounds of hawkers and engines all blended into a cacophony that added to my inability to think of even the simplest option.

All the while I felt the sharp pain in my back. About one thing I had no doubt: that this guy, this Dirt Devil, wouldn't refrain from using this knife. He'd already killed, so it would be so much easier to do it to me. One shove and any number of organs would be pierced. Before anyone even realized what happened, I would be history. What would Kiera do without me? I wouldn't be there to see her graduate and marry. I had to get away, but I had to do it without getting wounded. I tried to remember anything I could about Clive that I could use to say or do something. The all-encompassing crowd noise enveloped me.

"Move faster," he grunted. His voice was low and harsh, and I strained to hear.

I clutched at straws. Maybe if I drew him out, I could figure out some strategy. Even though I was stumbling, I had to find my courage. "What do you want with me?" I squeaked. Did he laugh or was it just background noise? No answer, just the knife pushed a little harder. *Did that mean to shut up?*

He propelled me towards the parking lot beside the arena and away from the crowds. I would lose my chance to escape when we moved away from the track. I had to engage him. The noise muted somewhat as we moved past the crowd, and the numbers thinned. I could finally hear myself think, if only I could think. "People will be looking for me," I blurted out.

"And they'll find you." *What does that mean? They'll find my body?*

"You won't get away with it. The Sheriff is on to you."

His grip on my elbow tightened. Maybe that wasn't the right thing to say.

"I have so far." Damn, he sounded cocky.

As we moved further into the darkness, fear kept my heart rate pounding wildly. Do something, I thought. "Why me?" I rasped. I held back tears.

"I told you to back off, but you didn't listen." *He sent the note.*

"Did you throw the rock and slash my tires?"

"Yes, and this is the last message!" *Oh my God, I am going to die. I have to do something.*

"I'm listening now. I swear. I'll back off. No more investigating." I pleaded for my life.

"It's way too late. I warned you, but you didn't listen. You just barged in, interviewing everyone. Then today I saw you when they announced the contestants. I knew you were looking for me."

"I was looking for the Dirt Devil."

"I know. Everything was perfect. But then I saw you madly looking around at the ATV drivers. I knew it was about more than just the race. I put two and two together. That meddling bitch Candi must have mentioned my nickname. You should have left her alone!"

Something wasn't right. I saw him put on his helmet. I didn't think he saw me. "How did you get over to the stands so fast?" I asked, confused.

"I never went to the start. I watched from the sidelines when I saw you looking and phoning."

"But Clive, I saw you."

"Oh, that's sick." He laughed insanely. "Clive is a dope head. He's an out-of-date old dude. Clive and his Green Machine. That is so whack." My insides churned. This guy talked like a kid. I didn't have any kids on my list. There were all old dudes and a couple of women. Oh God. It couldn't be. I had asked him to look out for Kiera. I'd told her to keep him close. What a fool I'd been.

I stopped. "But you're a kid!" I exclaimed. He roughly shoved me ahead.

"That's exactly what my grandfather said. Everyone always underestimated me. Let Marco brush the horses; that's all he's good for."

"Marco, don't tell me. Not your grandfather." I didn't stand a chance with a kid who had killed one of his own family. He had to be psycho.

"You didn't know my grandfather. He was brutal. When he discovered the weed in the field, he decided to sell the stables. I was disinherited. He had promised me that one day that property would be mine, and I could run the stables."

So, that was the real reason Bruno was selling the farm. It had nothing to do with Nacho. "When was this?" I tried to keep him talking so we would slow down. Soon, I would be out of earshot of the crowd, if I wasn't already. Then, there would be a dead reckoning.

"The last night I saw him alive. He told me then. I asked him for another chance ... that I could do better. He laughed. Said I would never amount to anything. I was just a big, dumb screwup. I swore and he backhanded me. The tranquillizer syringe for Dante was in my hand. I stabbed him in the neck."

"Then it wasn't premeditated. It was an argument that got out of control," I said, hoping to calm him. I thought back to Tanya and her fear of the family. "Why stage it to look like suicide?"

I must have hit a raw nerve. He hurt me more as he pushed me into the parking lot. I hoped I had bought a few precious minutes. Maybe someone saw us leave and was looking for me. By now his emotions were raw. "You don't know my dad. He would have killed me, especially when he found out about the weed. We're supposed to be squeaky clean, not an embarrassment to the family."

"And Carl?" I asked, stalling as much as I could.

"He figured it out. He knew I was going to the barn the night Grandpa died. We usually met on Friday nights after Grandpa rode, to exchange dope for the weekend. He figured when I didn't show that Friday that I was involved in what happened. Like a moron, he told his bitch of a girlfriend. He wanted to pull out of our dope business. I couldn't trust him not to go to the cops."

"But why Candi? She didn't even know you."

"Are you kidding? Numb-nuts Carl told her everything. That's why he was going straight and all that going back to school BS. It was all her fault. I didn't trust her. Then she talked to you!"

"How did you know? Did you follow me?" I snapped, feeling guilty all over again.

"Your hot friend left a trail with all her stupid tweets. She gave the times and locations with every tweet. I didn't have to follow you. I always knew where the two of you were."

Shit. All my efforts to be so careful were for nothing. "So that's why you were able to use all your scare tactics on me."

"Not that any of it worked."

"And Morty?" I asked, both fishing and trying to buy time.

"Morty who?" he asked, and pushed me hard enough that I almost fell.

By the time we reached the parking lot he had worked himself into a frenzy. He was ranting about everyone who had betrayed him. When I saw his ATV parked, I knew all hope would soon be lost. "You can't hurt me. It would destroy Kiera, and she's your friend!"

"Was a friend, but she's loyal to my ex, her best friend Heather, who turned out to be like all the rest, always bitching about everything!"

This was news. If Heather and he were over, then so was I. We stopped at the ATV. Surely, Adam or Cyn had heard the Dirt Devil announcement and maybe figured out what happened. I had to hold on to the hope they were looking for me.

"Get on," he barked, dragging me onto the ATV so I was almost sidesaddle. Whatever he had in mind, I knew it was going to be bad. By now, the crowd was far behind. Darkness had descended, leaving the only illumination a few dim lights in a corner of the lot. I could hear noise drifting over the parking lot. It sounded as if the second heat had already begun. The walk over had felt like hours. No one would notice us or care if we zipped away. If I was going to make a move, I had to do it before we got behind the arena. I willed myself to think.

He mounted the ATV behind me, locking me in a death grip. His muscular arms pinned me tight when he put his hands on the handlebars. I squirmed as I felt him crush me. Sharp pain pierced my chest where my rib was broken. *Don't pass out. Keep alert.* Where was the knife? He couldn't drive and hold a knife. He must have let go while he kick-started the ATV. We zoomed towards the back of the arena. My ribs screamed in agony at the pressure. I had to come up with an idea. My life depended on it.

The back of the arena meant no people, no witnesses, no one to hear. *It is a great place to toss a dead body.* I had only one chance. We left the parking lot and slowed slightly when we hit the softer turf of the field behind the arena. The terrain became uneven. My ribcage felt as if it would explode with each bump. He had to pay more attention to his driving.

I squirmed from the pain while I quietly manoeuvred my legs onto something that could give me some leverage. "Stop wiggling!" he shouted. Momentarily he loosened his grip to switch gears. It was now or never. There was no time to lose. I grabbed the handlebars and abruptly turned the machine sharply to the right. The machine's two left wheels lost traction and became slightly airborne. He yelled and swore. He fought for control of the wayward machine while trying to keep his grip on me. I grabbed the handlebars again and the ATV teetered. Adrenaline pumped through me. Ignoring the pain, I smashed his helmet with my elbow. Pain shot up my arm. In a split second, he lost control. The machine started to flip. I pushed off with both my arms and legs with all my might. I launched and twisted myself as far from the machine as I could. I heard a scream. I hurtled into the air and smashed into the ground with a thud. The collision knocked the air out of me. I clenched my teeth to stop from screaming in pain. The ground beside me shook. Above the grind of gears and motor noise was a sound like an animal in agony.

I lay still for a second, trying to catch my breath. I felt frozen in time, with no idea how long I lay there. The dark disoriented me, but gradually I was aware of the sounds of the motor. With that realization, adrenaline pumped once more. Where was he? Where was the ATV? Did he get it upright again? With that consciousness also came pain. It radiated everywhere.

My head throbbed, and stars like big bursts of fireworks flashed in my eyes. Roll, I thought. Get away! It took everything in me to roll. I tried to scramble to my feet and sunk down again in pain. Something trickled down my face. Had I been stabbed? Did I smash my skull? Headlights bounced erratically in front of me. He was coming for me. The lights grew brighter. The noise of a motor sounded very close. Lights flashed in the grass. How could he have found me?

"No!" I screamed, my voice alien to my ears. I tried again to rise to flee but stumbled and fell. I pushed myself to keep rolling. I didn't have the strength to stand. I grimaced with acute pain. *Don't scream any more, or he'll find you.* I rolled through long grass, desperate to get away from the noise and the lights closing in.

A voice carried over the field. Was it real? Was it my name being called? I felt sick. He was right on top of me. *I'm going to die!* "Help!" I screeched, and then he grabbed me again and held on. Now, I screamed with everything I had. My arms were the only thing I could move, and I flailed away at him trying to break his hold, even though pain shot through me like lightning bolts.

"Stop!" he commanded. I lashed out, pushing him away. I hardly had any strength left.

"For heaven's sake, it's me, Adam," the voice said. I was confused; my body wrecked. I was close to passing out. A face appeared in the flashlight. Adam's? An arm clothed in a uniform—a police uniform—reached around me. I collapsed. Tears flooded down my face. *I'm not dead.* Adam carefully wrapped me in his arms. "It's over," he whispered.

TWENTY-EIGHT

A uniformed officer arrived and handed Adam a foil blanket. Gingerly he wrapped it around me, careful of my many scrapes and bruises. He turned to the officer. "Take care of her. Get her out of harm's way," he said, then he ran.

I gave my head a shake, as if that could remove the cobwebs and start my brain again. I became more aware of my surroundings. Sounds that had been muffled poured in. Shouts erupted all around me, but I couldn't make out what anyone was saying. I heard the whine of the engine, the explosive sounds of more cars and ATVs, and the screech of tires on gravel. Horns blared, and sirens screeched, getting louder with every second. I wanted to put my hands over my ears. As I raised my head, lights flashed everywhere— blue and red strobe lights; headlights flashing and bouncing in the distance; and red lights twirling. Excessive screaming, full of pain and fury rose above the din, as if some trapped animal was in its death throes.

I stumbled, and the officer held me tighter. "Sorry,' he said. I didn't know why he was apologizing, and then in seconds we were out of the grass. My knees buckled. There was the overturned ATV, engine whining, wheels turning, and the horrifying source of the screaming. A posse of men were around each corner of the ATV as a figure on the ground writhed in pain, legs trapped under the thundering machine. Adam was off to one side, illuminated by headlights.

Adam yelled to the cops, "Shut the damn engine off."

An officer reached in and turned off the engine as the cops braced to lift the ATV off Marco's legs. The officer had nowhere to go with me, except try to skirt around the horrific scene. Part of me was terrified that this monster was still alive. I couldn't take my eyes away. The screaming stopped.

"You bitch!" Marco spat as his eyes met mine. I whimpered, and then felt the officer increase his hold on me.

Adam stared at Marco, his face hard and stony, and unlike Adam altogether. "Shut up!"

I wrapped the blanket tighter around myself. *He almost succeeded. He almost killed me.*

On the count of three, the officers lifted the ATV. In a burst of adrenalin, Marco pulled himself up on his arms and started scrambling towards me, hands clawing and scraping at the dirt, his legs dragging uselessly behind him. I froze, terrified.

"I'll kill you," he seethed. He madly grabbed at anything he could get his hands on and hurled gravel and dirt in my direction. I couldn't move as the officer did his best to try to budge me. "You nosy bitch … poking your nose where …" An "oomph" cut off the words.

Adam grabbed Marco from behind and pinned him face down in the dirt. He pulled Marco's hands roughly behind his back, swiftly producing cuffs and clapping them on his wrists. "You're under arrest." He stood up and turned to the waiting officers. "Read him his rights and get that gurney from the ambulance over here."

I was so shell-shocked from seeing Marco and reliving the terror all over again, I hadn't noticed that I was also the center of attention. Only the buzz from what I could now see was a gathering crowd of gawkers alerted me to the chaotic scene amidst the strobing lights. A crowd that had gathered by the ambulance and cop cars were being held back by uniformed police. Other cops were putting up yellow crime scene tape to keep back the growing numbers running and driving up to the scene. I saw people holding up their cellphones, probably taking videos, and flashes as people took pictures. How did they all get here, and so fast, I wondered. Here I thought I was going to die, isolated in a field by a madman, and minutes later a whole peanut gallery was taking up all available space. How were they alerted and by whom? As I was gazing, I heard a voice above the din. "Mom, Mom, over here."

The cop was leading me over to a police car when I spotted Kiera and Heather in the direction of the crowd. Kiera was frantically waving and alternately arguing with a cop. "It's my daughter," I sobbed to the cop who was escorting me. "Please let her and her friend by. Please."

The cop shouted over to the one arguing with Kiera and gave the okay. The kids made a run for it, and the next thing I know Kiera was wrapping her arms around me. Tears streamed down her face.

"I'm okay." I patted her on the back even though I winced from the pain. "How did you find me?" I asked, then winced and reached down to cradle my ribs.

"Mom. Look. The lights, the sirens. And Cyn called …"

"Oh my god, that looks like Marco; he's hurt!" interrupted Heather, catching sight of Marco being placed onto a stretcher.

"WTF! What's going on? Heather, he's a jerk!" snapped Kiera.

Heather started to run anyway, but I grabbed an arm to stop her. "Heather, no, stop." I held on to her and looked her in the eye. "He tried to kill me. Do you understand?"

Heather and Kiera simultaneously yelled, "What?" Obviously, only I and maybe Adam knew exactly what had happened here.

"He had a knife at my back. He abducted me. He was the killer. Of his grandfather … of all of them. I was to be next!"

Kiera cut in. "What the hell, the bastard. He had a knife on you! He tried to kill you!" And then her eyes opened wide. "Oh my God, he was the one protecting me. I was with the killer all along?" She shuddered. Heather stood there, mouth open, as if her brain had ceased functioning. Shock.

I winced. "If I'd known he was the Dirt Devil, we could have connected the dots earlier."

"Dirt Devil? I could have told you Marco's racing name is Dirt Devil," Kiera erupted.

It seems I had underestimated Kiera as well as Marco. I thought I was sheltering her all along by not sharing what I knew. Instead, I'd put her in harm's way by asking him to stay close to her. This was a harsh awakening to the fact Kiera was growing up, and I should have treated her more like an adult than a child. I could have saved us all some suffering and maybe saved Candi. I thought for a moment, then realized there was no way I could have saved Candi. Her fate was sealed by Carl, who should have gone to the police as soon as he had figured it out. Maybe they'd both be alive today.

"It's not possible," Heather muttered. "Killed his grandfather and who else?"

Where do I start? Let me count the bodies. "He killed his grandfather, the guy found at the barn, and the girl blown up in the trailer park."

"Can't be. He has an alibi," Kiera said. "He was at the movies with Heather."

"Oh," Heather interrupted. "I never really thought about it."

"Thought about what?" Kiera asked, confused.

"We did go to the movies. But now that I think about it more carefully, he was late. We saw the movie, but we got there when it had already started. We missed all the trailers."

"Those things run forever. That gave Marco an extra thirty minutes or so to kill his grandfather and still get to the show in time," Kiera said with authority. "And then just sit and eat popcorn with you, Heather … sick."

I was shivering by now. I wasn't the only one. Heather was shaking. "Heather, you need to tell this to Sheriff Armstrong as soon as possible."

Before I could continue, we heard a familiar voice.

"Hello, Ham Sandwich. You alive?" There, in all her hoedown finery, with her press pass flashing around her neck, was Cyn, carefully balancing in her heels and stepping through the gravel as if it were quicksand. She arrived breathless. "You are lighting up the night more than the Midway!"

"Oh my God, Cyn. You won't believe it. Marco was the killer! I'm so glad Adam arrived so fast. I don't even know how he knew." I paused when a thought occurred to me. "Maybe we've developed some weird telepathic ability with each other. I've never had this kind of connection with a man."

"You must have hit your head hard. You are not telepathic, you silly old coot," Cyn said, reaching up to brush hair and dirt off my face, and inspect me for injuries. "It was the phone. That and a bit of luck, really. I was in the stands, and I had tried to call you when I heard an announcement that referred to 'Dirt Devil'. I couldn't get an answer. I didn't know if you didn't have reception or if something had happened."

"I was hoping someone might have seen me," I answered.

"I actually did. I scanned the crowds before the race with my telephoto lens. I caught sight of you, and it looked as if you were being led away by a guy in a helmet. You looked scared out of your mind, and he was practically glued to you," she continued. "I figured he could be Dirt Devil."

"He had a knife at my back."

She gasped. "That I didn't see, but I had enough bars, so I called the Sheriff. I told him about the Dirt Devil announcement, and you and the guy in the helmet."

Adam walked up, eyes on me only.

"I hate to break the party up, ladies. Darcy needs medical attention, and I need to get statements." The ladies nodded. "And thank you, Cyn, for your quick thinking." She beamed.

"I'm fine," I protested. "I need to be with Kiera and my peeps. Heather has some information for you as well." I wobbled, and Adam reached out to steady me.

"Easy, this is not optional; you are going to go to the hospital and get some much-needed medical attention." He reached out and wrapped the blanket tighter around me, pulling it up around my shoulders more. His hand brushed my cheek.

"Don't worry about the girls," Cyn said, interrupting the moment. "I'm on it. We'll meet you at the hospital."

"Cyn, at some point we'll need to talk officially about what you witnessed. And Heather, give me your cell number, and when I get everything cleared up, I will give you a call," Adam interjected before Cyn could lead them away. They hurriedly got numbers before Adam escorted me to a waiting cop car, away from all the prying eyes.

"Is Marco going to live?" I asked Adam.

"Yes, but I'm not sure of the prognosis for his legs. They were crushed under the weight of the ATV when it flipped over, but he'll live."

"He did it," I gushed. "All of it. He confessed to me when he had the knife at my back. More like boasted. I was so blind. I had him watching Kiera at the barn. I put her under the protection of the killer, the one person I wanted her safe from. What kind of mother am I …"?

"The best kind," Adam cut in. "Don't feel guilty; he had us all fooled." He wrapped his arms around me and pulled me into his chest. I felt safe.

The second ambulance arrived on the scene, backing up towards us with a loud beep, beep, beep. *Talk about killing the moment!* Adam abruptly pulled out of the hug and became all business again.

"First things first. We need to get you to the hospital, Darcy. I'll come see you after I am done here and take your statement there."

He waved over the paramedics and the officer who had accompanied me. The paramedics quickly took charge. They felt around the matted hair on my head and peered into my eyes with bright lights, lifting my eyelids to see more. They buckled me onto the waiting stretcher and hoisted me into the ambulance. I winced in pain as the stretcher jostled. Adam gave me one last look and tipped his hat. "Take good care of her," he said, and then he was off to meet up with the other officers on scene.

The ambulance door closed with a loud thud, and the paramedic signaled to the driver to proceed. *Could it really all be over?*

Twenty-Nine

After a night in the hospital, I was discharged, and a day later gratefully lay on my couch with a blanket draped over me. Adam sat in a chair across from me, and Cyn was in the kitchen making coffee. I hoped she'd add a little something extra, like Bailey's. I had more bruises and scrapes on top of the ones that were already starting to heal from the car crash. I was not a pretty sight. My rib was still broken and my chest was taped. There wasn't much more they could do for me, so they sent me home with pain killers and instructions to take it easy.

"Well, was my statement enough to lock him up?" I asked.

"It was enough to give us a search warrant. That, Heather's statement, and a lack of an alibi helped seal Marco's fate."

"How so?"

"When we searched his place, we found the missing machete that tied him to Carl's death. As for Bruno's murder, the only prints on the syringe found in Dante's stall were those of Bruno, and we know Bruno couldn't have injected himself, so that was staged. Reena had cleaned the stall not long before she left that day, so the syringe had to be new. We also know Marco had time to go to the barn on that Friday night, as he told you."

"But how did Bruno's prints get on the syringe?"

"He put Bruno's hand on the syringe after he was deceased."

"Eww."

"Murder isn't pretty, Darcy." He shrugged while I shivered.

"And what about Candi?"

"Along with the fire department, we are still processing the scene at her trailer and building evidence, but there were items in his SUV consistent with building a Molotov cocktail. We'll get him on all three counts; I'm sure of it."

"Can I quote you on that?" I asked with a grin. Lorne had called earlier. My trial period was over, and he wanted me back on the job after a few days of ordered rest. Even Simon had sent me an email letting me know that I could have the full front page, this time only. A one-shot deal, he had assured me. I shouldn't get used to it. I breathed a sigh of relief. It really was all over?

That reminded me of Morty's death. "Is there are a connection between Morty's death and Marco? When I bought it up to Marco, he didn't know what I was talking about."

"Morty died of an overdose of his heart medication. Bruno was also on the exact same heart medication we found in Morty's system. I have nothing concrete, only circumstantial. We think Bruno was in Morty's office just before he died, but we have no one who can corroborate that, and of course, we can't ask Bruno."

"What about the notation I found in his calendar. The *BM?*"

"There's no proof that he wrote it, or what it referred to. We will never have conclusive evidence in Morty's death, even though Bruno could have slipped him the medication to keep him quiet. Could be Morty knew about Marco and the weed. Who knows …?" Adam answered. "All we can do is label it an accidental overdose since we will never know with 100 percent certainty how it happened."

I nodded my head in understanding and sighed in relief. The nightmare had really ended.

Cyn came back into the room and handed me my coffee. I took a sip and smiled up at her. Cyn winked. She certainly knew what I needed.

"Oh, Amelia sent over a sandwich for you; she hopes to see you back in the café soon," Cyn said, handing me a sandwich wrapped in waxed paper. I opened it up to reveal an avocado and sprout sandwich. I frowned.

"What I don't get is how Marco always knew where we were." Cyn said.

"He was one of your followers," I provided.

"What? One of my tweet peeps from Twitter?"

"Yes, Twitter Queen. Marco told me all your tweets were set to stamp with your location and time data. He knew that the likelihood was we would be together. You left a trail of digital bread crumbs everywhere you went."

"Sorry, Darcy, I never thought," she said, giving me a sheepish look as she retrieved her phone from her purse.

"That's how he knew where to find you when he ran you off the road. His black Escalade has paint matching the scrapes of paint we found on your back bumper," Adam added.

Kiera bounded down the stairs by twos, with a large thump as she hit each step. "I'm off to the stables. Everything is getting back to normal at the barn. People are already in touch and starting to return. We have some catching up to do with our training, but everything should be on track for The Fall Classic." She grabbed the car keys off the front hall table, then turned to me again. "Dad called," she said. I gulped. Would he be coming back to York Ridge to exert his fatherly rights? "He's staying in Florida," Kiera continued. "Some big charity horse show is coming up, and he doesn't want to interrupt his training routine. He says 'get well' though."

I smiled. Yep, things were returning to normal.

The doorbell rang so Kiera answered it on her way out. She passed something to Cyn, who promptly removed the packaging.

"Oh, flower delivery." Cyn sashayed over to me with a beautiful bouquet in her arms. She plucked the card from between the flowers and read, "Mi Amiga: You saved my business, my reputation, my life. Let me know when you are well enough for me to show my appreciation. Hopefully, new owner of Maple Lane Stables, Nacho."

She stuck the card back in the flowers and set them on a side table next to me. A little smile played about her lips. Adam's eyebrows rose as he cut a glance my way. I blushed and looked down at my hands.

"What does Macho Nacho mean by 'new owner'? Is Frank selling?" asked Cyn.

"It's not yet official. Nacho called me earlier. The family want nothing to do with the horse or the stables. Too many horrid memories."

"That will be a relief to you and Kiera, as well as Nacho … I was wondering …" Adam said, shifting forward in his seat, "could I show a little appreciation myself by taking you out for coffee sometime?"

Coffee? Oh, surely he couldn't mean going to The Blackbird, could he? I squirmed uncomfortably and shot an uneasy look at my discarded sandwich on the side table. Not exactly the confidence-building atmosphere for a first date. Was I jumping to conclusions? Was he asking me on a date? I realized belatedly that I had left Adam hanging.

"Or not, if that would make you uncomfortable?" Adam said, misunderstanding my reticence.

To hell with it. I had a life to live, and a life I almost lost. "Not at all, I'd love to join you," I said with a big smile. Things were looking up. Maybe taking the job of a dead guy wasn't bad luck after all. I winced from a shot of pain from my rib … then again.

Acknowledgements

We are grateful to have lived in wonderful King Township, Ontario among the gorgeous, wooded hills, ravines and streams of the Oak Ridges Moraine, as well as all the glorious and unique towns in the township, specifically Schomberg, for their delightful fall fair and scarecrow contest. Schomberg is also the location of the original Grackle, a true one-of-a-kind café that became with some exaggeration the inspiration for The Blackbird Café, while the township was an ideal model for Yorkdale County. Our love for the equestrian township with horse farms down every road made it the perfect venue for our murder mystery, and the book would be a far different tale if not for being members of that community.

Thanks to the people who gave their time and expertise while we were writing this novel, such as coach and owner of Standalone Farms, Neil Badcock, for his expertise on all things horsey; Terra Ciolfe, editor of the King Weekly for generously sharing her knowledge and taking us behind the scenes; author, Kim McDougall of Castelane Inc. for her fabulous mentoring; writer and editor, Lois Gordon, for her sharp eyes proofreading our book; and our families for their insight, inspiration and patience.

GIVE US YOUR FEEDBACK

Tell us what you think of Groomed for Death!

As this is the first in a new series, we would love to hear what you think. Here are a few ways you can provide your review:

- Leave a comment or a detailed review on the site where you purchased
- Tag us on social media with #GroomedforDeath and/or #Wollison&Cooke
- Submit a review on our site at https://www.blackashbooks.com/review

Subscribe on our website for behind-the-scenes info and to get the latest information on new releases: www.blackashbooks.com

About the Authors

Photo by Robert Brown

Mary Anne Wollison has been a successful national magazine editor, authored hundreds of magazine articles for North American markets, as well as, published three non-fiction books that have been translated and distributed internationally A former English curriculum leader and provincial education officer she has published five award winning middle school and YA graphic novels and two literacy anthologies for the international educational market.

Michelle Cooke is a senior marketing manager with over 20 years in the IT industry. When not busy with marketing strategy she reads and writes mysteries and runs a graphic design and illustration company called Quick Brown Fox Canada where she sells her art on merchandise worldwide.

Find us at: http://blackashbooks.com.

CPSIA information can be obtained
at www.ICGtesting.com
Printed in the USA
LVHW010116090222
710560LV00004B/387